THE OLD CURIOSITY SHOP

Published by Priory Books,
© Peter Haddock Publishing,
United Kingdom, YO16 6BT.

THE OLD CURIOSITY SHOP

CHAPTER 1

One night I was walking slowly in the city when I was stopped by a soft voice asking me something. I turned and found at my elbow a pretty little girl, who begged to be directed to a street in another part of town.

"That is far from here," said I.

"I know that, sir," she replied timidly. "For I came from there tonight."

"Alone?" said I, in some surprise.

"Oh, yes, but I am a little frightened now, for I am lost."

"And what made you ask me? Suppose I tell you wrong?"

"I am sure you will not do that," said the little creature. "You are such a very old gentleman, and walk so slow yourself."

I cannot describe how much I was impressed by this request.

"Come," said I, "I'll take you there."

She put her hand in mine as if she had known me from her cradle, and we trudged away together; the little creature accommodating her pace to mine. Every now and then she looked at my face, as if to be sure that I was not deceiving her.

My curiosity was equal to the child's, for child she certainly was, although I felt her very small and delicate frame imparted a peculiar youthfulness to her appearance. She was dressed with perfect neatness, and betrayed no marks of poverty or neglect.

"Who sent you so far by yourself?" said I.

"Someone who is very kind to me, sir."

"And what have you been doing?"

"That, I must not tell," said the child firmly.

I wondered what kind of errand made her prepared for questioning. She seemed to read my thoughts, for she added that there was no harm in what she had been doing, but it was a great secret – a secret that she did not even know herself.

She walked on as before, talking cheerfully, but she said no more about her home, beyond remarking that we were taking a new road and asking if it were a short one.

While walking, a hundred different explanations of the riddle came into my mind. I had felt pleased at first by her confidence and now determined to deserve it.

There was no reason why I shouldn't see the person who had inconsiderately sent her so great a distance by night alone. It was not unlikely that if she found herself near home she might leave me, depriving me of the opportunity, so I avoided the most frequented ways and took the most intricate. It wasn't until we arrived in the street itself that she knew where we were. Clapping her hands with pleasure, she ran on before me, waiting on the step till I came up, knocking when I joined her.

All was dark and silent within, and I was anxious (as indeed the child was also) for an answer. When she had knocked twice or thrice there was a noise as if someone were moving inside. At length a faint light appeared through the glass. It approached very slowly, the bearer having to make his way through a great many scattered articles.

It was an old man with long grey hair. Though much altered by age, I fancied I could recognize something of that delicate mould which I had noticed in the child. Their bright blue eyes were certainly alike, but his face was so deeply furrowed and so very full of care, that here all resemblance ceased.

The place was one of those receptacles for old and curious things that seem to crouch in odd corners of this town. There were suits of mail standing like ghosts in armour here and there, fantastic carvings brought from monkish cloisters, rusty weapons of various kinds, distorted figures in china and wood and iron and ivory; tapestry and strange furniture that might have been designed in dreams. The haggard aspect of the little old man was wonderfully suited to the place. There was nothing in the whole collection but was in keeping with himself; nothing that looked older or more worn than he.

As he turned the key, he surveyed me with some astonishment. The child addressed him as grandfather, and told him how we had met.

"Why, bless thee, child," said the old man, patting her on the head, "how couldst thou miss thy way? What if I had lost thee, Nell!"

"I would have found my way back to *you*, grandfather," said the child boldly; "never fear."

The old man kissed her, then turned to me, begging me to walk in. I did so. The door was closed and locked. He led me through to a small sitting-room, in which another door opened into a kind of closet, where I saw a little bed that a fairy might have slept in, it looked so very small and was so prettily arranged. The child tripped into this little room, leaving the old man and me together.

"You must be tired, sir," said he, placing a chair near the fire, "how can I thank you?"

"By taking more care of your grandchild another time, my good friend," I replied.

"More care!" said the old man in a shrill voice. "Why, whoever loved a child as I love Nell?"

He said this with such surprise that I was lost for an answer. The more so because, coupled with something feeble and wandering in his manner, there were in his face marks of deep and anxious thought which convinced me that he could not be, as I had at first thought, in a state of dotage or imbecility.

"I don't think you consider – " I began.

"I don't consider!" cried the old man interrupting me. "Ah, how little you know of the truth! Little Nelly!"

It would be impossible for any man to express more affection than the dealer in curiosities did, in these two words. I waited for him to speak again, but he rested his chin upon his hand and shaking his head, gazed upon the fire.

While we sat thus in silence, the child returned, her light brown hair hanging loose about her neck, and her face flushed with the haste she had made to rejoin us. She busied herself in preparing supper, and while she did so I remarked that the old man watched me more closely than he had done yet. I was surprised to see that everything was done by the child, and that there appeared to be no other persons in the house. When she was absent a moment I ventured a hint on this point. The old man replied that there were few grown persons as trustworthy or as careful as she.

"It always grieves me," I observed, roused by what I took to be his selfishness, "to contemplate the initiation of children into the ways of life, when they are scarcely more than infants. It checks their confidence and simplicity and demands that they share our sorrows before they are capable of entering into our enjoyments."

"It will never check hers," said the old man looking steadily at me, "the springs are too deep. Besides, the children of the poor know but few plea-

5

sures. Even the cheap delights of childhood must be bought and paid for."

"But – forgive me – you are surely not so very poor," said I.

"She is not my child, sir," returned the old man. "Her mother was, and she was poor. I save not a penny – though I live as you see, but – " he leant forward to whisper – "she shall be rich one of these days, and a fine lady. Don't think ill of me because I use her help. She gives it cheerfully as you see, and it would break her heart if anybody else did for me what her little hands undertake. I don't consider!" he cried waveringly, "why, God knows that this one child is the object of my life, and yet he never prospers me – never!"

At this point, the subject of our conversation returned, and the old man motioned me to the table, and said no more.

We had scarcely begun our meal when there was a knock at the door, and Nell bursting into a hearty laugh, which I rejoiced to hear for its childlike quality, said it was no doubt dear old Kit coming back at last.

"Foolish Nell!" said the old man fondling her hair. "She always laughs at poor Kit."

The child laughed again more heartily than before, and I could not help smiling. The little old man went to open the door. He returned with Kit at his heels.

Kit was a shock-headed, shambling, awkward lad with an uncommonly wide mouth, very red cheeks, a turned-up nose, and certainly the most comical expression of face I ever saw. He stopped at the door on seeing a stranger, twirled in his hand a perfectly round old hat, and rested himself now on one leg and now on the other. I entertained a grateful feeling towards the boy, for I felt that he was the comedy of the child's life.

"A long way, wasn't it, Kit?" said the little old man.

"Why, it was a goodish stretch, master," returned Kit.

"You have come back hungry?"

"I do consider myself rather so, master," was the answer.

He then carried a large slice of bread and meat and a mug of beer into a corner, and applied himself to disposing of them.

"Ah!" said the old man turning with a sigh, as if I had spoken but that moment, "you don't know what you say when you tell me that I don't consider her."

"You must not pay too much attention to a remark founded on first appearances, my friend," said I.

"No," returned the old man thoughtfully. "Come hither, Nell."

The little girl hurried over, and put her arm about his neck.

"Do I love thee, Nell?" said he. "Or no?"

The child answered with her caresses.

"Why dost thou sob?" said the grandfather, pressing her closer to him and glancing towards me. "Is it because thou know'st I love thee, and feel that I doubt it by my question? Well, let us say I love thee dearly."

"Indeed you do," replied the child, "Kit knows you do."

Kit stopped short in swallowing his food on being thus appealed to, and bawled, "Nobody isn't such a fool as to say he doesn't," after which he managed to avoid further conversation by taking a bite of the sandwich.

"She is poor now," said the old man, patting the child's cheek, "but I repeat that she shall be rich. It has been a long time coming, but it must come at last. It has come to other men who do nothing but waste. When *will* it come to me!"

"I am very happy as I am, grandfather," said the child.

"Tush, tush!" returned the old man, "thou dost not know – how should'st thou!" Then he muttered again between his teeth, "The time must come, it will be all the better for coming late." And then he sighed and fell into his former musing state. By this time it was almost midnight and I rose to go.

"One moment, sir," he said. "Now, Kit – near midnight, boy, and you still here! Get home, and be on time in the morning, for there's work to do. Good night! There, bid him good night, Nell!"

"Good night, Kit," said the child, her eyes lighting up.

"Good night, Miss Nell," returned the boy.

"And thank this gentleman," interposed the old man, "but for whose care I might have lost my little girl tonight."

"No, no, master," said Kit, "that won't do. I'd have found her. I'll bet that I'd find her if she was above ground, I would, as quick as anybody, master!"

When he had gone, and the child was occupied in clearing the table, the old man said: "I do thank you humbly and heartily, for what you have done tonight, and so does she. I should be sorry that you went away, and thought I was unaware of your goodness, or careless of her – I am not indeed."

I was sure of that, I said, from what I had seen. "But," I added, "may I ask you a question?"

"Ay, sir," replied the old man. "What is it?"

"This delicate child," said I, "has she nobody to care for her but you? Has she no other companion or adviser?"

"No," he returned, looking anxiously in my face, "and she wants no other."

"But are you not fearful," said I, "that you may misunderstand a charge so tender? Are you quite certain that you know how to execute such a trust as this? I too am an old man, and it is an old man's concern in all that is young and promising that moves me."

"Sir," rejoined the old man after a moment's silence. "I shouldn't feel hurt at what you say. In many respects I am the child, and she the grown person – that you have seen already. But she is the one object of my care, and if you knew how much, you would look at me with different eyes. Ah! It's a weary life for an old man – but there is an end to gain and that I keep before me."

I turned to put on my outer coat, meaning to say no more. I was surprised to see the child standing patiently by with a cloak, a hat, and a stick.

"Those are not mine, my dear," said I.

"No," returned the child, "they are grandfather's."

"But he is not going out tonight."

"Oh, yes, he is," said the child, with a smile.

"And what becomes of you, my pretty one?"

"I stay here of course. I always do."

I looked in astonishment towards the old man, but he was busy in the arrangement of his dress. From him I looked back to the slight gentle figure of the child. Alone! In that gloomy place all night.

She cheerfully helped the old man with his cloak, and then took a candle to light us out. Finding that we did not follow she looked back with a smile, waiting. The old man showed that he plainly understood why I hesitated, but he merely nodded to me to leave the room before him, and remained silent. I had to comply.

When we reached the door, the child set down the candle and raised her face to kiss me. Then she ran to the old man, who folded her in his arms and bade God bless her.

"Sleep soundly, Nell," he said in a low voice, "and angels guard thy bed! Do not forget thy prayers, my sweet."

"No, indeed," answered the child fervently.

"Bless thee a hundred times!" said the old man. "Early in the morning I shall be home."

"You'll not ring twice," returned the child. "The bell wakes me, even in the middle of a dream."

With this, they separated. The child opened the door, and with another farewell whose clear and tender note I have recalled a thousand times, held it until we had passed out. The old man paused a moment, satisfied that it was closed, and walked on at a slow pace. At the street-corner he stopped, and giving me a troubled look said that our ways were widely different and that he must take his leave. I would have spoken, but he hurried away. The darkness soon hid him.

I remained, unwilling to depart, and yet not sure why I should stay. I looked wistfully into the street, and after a while walked that way. I passed the house, and stopped and listened at the door; all was dark, and silent as the grave.

Still I lingered, unable to tear myself away, thinking of all possible harm that might befall the child – fires, robberies – even murder. The closing of a door or window took me to the curiosity dealer's again. I crossed the road, looking up at the house to be sure the noise had not come from there. No, it was still black and lifeless.

There were few people astir. The clocks struck one. Still I paced, promising myself that every time should be the last.

I recalled the old man's haggard face, his restless anxious looks. His affection for the child was in itself an extraordinary contradiction, or how could he leave her thus? I was inclined to think badly of him, but I never doubted his love for her. I remembered the tone of voice when he had called her name.

"Stay here of course," the child had said in answer to my question. What could take him from home every night? I called up all the strange tales I had ever heard of dark and secret deeds committed in great towns and escaping detection for a long series of years.

Rain began to fall; overcome by fatigue I engaged the nearest coach home. A cheerful fire was blazing on the hearth, the lamp burnt brightly; everything was cheering, and in contrast to the darkness I had quitted.

9

But all that night, I had before me the old, murky rooms – the gaunt suits of mail with their ghostly silent air – and alone in the midst of all this decay, the beautiful child, smiling through her light and sunny dreams.

CHAPTER 2

For nearly a week I fought the urge to revisit the place, but I finally gave in. This time I would present myself by the light of day.

I walked past the house several times, naturally hesitant, conscious that the visit would be unexpected. However, the door was shut, and it did not appear likely that I should be recognized if I continued merely to pass up and down before it. I soon conquered this irresolution, and entered the Curiosity Dealer's warehouse.

The old man and another person were together in the back, and their voices were raised to a very high pitch, which suddenly stopped on my entering. The old man advanced hastily towards me, saying in a tremulous tone that he was very glad I had come.

"You interrupted us at a critical moment," said he, pointing to the man with him, "this fellow will murder me one of these days. He would have done so, long ago, if he had dared."

"Bah! You would swear away my life if you could," returned the other. "We all know that!"

"I almost think I could," cried the old man, turning feebly upon him. "If prayers, or words, could rid me of you, they should. I would be quit of you, glad if you were dead."

"I know it," returned the other. "But neither oaths, prayers, nor words, *will* kill me, and therefore I live, and mean to live."

He stood lounging, his foot upon a chair, and regarded him with a contemptuous sneer. He was young, about twenty-one years old. He was certainly handsome, but his expression was insolent and repelled one.

"Justice or no," said the young fellow, "here I am and here I shall stop until I'm ready to go, unless you send for help to put me out – which you won't do. I tell you again – I want to see my sister."

10

"*Your* sister!" said the old man bitterly.

"Ah! You can't change the relationship," returned the other. "Or you'd have done it long ago. I want to see my sister, that you keep cooped up here, poisoning her mind with your sly secrets. I want to see her; and I will."

"Here's a moralist to talk of poisoned minds!" cried the old man, turning from him to me. "A profligate, too, sir, who has forfeited every claim upon his relatives. A liar," he added, as he drew closer to me, "who knows how dear she is to me, and seeks to wound me even there, because there is a stranger nearby."

"Strangers are nothing to me, grandfather," said the young fellow catching at the word, "nor I to them, I hope. The best they can do is mind their business and leave me to mine. I've a friend waiting outside, and as it seems that I may have to wait some time, I'll call him in, with your leave."

Saying this, he stepped to the door, and beckoned several times to some unseen person. At length there sauntered up, on the opposite side, a figure conspicuous for its dirty smartness, which came into the shop.

"There. It's Dick Swiveller," said the young fellow, pushing him in. "Sit down, Swiveller."

"But is the old man agreeable?" said Mr Swiveller in an undertone.

"Never you mind," replied his friend.

"Quite right," said Mr Swiveller, "caution is the word, and caution is the act." With that, he winked, folded his arms, leaned back in his chair, and looked up at the ceiling with profound gravity.

It was clear that Mr Swiveller had been drinking. His attire suggested that he had gone to bed in it. It consisted of a brown body-coat with a great many brass buttons up the front and only one behind, a bright check neckerchief, a plaid waistcoat, soiled white trousers, and a very limp hat. His dirty wristbands were pulled on as far as possible and ostentatiously folded back over his cuffs. Mr Swiveller leant back, eyes fixed on the ceiling.

The old man sat in a chair, and with folded hands, looked sometimes at his grandson and sometimes at his strange companion. The young man reclined against a table at no great distance from his friend, in apparent indifference to everything that had passed. I pretended to examine some of the goods ready for sale, and to pay little attention to anyone before me.

"Fred," Mr Swiveller whispered, "is the old man friendly?"

"What does it matter?" returned his friend peevishly.

"No, but *is* he?" said Dick.

11

"Yes, of course. What do I care whether he is or not?"

"It's a devil of a thing, gentlemen," said Mr Swiveller, "when relations fall out and disagree. Why should a grandson and grandfather peg away at each other with mutual wiolence when all might be bliss and concord. Why not jine hands and forget it?"

"Hold your tongue," said his friend.

"Sir," replied Mr Swiveller. "Don't interrupt the chair. Gentlemen, how does the case now stand? Here is a jolly old grandfather – I say it with the utmost respect – and here is a wild, young grandson. The jolly old grandfather says to the wild young grandson, 'I have brought you up and educated you, Fred; I have helped you get on in life. You have gone a little off course, as young fellows often do.' The wild young grandson makes answer to this and says, 'You're as rich as rich can be; you have been at no uncommon expense on my account. You're saving piles of money for my little sister who lives with you in a secret, hugger-muggering way, with no kind of enjoyment. Why can't you stand a trifle for your grown-up relation?' The jolly old grandfather answers that he declines to fork out with that cheerful readiness which is always so agreeable and pleasant in a gentleman of his time of life. The plain question is, an't it a pity that this state of things should continue. How much better would it be for the gentleman to hand over a reasonable amount of tin, and make it all right and comfortable?"

Having delivered this oration, Mr Swiveller abruptly thrust the head of his cane into his mouth.

"Why do you hunt and persecute me, God help me!" said the old man turning to his grandson. "Why do you bring your profligate companions here? How often must I tell you that my life is one of care and self-denial, and that I am poor?"

"How often am I to tell you," returned the other, "that I know better?"

"You have chosen your own path," said the old man. "Follow it. Leave Nell and me to work."

"Nell will be a woman soon," returned the other, "who will forget her brother unless he shows himself sometimes."

"Take care," said the old man with sparkling eyes, "that she does not forget you when you would have her memory keenest. Take care that the day don't come when you walk barefoot, and she rides in a gay carriage of her own."

"You mean when she has your money?" retorted the other. "How like a poor man he talks!"

"And yet," said the old man dropping his voice, "how poor we are, and what a life it is! The cause is a young child's, guiltless of all harm or wrong, but nothing goes well with it! Hope and patience!"

These words were uttered too quietly to reach the ears of the young men. Moments later, the door opened, and the child herself appeared.

CHAPTER 3

She was closely followed by a man of remarkably hard features and forbidding aspect. He was as short as a dwarf. His black eyes were restless and cunning; his mouth and chin were bristly and his complexion was neither clean nor wholesome. What added most to the grotesque expression was the ghastly mirthless smile that constantly revealed the few discoloured fangs yet scattered in his mouth. His dress consisted of a large high-crowned hat, a worn dark suit, a pair of capacious shoes, and a dirty white neckerchief. His hair was grizzled black, cut short and hanging in a frowzy fringe about his ears. His hands were very dirty, his fingernails crooked, long, and yellow.

There was ample time to note these particulars as some moments elapsed before anyone spoke. The child advanced timidly towards her brother and put her hand in his, the dwarf (if we may call him so) glanced keenly at all present, and the curiosity-dealer, who plainly had not expected his uncouth visitor, seemed disconcerted.

"Ah!" said the dwarf, who had been surveying the young man attentively, "that should be your grandson, neighbour!"

"Say rather that he should not be," replied the old man. "But he is."

"And that?" said the dwarf, pointing to Dick Swiveller.

"Some friend of his, as welcome as he," said the old man.

"And that?" inquired the dwarf, pointing straight at me.

"A gentleman good enough to bring Nell home the other night when she lost her way, coming from your house."

The little man turned to the child, but as she was talking to the young man, held his peace, and bent his head to listen.

"Well, Nelly," said the young fellow aloud. "Do they teach you to hate me?"

"No. For shame. Oh, no!" cried the child.

"To love me, perhaps?" pursued her brother.

"To do neither," she returned. "They never talk to me of you."

"I believe you there," he said, darting a bitter look at the grandfather.

"But I love you dearly, Fred," said the child.

"No doubt!"

"I do indeed, and always will," the child repeated with great emotion, "but if you would stop vexing him, then I could love you more."

"I see!" said the young man, as he stooped carelessly over the child. Having kissed her, he pushed her away. "There, away now you have said your lesson. We part good friends."

He watched her until she had gained her room and closed the door. He then turned to the dwarf, saying abruptly, "Harkee, Mr Quilp. You have some influence with my grandfather there."

"Some," said Mr Quilp emphatically.

"And are in a few of his mysteries and secrets."

"A few," replied Quilp, with equal dryness.

"Then tell him once for all, that I will come and go from this place as often as I like, so long as Nell is here, and that if he wants to be quit of me, he must first be quit of her. He'll tell you that I care no more for Nell, than I do for him. I *will* see her when I please. I came here today to remind her, and I'll come again fifty times with the same object. I said I would stay till I had gained it. I have done so, and now my visit's ended. Come, Dick."

Mr Swiveller cast himself upon his friend's track, and vanished also.

"Humph!" said the dwarf with a sour look and a shrug of his shoulders, "so much for dear relations. Thank God I acknowledge none."

"What would you have me do?" the old man retorted in a kind of helpless desperation. "It is easy to talk and sneer."

"What would I do if I was in your case?" said the dwarf.

"Something violent, no doubt."

"You're right there," returned the little man, highly gratified by the compliment. "Ask Mrs Quilp, pretty Mrs Quilp, obedient, timid, loving Mrs Quilp. But that reminds me – I have left her alone, and she will be anxious till I return. Oh! Well-trained Mrs Quilp."

The creature rubbed his hands slowly round, and round again.

14

"Here," he said, sidling up to the old man as he spoke. "I brought it myself for fear of accidents, as, being in gold, it was too heavy for Nell to carry. She will have to get used to such weights though, for she will carry them when you are dead."

"Heaven send she may! I hope so," said the old man with a groan.

"Hope so!" echoed the dwarf, approaching close to his ear. "Neighbour, I wish I knew where you invested all this. But you keep your secret close."

"My secret!" said the other with a haggard look. "Yes, you're right – I – I – keep it close – very close."

He said no more, but taking the money turned away with a slow, uncertain step. The dwarf watched him sharply, while he locked it in an iron safe. After musing for a short space, he prepared to take his leave, observing that unless he was quick, Mrs Quilp would certainly be in fits on his return.

"And so, neighbour," he added, "I'll head for home, leaving my love for Nelly and hoping she may never lose her way again." With that he bowed and leered at me, and with a keen glance around, went his way.

The old man begged me to remain and I yielded to his persuasions, and sat, pretending to examine some curious miniatures he placed before me. I needed no persuasion, for my curiosity was not diminished now.

Nell joined us with some needlework and sat by the old man's side. It was pleasant to observe the fresh flowers in the room, the breath of freshness and youth which seemed to rustle through the old dull house and hover round the child. It was curious, but not so pleasant, to turn from the beauty and grace of the girl, to the stooping figure and care-worn face of the old man. As he grew weaker, what would become of this lonely little creature? Poor protector as he was, what would be her fate if he died?

The old man almost answered my thoughts, as he laid his hand on hers, and spoke aloud.

"I'll be of better cheer, Nell," he said; "there must be good fortune in store for thee!"

She looked cheerfully into his face, but made no answer.

"When I think," said he, "of the years that thou has lived with me; of my monotonous existence, with no childish pleasures; of the solitude in which thou hast lived apart; I sometimes fear I have dealt hardly by thee, Nell."

"Grandfather!" cried the child in unfeigned surprise.

15

"Not on purpose," said he. "I always look forward to when you will be able to mix among the gayest and prettiest, and take thy station with the best. But I still look forward, Nell, and if I should be forced to leave thee, meanwhile, how have I fitted thee for struggles with the world? Hark! I hear Kit outside. Go to him, Nell, go to him."

She rose, and put her arms about the old man's neck, then left him and hurried away – but quickly, to hide her falling tears.

"A word in your ear, sir," said the old man in a hurried whisper. "Your words the other night have made me uneasy and I can only plead that I have done all for the best and that I hope to triumph yet. All is for her sake. I have borne great poverty myself, and would spare her those particular sufferings. I would spare her the miseries that brought her mother, my own dear child, to an early grave. I would leave her – not with resources that could be easily spent or squandered away, but placed beyond the reach of want forever. She shall have no pittance, but a fortune. Hush! I can say no more than that! She is here again!"

The eagerness with which all this was poured into my ear led me to suppose that he was a wealthy man. I wondered if he were one of those miserable wretches who, having succeeded in amassing great riches, was constantly tortured by the dread of poverty, and beset by fears of loss and ruin. Many things he had said made me think this way, and at length I concluded that beyond all doubt he was one of this unhappy race.

The child came directly, and prepared to give Kit a writing lesson, of which it seemed he had a couple every week, to the great mirth and enjoyment both of himself and his instructress. From the very first moment of holding the pen, he began to wallow in blots. At every fresh mistake, there was a fresh burst of merriment from the child and a louder and not less hearty laugh from poor Kit himself, but there was all the way through, a gentle wish on her part to teach, and an anxious desire on his to learn. Evening passed and night came on, the old man again grew restless and impatient, leaving the house secretly at the same hour as before. The child was again left alone within its gloomy walls.

And now that I have introduced these people, I shall now detach myself, and leave those with prominent and necessary parts to speak and act for themselves.

CHAPTER 4

Mr and Mrs Quilp resided on Tower Hill, where Mrs Quilp was left to pine the absence of her lord, when he left her on business.

Mr Daniel Quilp could scarcely be said to be of any particular trade, though his pursuits were diversified. He collected the rents of whole colonies of filthy streets and alleys by the waterside, advanced money to the seamen of merchant vessels, and smoked his smuggled cigars under the very nose of the Custom House. On the Surrey side of the river was a small rat-infested yard called "Quilp's Wharf," in which were a little wooden counting house, a few fragments of rusty anchors, several large iron rings, piles of rotten wood, and two or three heaps of old sheet copper, crumpled, and battered. On Quilp's Wharf, Daniel Quilp was a ship-breaker, yet by these appearances he was either a ship-breaker on a very small scale, or he broke his ships up very small indeed. Its only human occupant was an amphibious boy in a canvas suit, who either threw stones into the mud when the tide was out, or stood gazing at the bustle of the river at high-water.

The dwarf's lodging on Tower hill comprised, besides accommodation for himself and Mrs Quilp, a small sleeping-closet for that lady's mother. Over nobody had he such complete ascendance as Mrs Quilp herself – a pretty mild-spoken, blue-eyed woman, who having married the dwarf in one of those strange infatuations of which there are many examples, paid penance for her folly, every day of her life.

Mrs Quilp had company – there were present some half-dozen ladies of the neighbourhood who had happened to drop in one after another, just about tea-time. The ladies felt inclined to talk and linger, especially when fresh butter, new bread, shrimps, and watercress were put on the table.

A stout lady opened the proceedings by inquiring how Mr Quilp was; whereunto Mr Quilp's wife's mother replied sharply, "Oh! He was well enough – ill weeds were sure to thrive." The ladies sighed, shook their heads gravely, and looked at Mrs Quilp as a martyr.

Poor Mrs Quilp, looked helplessly from one to another, coloured, smiled, and shook her head doubtfully. This was the signal for a general clamour, which beginning in a low murmur gradually swelled into a great noise. The noise was at its height, and half the company had raised their voices into a perfect shriek in order to be heard, when Mrs Quilp's mother Mrs Jiniwin suddenly changed colour and shook her forefinger stealthily, as if exhorting them to silence. Then, they realized Daniel Quilp was in the room, looking on and listening.

"Go on, ladies, go on," said Daniel. "Mrs Quilp, pray ask the ladies to stop to supper, and have a couple of lobsters and something light and palatable."

"I – I – didn't ask them to tea, Quilp," stammered his wife.

"These accidental parties are always the pleasantest," said the dwarf, rubbing his hands. "What! Not going, ladies, surely!"

His fair enemies tossed their heads slightly as they sought their respective bonnets and shawls, but left all verbal contention to Mrs Jiniwin.

"And why not stop to supper, Quilp," said the old lady, "if my daughter had a mind? There's nothing dishonest or wrong in a supper, I hope?"

"Surely not," returned the dwarf.

"My daughter's your wife, Mr Quilp, certainly," said the old lady.

"So she is, certainly," observed the dwarf.

"And she has a right to do as she likes, I hope, Quilp," said the old lady trembling.

"Hope she has!" he replied. "Oh! Don't you know she has?"

"I know she ought to have, Quilp, and would have, if she was of my way of thinking."

"Why an't you of your mother's way of thinking, my dear?" said the dwarf, turning round and addressing his wife, "why don't you always imitate your mother, my dear? She's the ornament of her sex – your father said so every day of his life. I am sure he did."

The old lady gave a gasp. Quilp resumed, with the same malice and sarcasm. "You look ill, Mrs Jiniwin; I know you have been exciting yourself too much – talking perhaps, for it is your weakness. Go to bed. Do go to bed."

"I shall go when I please, Quilp, and not before."

"But please go now," said the dwarf.

The old woman looked angrily at him, but retreated and suffered him to shut the door upon her and bolt her out among the guests, who were by this time crowding downstairs. The little man planted himself before his trembling wife. He looked steadily at her without speaking.

"Mrs Quilp," he said at last.

18

"Yes, Quilp," she replied meekly.

"If ever you listen to these beldames again, I'll bite you."

With this laconic threat, which he accompanied with a snarl that gave him the appearance of being particularly in earnest, Mr Quilp bade her clear the teaboard away, and bring the rum. He then settled himself in an armchair with his little legs on the table.

"Now, Mrs Quilp," he said. "I feel in a smoking mood, and shall probably blaze away all night. But sit where you are, if you please, in case I want you."

His wife could only say, "Yes, Quilp," and the small lord of the creation took his first cigar and mixed his first glass of grog. The sun went down and the stars peeped out and still Mr Quilp went on smoking and drinking in the same position, and staring out of window with the dog-like smile always on his face, save when Mrs Quilp made some involuntary movement of restlessness or fatigue; and then it expanded into a grin of delight.

CHAPTER 5

At length day broke, and poor Mrs Quilp, shivering with the cold of early morning and harassed by fatigue and want of sleep, was still sitting patiently on her chair, looking up at intervals in mute appeal to the compassion and clemency of her lord. But it was not until the sun had some time risen, and the activity and noise of city day were rife in the street, that he deigned to recognize her presence. He might not have done so even then, but for certain impatient tapping at the door.

"Why dear me!" he said looking round with a malicious grin, "it's day. Open the door, sweet Mrs Quilp!"

His obedient wife withdrew the bolt, and her lady mother entered. Mrs Jiniwin stopped short, in some embarrassment.

Nothing escaped the ugly little man, and he perfectly understood what passed in the old lady's mind. He bade her good morning.

"Why, Betsy," said the old woman, "you haven't been – "

"Sitting up all night?" said Quilp, giving the end of the sentence. "Yes she has!"

"All night?" cried Mrs Jiniwin.

"Ay, all night. Is the dear old lady deaf?" said Quilp, with a smile. "Who says man and wife are bad company? The time has flown."

"You're a brute!" exclaimed Mrs Jiniwin.

"Come come," said Quilp, wilfully misunderstanding her. "You mustn't call her names. She's married now, you know. Bless you for a dear old lady. Here's to your health!"

"I am much obliged to you," returned the old woman, struggling not to shake her matronly fist at her son-in-law.

"Grateful soul!" cried the dwarf. "Mrs Quilp."

"Yes, Quilp," said the timid sufferer.

"Help your mother to get breakfast, Mrs Quilp. I am going to the wharf this morning – so be quick."

Mr Quilp withdrew to the adjoining room, and proceeded to smear his face with a damp grimy towel. But, still he often stopped to listen for any conversation in the next room, of which he might be the theme.

"Ah!" he said after a short effort of attention, "I'm a little hunchy villain and a monster, am I, Mrs Jiniwin? Oh!"

The pleasure of this discovery called up the old dog-like smile. When he had quite done with washing, he shook himself in a dog-like manner, and rejoined the ladies.

After his breakfast, Mr Quilp left them reduced to a very obedient and humbled state, and betook himself to the riverside, where he took boat for Quilp's wharf.

It was flood tide when he sat down in the ferry. On either hand were long black tiers of colliers; between them vessels slowly working out of harbour with sails glistening in the sun. The water and all upon it was in active motion, dancing and buoyant; while the old grey Tower and piles of building on the shore, with many a church-spire shooting up, looked coldly on.

Daniel Quilp, not much affected by a bright morning, was put ashore by the wharf. The first object to present itself to his view was a pair of very imperfectly shod feet as the boy, having a natural taste for tumbling, was now standing on his head and contemplating the river from this position. He was speedily brought on his heels by the sound of his master's voice, and as soon as his head was in its right position, Mr Quilp "punched it" for him.

"You let me alone," said the boy, parrying Quilp's hand with both his elbows alternately.

"You dog," snarled Quilp, "I'll beat you with an iron rod if you talk to me – I will."

With these threats he clenched his hand again, and dextrously gave the boy's head three or four hard knocks. He then left off. "Now, stand still," said Quilp. "I won't do it again, because I've done it as often as I want. Here. Take the key."

"Why don't you hit one of your size?" said the boy, approaching very slowly.

"Where is there one of my size?" returned Quilp. "Take the key, or I'll brain you with it. Now, open the counting house."

The boy sulkily complied, muttering. Here it may be remarked, that between this boy and the dwarf there existed a strange kind of mutual liking. Quilp would certainly suffer nobody to contradict him but the boy, and the boy would never have submitted to be knocked about by anybody but Quilp.

"Now," said Quilp, passing into the counting house, "you mind the wharf."

It was a dirty little box, the counting house, with nothing in it but an old ricketty desk and two stools, a hat-peg, an ancient almanack, an ink stand with no ink and the stump of one pen, and an eight-day clock which hadn't gone for eighteen years at least. Daniel Quilp pulled his hat over his brows, climbed on to the desk, and stretching his short length upon it went to sleep, intending, no doubt, to make up for the lack of last night's sleep.

He had not been asleep a quarter of an hour when the boy opened the door and thrust in his head. Quilp started up directly.

"Here's somebody for you," said the boy.

"Who?"

"I don't know."

"Ask!" said Quilp.

Not caring to venture in again, the boy discreetly sent in the cause of the interruption, who now presented herself at the door.

"What, Nelly!" cried Quilp.

"Yes," said the child, hesitating at the door, for the dwarf just roused, was something fearful to behold. "It's only me, sir."

21

"Come in," said Quilp, without getting off the desk. "Come in. Stay. Just look out into the yard, and see whether the boy's standing on his head."

"No, sir," replied Nell. "He's on his feet."

"You're sure?" said Quilp. "Well. Come in and shut the door. What's your message, Nelly?"

The child handed him a letter. Mr Quilp turned over a little more on his side and rested his chin on his hand, then proceeded to read.

CHAPTER 6

Little Nell stood timidly by, her eyes raised to Mr Quilp as he read the letter.

That Mr Quilp was perplexed by the contents of the letter, was sufficiently obvious. Before he had got through the first few lines he opened his eyes very widely and scratched his head and at the conclusion he gave a long dismal whistle of dismay. After folding and laying it down beside him, he bit the nails of all his ten fingers, then taking it up sharply, read it again. The second perusal seemed as unsatisfactory as the first.

"Well, Nelly!" he said at length, in a voice, and with a suddenness, which made the child start. "Do you know what's inside this?"

"No, sir!"

"Are you quite sure, upon your soul?"

"Quite sure, sir."

"Well!" muttered Quilp at her earnest look. "I believe you. Humph! Gone already? Gone in twenty-four hours! What the devil has he done with it, that's the mystery!"

This reflection set him scratching his head once more. When the child looked up again he was regarding her with extraordinary favour.

"You look very pretty today, Nelly. Are you tired, Nelly?"

"No, sir. I'm in a hurry to get back, for he will be anxious."

"There's no hurry, little Nell," said Quilp. "How should you like to be my number two, Nelly?"

"To be what, sir?"

"My number two, my second, my Mrs Quilp," said the dwarf.

The child looked frightened, but seemed not to understand him. Mr Quilp hastened to make his meaning more clear.

"To be Mrs Quilp the second, when Mrs Quilp the first is dead, sweet Nell," said Quilp, wrinkling up his eyes and luring her towards him with his bent forefinger, "to be my wife, my little cherry-cheeked, red-lipped wife. Say that Mrs Quilp lives five years, or only four, you'll be just the proper age for me. Ha ha! Be a very good girl, Nelly, and see if one of these days you don't come to be Mrs Quilp of Tower Hill."

The child shrank from him, trembling violently. Mr Quilp, either because frightening anybody gave him huge delight, or because it was pleasant to contemplate the death of Mrs Quilp number one, and the elevation of a new Mrs Quilp, only laughed, pretending not to notice her alarm.

"You shall come with me to Tower Hill and see Mrs Quilp that is," said the dwarf. "She's very fond of you, Nell, though not so fond as I am. You shall come home with me."

"I must go back indeed," said the child. "He told me to return directly I had the answer."

"But you haven't it, Nelly," retorted the dwarf, "and won't have it, until I have been home, so to do your errand, you must go with me." With that, Mr Quilp rolled gradually off the desk until his short legs touched the ground. He then led the way to the wharf outside, where they saw the boy and another young gentleman of about his own stature, rolling in the mud together, locked in a tight embrace, and cuffing each other.

"It's Kit!" cried Nelly, clasping her hands. "He came with me! Oh, pray stop them, Mr Quilp!"

"I'll stop 'em," cried Quilp, grabbing a thick stick, "I'll stop 'em. Now, my boys, fight away. I'll fight you both, both together!"

The dwarf flourished his cudgel, and dancing round the combatants laid about him, now on one and now on the other, always aiming at their heads. The two belligerents soon scrambled to their feet and called for quarter.

"I'll beat you to a pulp," said Quilp, vainly endeavouring to get near either of them for a parting blow. "I'll bruise you until you're copper-coloured, I'll break your faces till you haven't a profile between you."

23

"Well, see if ever I offer to strike anybody again because they say you're an uglier dwarf than can be seen anywheres for a penny, that's all."

"Do you mean to say I'm not, you dog?" returned Quilp.

"No!" retorted the boy.

"Then why fight on my wharf, you villain?" said Quilp.

"Because he said so," replied the boy, pointing to Kit, "not because you an't."

"Why did he say," bawled Kit, "that Miss Nelly was ugly, and that she and my master was obliged to do whatever his master liked? Why did he say that?"

"He said that because he's a fool," said Quilp, with quiet malice about his eyes and mouth. "Here's sixpence for you, Kit. Always speak the truth. Lock the counting house, you dog."

The other boy did as he was told. Then Mr Quilp departed with the child and Kit in a boat, and the boy revenged himself by dancing on his head on the edge of the wharf, while they crossed the river.

There was only Mrs Quilp at home, and she, little expecting the return of her lord, was just settling for a nap. She had barely time to gather her needlework, when he entered, accompanied by the child. Kit was downstairs.

"Here's Nelly Trent, dear Mrs Quilp," said her husband. "She'll sit with you, my soul, while I write a letter."

Mrs Quilp looked tremblingly in her spouse's face wondering what this unusual courtesy might mean, and followed him into the next room.

"Mind what I say," whispered Quilp. "See if you can get out of her anything about her grandfather, or what they do, or how they live. You women talk more freely to one another than you do to us, and you have a soft, mild way with you. Do you hear?"

"Yes, Quilp."

"Go then. What's the matter now?"

"Dear Quilp," faltered his wife. "I love the child – if you could do without making me deceive her – "

The dwarf muttering a terrible oath, looked round as if for some weapon with which to punish his disobedient wife. The submissive little woman hurriedly begged him not to be angry, and promised to do as he asked.

"Worm your way into her secrets," whispered Quilp, pinching her arm.

"I know you can. I'm listening. If you're not sharp enough, I'll creak the door, and woe betide if I have to creak it much. Go!"

Mrs Quilp departed, and her amiable husband ensconced himself behind the partly opened door, and began to listen.

Poor Mrs Quilp was wondering, however, how to begin. The door creaking in a very urgent manner warned her to proceed and the sound of her voice was heard.

"How very often you have come backwards and forwards lately to Mr Quilp, my dear."

"I have said so to grandfather, a hundred times," returned Nell innocently.

"And what does he say?"

"He sighs and seems so sad that it would make you cry. How that door creaks!"

"It often does," returned Mrs Quilp, with an uneasy glance towards it. "But your grandfather – he wasn't always so wretched?"

"Oh, no!" said the child eagerly, "So different! We were once so happy and he so contented! You cannot think what a sad change has fallen on us since."

"I am truly sorry, to hear you speak like this, my dear!" said Mrs Quilp. And she spoke the truth.

"Thank you," returned the child, kissing her cheek. "You are always kind, and it is a pleasure to talk to you. I can speak to no one else about him, but poor Kit. You cannot think how it grieves me sometimes to see him alter so."

"He'll alter again, Nell," said Mrs Quilp, "and be as he was before."

"Oh, if God would only let that come about!" cried the child. "But it is a long time now, since he first began to – I thought I saw that door moving!"

"It's the wind," said Mrs Quilp, faintly. "Began to – "

"To be so thoughtful and dejected, and to forget our old ways," said the child. "I used to read to him by the fireside, and he sat listening. We would talk, he told me about my mother, and how she once looked and spoke just like me when she was young – we were very happy once!"

"Nelly, Nelly!" said the poor woman. "I can't bear to see one as young as you so sorrowful. Pray don't cry."

"I do so very seldom," said Nell, "but I have kept this to myself a long

25

time, and I am not quite well, I think, for I cannot stop the tears. I don't mind telling you my grief, for I know you will not tell anyone."

Mrs Quilp turned away, making no answer.

"Then," said the child, "we often walked in the fields and among the green trees, and when we came home at night, we liked it better for being tired. But now we never have these walks, and though it is the same house it is darker and more gloomy!"

She paused, but though the door creaked more than once, Mrs Quilp said nothing.

"Mind you," said the child, "I think he loves me more every day, and is kinder and more affectionate than he was the day before."

"I am sure he loves you dearly," said Mrs Quilp.

"Indeed he does!" cried Nell, "as dearly as I love him. But I have not told you the greatest change of all, and this you must never breathe to any one. Every night and nearly all night long he is away from home."

"Nelly!"

"Hush!" said the child, laying her finger on her lip and looking round. "When he comes home it's generally just before day. Last night he was very late, and it was quite light. His face was pale, his eyes were bloodshot, and his legs trembled. When I had gone to bed again, I heard him groan. I ran back to him, and heard him say, that he could not bear his life much longer, and if it were not for the child, would wish to die. Oh! What shall I do?"

The child, overpowered by the weight of her sorrows and anxieties, and the sympathy with which her little tale had been received, hid her face, and burst into tears.

A few minutes later Mr Quilp returned, and expressed the utmost surprise to find her in this condition.

"She's tired you see, Mrs Quilp," said the dwarf. "It's a long way from her home to the wharf, and then she was alarmed to see a couple of young scoundrels fighting. It has been too much for her."

Mr Quilp unintentionally helped the speedy recovery of his young visitor, by patting her on the head. The child shrank from his touch and wishing to get beyond his reach, she rose, declaring herself ready to return.

"You should wait, and dine with us," said the dwarf.

"I have been away too long, sir," returned Nell, drying her eyes.

"Well," said Mr Quilp, "off you go then, Nelly. Here's the note. It just says that I shall see him tomorrow or maybe next day, and that I couldn't do that little business for him this morning. Good-bye, Nelly. Here, you sir; take care of her!"

Kit, who appeared at the summons, made no reply to so needless an order, wondering whether Quilp might be the cause of Nelly's tears. He turned about and followed his young mistress, who had by this time taken her leave of Mrs Quilp and departed.

"You're a keen questioner, an't you, Mrs Quilp?" said the dwarf, turning upon her as soon as they were alone.

"What more could I do?" returned his wife mildly.

"What more could you do!" sneered Quilp, "couldn't you have done something less? Couldn't you have done what you had to do?"

"I am very sorry for the child, Quilp," said his wife. "I've led her on to tell her secret when she supposed we were alone, God forgive me."

"You led her on!" said Quilp. "What did I tell you about making me creak the door? It's lucky for you that I've got the clue I want."

Mrs Quilp made no reply. Her husband added with some exultation, "You may thank your fortunate stars – the same stars that made you Mrs Quilp – that I'm upon the old gentleman's track. Let me hear no more about this matter, and don't get anything too nice for dinner, for I shan't be home to it."

So saying, Mr Quilp put his hat on and left, and Mrs Quilp, upset at the part she had just acted, shut herself in her chamber.

CHAPTER 7

Mr Richard Swiveller's apartments were close to Drury Lane, over a tobacconist's shop. His single chamber was always mentioned in a plural number, as in its disengaged times the tobacconist had advertised it as "apartments" for a single gentleman. Mr Swiveller, following up the hint, never failed to speak of it as his rooms or his lodgings, leaving his listeners to imagine suites of lofty halls.

"Fred!" said Mr Swiveller. "Pass the rosy." This, a glass of gin and water.

"Dick!" said the other, returning to his seat, "will you talk seriously for two minutes, if I show you how to make your fortune?"

"You've shown me before," returned Dick, "and nothing has come but empty pockets – "

"You'll tell a different story this time," said Fred, drawing his chair to the table. "You saw my sister Nell?"

"What about her?" returned Dick.

"She's pretty, is she not?"

"Why, certainly," replied Dick. "I must say there is no great likeness between her and you. What of it?"

"I'll tell you," returned his friend. "It's obvious the old man and I will remain at daggers drawn to the end of our lives, and that I can expect nothing from him. It's equally plain that the money will all be hers, is it not?"

"I should say it was," replied Dick.

"Now look here," returned the other, "Nell is nearly fourteen."

"Fine girl of her age, but small," observed Richard Swiveller.

"Be quiet for one minute," returned Trent, fretting at the slight interest the other appeared to take in the conversation. "I'm coming to the point."

"Right," said Dick.

"The girl may, at her age, be easily influenced. If I take her in hand, I will be bound by a very little coaxing and threatening to bend her to my will. So what's to prevent your marrying her?"

Richard Swiveller cried, "What!"

"I say, what's to prevent," repeated the other with a steadiness of manner, the effect of which upon his companion he was well assured by long experience, "your marrying her?"

"And she 'nearly fourteen'!" cried Dick.

"I don't mean now," returned the brother angrily. "Say in two years' time, three, four. Does the old man look like a long-liver?"

"He don't look like it," said Dick shaking his head, "but these old people – there's no trusting them, Fred."

"Look at the worst side then," said Trent, keeping his eyes upon his friend. "Suppose he lives and I persuaded, or if the word sounds more feasible, forced Nell to a secret marriage with you. What do you think would come of that?"

"A family and an annual income of nothing to keep 'em on," said Richard Swiveller after some reflection.

"I tell you, that he lives for her, that he would no more disinherit her for an act of disobedience than he would take me into his favour again. He could not do it."

"It seems improbable certainly," said Dick, musing. "I suppose there's no doubt about his being rich."

"Doubt! Did you hear what he let slip the other day when we were there?"

Vanity, interest, poverty, and every spendthrift consideration urged Dick to look upon the proposal with favour. To these impulses must be added the complete ascendancy that his friend had long held over him.

CHAPTER 8

The child, in her confidence with Mrs Quilp, had barely talked about her worries. It was so very difficult to give anyone not intimately acquainted with the life she led, an adequate sense of its gloom and loneliness. A constant fear of in some way injuring the old man whom she so dearly loved, had restrained her, even in the midst of her heart's overflowing, and made her wary of the main cause of her anxiety and distress.

To see the old man struck down beneath some hidden grief, to mark his wavering state, to be afraid that his mind was wandering; to watch and wait and listen for confirmation of these things day after day, and to know that, whatever happened, they were alone in the world with no one to help or advise – these might have sat heavily on an older breast, but how heavily they sat on the mind of a young child to whom they were ever present!

And yet, to the old man, Nell was still the same. When he could briefly disengage his mind from the phantom that haunted him, there was his young companion with the same smile for him, the same merry laugh, the same love and care that, sinking deep into his soul, seemed to have been there through his whole life. He little knew the troubles deep within her.

She had been happy once. She had gone singing through the dim rooms, and moving with light steps among their dusty treasures. But, now, the chambers were cold and gloomy.

In one of these rooms was a window onto the street, where the child sat, many a long evening, and often far into the night, alone and thoughtful.

She would take her station here, at dusk, and watch the people as they passed in the street, or appeared at the windows of the opposite houses; wondering whether their rooms were as lonesome as hers. She was sorry when the man came to light the lamps in the street – for it made it late, and very dull inside. Then, she would draw in her head to look round the room and see that everything was in its place. If, one night, the old man should come home, and kiss and bless her as usual, and after she had gone to bed and had fallen asleep, he should kill himself and his blood come creeping, on the ground to her own bedroom door! These thoughts were too terrible to dwell upon, and again she would look back to the street. The shops were closing fast, and lights began to shine from the upper windows, as the neighbours went to bed.

When the night had worn away thus far, the child would close the window, and steal softly downstairs. After praying fervently and with many bursting tears for the old man, and the restoration of his peace of mind and the happiness they had once enjoyed, she would lay her head upon the pillow and sob herself to sleep, often starting up again, before daylight came, to listen for the bell.

One night, the third after Nell's interview with Mrs Quilp, the old man, who had been weak and ill all day, said he should not leave home. The child's eyes sparkled, but her joy subsided when she saw again his worn and sickly face.

"Two days," he said, "two whole, clear, days have passed, and there is no reply. What did he tell thee, Nell? That he would see me tomorrow or next day? That was in the note."

"Nothing more," said the child. "Shall I go to him again tomorrow? I can be there and back, before breakfast."

The old man shook his head, and drew her towards him.

"'Twould be of no use, my dear. But if he deserts me, Nell, at this moment – when I should, with his assistance, be recompensed for all the time and money I have lost, and all the agony of mind which makes me what you see, I am ruined. Worse than that – I'll have ruined thee, for whom I ventured all. If we are beggars – !"

"What if we are?" said the child. "Let us be beggars, and be happy."

"Beggars – and happy!" said the old man. "Poor child!"

"Dear grandfather," cried the girl with an energy which shone in her face, "we may beg, or work in open roads or fields, to earn a scanty living, rather than live as we do now."

"Nelly!" said the old man.

"Yes, yes, rather than live as we do now," the child repeated, more earnestly than before. "If you are sorrowful, let me know why and be sorrowful too. If you are poor, let us be poor together; but let me be with you; do not let me see such change and not know why, or I shall break my heart and die. Grandfather, let us leave this sad place tomorrow, and beg our way from door to door."

The old man covered his face with his hands, and hid it in the pillow of the couch on which he lay.

"Let us be beggars," said the child passing an arm round his neck, "I have no fear but we shall have enough, I am sure we shall. Let us walk through country places, and sleep in fields and under trees, and never think of money again, but rest at nights, and have the sun and wind upon our faces in the day, and thank God together! Let us never set foot in dark rooms or melancholy houses, any more, but wander up and down wherever we like to go."

The child's voice was lost in sobs as she dropped upon the old man's neck; nor did she weep alone.

These were not words to be overheard, nor was it a scene for other eyes. And yet other ears and eyes were there, greedily taking in all that passed. Mr Daniel Quilp, who, having entered unseen when the child first placed herself at the old man's side, refrained from interrupting the conversation, and stood looking on with his accustomed grin. Standing, however, was a tiresome attitude for the dwarf, and he being one of those people who make themselves at home, spotted a chair, into which he skipped with uncommon agility. Here he could look on with greater comfort. So, he sat, one leg cocked carelessly over the other. And in this position the old man, who moments later looked that way, finally saw him – to his unbounded astonishment!

The child shrieked on beholding him, wondering if he were real, Daniel Quilp merely nodding twice or thrice. At length, the old man pronounced his name, and inquired how he came there.

31

"Through the door," said Quilp pointing over his shoulder with his thumb. "I'm not quite small enough to get through keyholes. I wish I was. I want to talk with you, and in private. Good-bye, little Nelly."

Nell looked at the old man, who nodded to her, and kissed her.

"Ah!" said the dwarf, smacking his lips, "what a nice kiss that was – just upon the rosy part. What a capital kiss!"

Quilp looked after her with an admiring leer, and when she had closed the door, complimented the old man upon her charms.

"Such a fresh, blooming, modest little bud, neighbour," said Quilp, nursing his short leg; "Such a chubby, rosy, cosy, little Nell!"

The old man forced a smile. It was not lost upon Quilp.

"She's so," he said, speaking very slowly, as if absorbed in the subject, "so small, so compact, so beautifully modelled, and such little feet, and such winning ways – but bless me, you're nervous! Why neighbour, what's the matter?"

"There's burning fever here," groaned the old man, clasping his head with both hands. "And something now and then to which I fear to give a name."

The dwarf said nothing, but watched his companion pace up and down the room. He returned to his seat where he remained, with his head bowed for some time, and then suddenly raising it, said,

"Once, and once for all, have you brought me any money?"

"No!" returned Quilp.

"Then," said the old man, looking up, "the child and I are lost!"

"Neighbour," said Quilp glancing sternly at him, "let me be plain with you, and play a fairer game than when you held all the cards. You have no secret from me now."

The old man looked up, trembling.

"You are surprised," said Quilp. "Well, perhaps that's natural. You have no secret from me now. For now I know, that all that money, all those loans, have found their way to – shall I say the word?"

"Aye!" replied the old man. "Say it, if you will."

"To the gaming table," rejoined Quilp. "Your nightly haunt. This was your precious scheme, was it? The secret, certain source of wealth, your inexhaustible mine of gold, eh?"

"Yes," cried the old man, turning upon him with gleaming eyes, "it was. It is. It will be, till I die."

"That I should have been blinded," said Quilp with contempt, "by a mere shallow gambler!"

"I am no gambler," cried the old man fiercely. "Heaven will witness that I never played for my gain, or love of play. Every piece I staked, I whispered that orphan's name and called on Heaven to bless the venture – which it never did. Whom did it prosper? Men who live by plunder, profligacy, and riot – squandering their gold in propagating vice and evil. My winnings would have been bestowed to the last farthing on a young sinless child whose life they would have sweetened and made happy."

"When did you first begin this mad career?" asked Quilp, his taunting subdued, for a moment, by the old man's grief.

"When did I first begin?" he rejoined, passing his hand across his brow. "When I began to think how little I had saved, how long a time it took to save at all, how short a time I might have at my age to live, and how she would be left to the rough mercies of the world, with barely enough to keep her from the sorrows that wait on poverty; then it was that I began to think about it."

"After you first came to me to get your precious grandson packed off to sea?" said Quilp.

"Shortly after that," replied the old man. "I found no pleasure – I expected none. It has brought me nothing but anxious days and sleepless nights, and loss of health and peace of mind!"

"You lost what money you had laid by, and then came to me. While I thought you were making your fortune, you were making yourself a beggar, eh? Dear me! So, I now hold every security you could scrape together, and a bill of sale upon the – upon the stock and property," said Quilp. He stood up, looking about, as if to be sure that nothing had been taken away. "But did you never win?"

"Never!" groaned the old man. "Never won back my loss!"

"I thought," sneered the dwarf, "that if a man played long enough he was sure to win at last, or, at the worst, not to come off a loser."

"And so he is," cried the old man, suddenly rousing himself, "So he is. I have always known it. I never felt it half so strongly as I feel it now. Quilp, I have dreamed, three nights, of winning the same large sum. I never could dream that dream before, though I have often tried. Do not desert me, now I have this chance. I have no resource but you; give me some help, let me try this one last hope."

The dwarf shrugged his shoulders and shook his head.

"See, Quilp, good tender-hearted Quilp," said the old man, drawing some scraps of paper from his pocket with a trembling hand. "Look at these figures, the result of long calculation, and painful experience. I *must* win. Just a little help once more, a few pounds, but two score pounds, dear Quilp."

"The last advance was seventy," said the dwarf. "Gone overnight."

"I know," answered the old man, "but the time had not come then. Quilp, consider that orphan child! If I were alone, I could die with gladness. But what I have done has been for her. Help me for her sake, I implore you!"

"I have an appointment in the city," said Quilp, looking at his watch with perfect self-possession, "or I should have been glad to have spent half an hour with you while you composed yourself."

"Nay, good Quilp," gasped the old man, catching at his skirts. "You and I have talked together, more than once, of her poor mother's story. Oh spare me the money for this one last hope!"

"I couldn't do it really," said Quilp with unusual politeness, "though I tell you what, I was so deceived by the penurious way in which you lived – "

"To save money for tempting fortune, and to make her triumph greater," cried the old man.

"Yes, yes, I understand that now," said Quilp. "I was going to say, I was so deceived by that, your miserly way, the reputation you had of being rich, and your repeated assurances that you would make of my advances treble and quadruple the interest you paid me, that I'd have advanced you, even now, what you want, on your simple note of hand, if I hadn't unexpectedly become acquainted with your secret way of life."

"Who is it," retorted the old man desperately, "that told you? Come. Let me know the name – the person."

The crafty dwarf stopped short. "Now, who do you think?"

"It was Kit, it must have been the boy; he played the spy, and you tampered with him?" said the old man, desperately.

"Why do you think of him?" said the dwarf in a tone of great commiseration. "Yes, it was Kit. Poor Kit!"

So saying, he nodded in a friendly manner, and left, stopping when he had passed the outer door a little distance, and grinning with extraordinary delight.

"Poor Kit!" muttered Quilp. "I think it was Kit who said I was an uglier dwarf than could be seen anywhere for a penny, wasn't it. Ha! Poor Kit!" And with that he went his way, still chuckling.

CHAPTER 9

Daniel Quilp neither entered nor left the old man's house, unobserved. In the shadow of an archway nearly opposite, there lingered someone.

This patient lounger's eyes were constantly directed towards the window at which the child would sit. Occasionally he glanced at a clock in some neighbouring shop, and then turned his sight once more to the window.

It was clear he didn't want to leave, but at length, he gave up for that night, and scampered off at his utmost speed, not once looking behind him lest he should be tempted back again.

Without slowing, or stopping to take breath, he dashed on through a great many alleys until he arrived in a square paved court. Here he made for a small house and lifted the latch and went in.

"Bless us!" cried a woman turning sharply, "who's that? Oh! It's you, Kit!"

"Yes, mother."

"Why, how tired you look, my dear!" said Mrs Nubbles.

"Old master an't gone out tonight," said Kit; "and so she hasn't been at the window at all." With which words, he sat down by the fire and looked very mournful.

The room in which Kit sat, in this condition, was an extremely poor and homely place, but with that air of comfort about it, which cleanliness and order can always impart. Late as it was, the poor woman was still hard at work, ironing. A young child lay sleeping in a cradle near the fire; and another, a sturdy boy of two or three years old, very wide awake, was sitting bolt upright in a clothes basket.

Kit felt out of temper, but looking at the youngest child, then his other brother, and from him to their mother, who had been at work without complaint since morning, he thought it would be a kinder thing to be good-humoured. So he rocked the cradle with his foot and stoutly determined to make himself agreeable.

"Ah, mother!" said Kit, falling upon bread and meat she had had ready for him, hours before. "What a one you are! There an't many such as you, I know."

"Your beer's down there by the fender, Kit."

"I see," replied her son, taking up the pot, "my love to you, mother."

"Did you just say that your master hadn't gone out tonight?" inquired Mrs Nubbles.

"Yes," said Kit, "worse luck!"

"You should say better luck, I think," returned his mother, "because Miss Nelly won't have been left alone."

"Ah!" said Kit, "I forgot that. I said worse luck, because I've been watching since eight o'clock, and seen nothing of her."

"I wonder what she'd say," cried his mother, stopping in her work, "if she knew that every night, while she's alone at that window, you watch from the open street for fear any harm should come to her, and that you never come home, till you think she's safe in her bed."

"Never mind that," replied Kit, with something like a blush. "She'll never know nothing, and consequently, she'll never say nothing."

Mrs Nubbles ironed away in silence for a minute or two, and coming to the fireplace for another iron, glanced stealthily at Kit while she rubbed it on a board and dusted it. She said nothing until she was back at her work.

"Some day I hope she may know, for I'm sure she would be very grateful to you. It's cruel to keep the dear child shut up there."

"He don't think it's cruel," said Kit, "and don't mean it to be so. I think, mother, that he wouldn't do it for all the gold in the world. I know him better than that."

"Then why does he do it, and why not tell you?" said Mrs Nubbles.

"That I don't know," returned her son. "But it was his getting me away at night and sending me off so much earlier, that first made me curious. Hark! What's that?"

"It's only somebody outside."

"It's somebody crossing over here," said Kit, standing up to listen, "and coming very fast too."

The footsteps drew nearer, the door opened and the child herself, pale and breathless, hurried into the room.

"Miss Nelly! What is the matter?" cried mother and son together.

"I cannot stay long," she returned, "grandfather has been taken very ill. I found him in a fit upon the floor – "

"I'll run for a doctor," said Kit, seizing his hat. "I'll be there directly, I'll – "

"No, no," cried Nell, "there's one there, you're not wanted, you – must never come near us any more!"

"What!" roared Kit.

"Never again," said the child. "Don't ask me why, for I don't know. Pray don't be vexed with me! I have nothing to do with it indeed!"

Kit looked at her with his eyes stretched wide.

"He complains and raves of you," said the child, "I don't know what you have done, but I hope it's nothing very bad."

"I've done?" roared Kit.

"He cries that you're the cause of all his misery," returned the child with tearful eyes. "They say you must not come near him or he will die. You must not return to us. I came to tell you. I thought it better that I should come than somebody quite strange. Oh, Kit, what have you done? You were almost the only friend I had!"

Poor Kit looked at his young mistress, with eyes growing wider, but was perfectly speechless.

"I have brought his money for the week," said the child, looking to the woman and laying it on the table. "And – and – a little more, for he was always good to me. I hope he will do well somewhere else. It grieves me to part like this, but it must be done. Good night!"

Tears streaming down her face, the child hastened to the door, and disappeared as rapidly as she had come.

The poor woman, who had no cause to doubt her son, was staggered that he had not offered one word in his defence. Visions of gallantry, knavery, robbery and the nightly absences from home flocked into her brain and rendered her afraid to question him. She rocked herself upon a chair, wringing her hands and weeping bitterly. Kit remained quite bewildered.

CHAPTER 10

Next morning, the old man was in a raging fever, and lay for many weeks in imminent peril of his life. There was watching enough in the house, now, but it was the watching of strangers.

Yet, in all the hurry and crowding, the child was more alone than ever before – alone in spirit, alone in her devotion to him who was wasting away upon his burning bed and alone in her unfeigned sorrow. Day after day, and night after night, found her still by the pillow of the unconscious sufferer, hearing those repetitions of her name and those anxieties and cares, which were ever uppermost among his feverish wanderings.

The house was no longer theirs. Even the sick chamber seemed occupied on the uncertain tenure of Mr Quilp's favour. The old man's illness had not lasted many days when he took formal possession of the premises and all upon them, in virtue of certain legal powers to that effect, which few understood and none presumed to question. He did this with the assistance of a man of law he brought with him. He also brought with him the boy from the wharf. The dwarf proceeded to establish himself in the house, as an assertion of his claim against all comers; and then set about making his quarters comfortable.

Mr Quilp shut up the shop. He looked out the handsomest and most commodious chair he could possibly find and took up his position in great state. The apartment was far removed from the old man's chamber, but Mr Quilp deemed it prudent, as a precaution against infection from fever, to smoke, without cessation. These arrangements completed, Mr Quilp looked round him with chuckling satisfaction.

His legal friend, whose melodious name was Brass, could not sit easy in his chair. It was very hard, angular, slippery, and sloping. But he was a creature of Mr Quilp's and had a thousand reasons for conciliating his good opinion, so he smiled and nodded his acquiescence with the best grace he could assume.

This Brass was an attorney of no very good repute. He had a cringing manner but a very harsh voice.

"Shall we stop here long, Mr Quilp?" he inquired.

"We must stop, I suppose, till the old gentleman upstairs is dead," returned Quilp.

"He, he, he!" laughed Mr Brass, "oh! Very good!"

The boy from the dock stood at the door. "Here's the gal a comin' down."

"The what, you dog?" said Quilp.

"The gal," returned the boy. "Are you deaf?"

"Oh!" said Quilp, "you and I will have such a settling presently. There's such a bruising in store for you, my friend! Aha! Nelly! How is he now, my duck of diamonds?"

"He's very bad," replied the weeping child.

"What a pretty little Nell!" cried Quilp.

"Oh beautiful, sir, beautiful indeed," said Brass. "Quite charming."

"Has she come to sit upon Quilp's knee," said the dwarf, in what he meant to be a soothing tone, "or is she going to bed in her own little room? Which is poor Nelly going to do?"

"What a remarkable pleasant way he has with children!" muttered Brass.

"I'm not going to stay at all," faltered Nell. "I want a few things, and then I – I – won't come down here any more."

"And a very nice little room it is!" said the dwarf, looking into it as the child entered. "Quite a bower! You're sure you're not going to use it, Nelly?"

"Never," replied the child, hurrying away, with a few clothes.

"She's very sensitive," said Quilp, looking after her. "The bedstead is much about my size. I think I shall make it *my* little room."

The dwarf threw himself on his back upon the bed with his pipe in his mouth, and then kicked up his legs, smoking violently. Mr Quilp determined to use it, both as a sleeping place by night and as a kind of Divan by day, so he remained where he was, and smoked his pipe out.

For the next few days, with the assistance of Mr Brass, a minute inventory of all the goods in the place was made. His avarice and caution being, now, thoroughly awakened, however, Quilp was never absent from the house at night.

Nell shrank timidly from all the dwarf's advances towards conversation, and fled from the very sound of his voice. One night, she had stolen to her usual window, and was sitting there when she thought she heard her name called. Looking out, she saw Kit.

"Miss Nell!" said the boy in a low voice.

"Yes," replied the child, wondering whether she should speak with the supposed culprit. "What do you want?"

"I have wanted to speak to you, for a while," the boy replied, "but the people below wouldn't let me see you. You don't believe – I hope you don't – that I deserve to be cast off as I have been, do you, miss?"

"I must believe it," returned the child. "Or why would grandfather have been so angry with you?"

"I don't know," replied Kit. "I'm sure I never deserved it from him. I can say that, with a true and honest heart, anyway."

"I didn't know you came," said the child.

"Miss Nell," cried the boy coming under the window, and speaking in a lower tone, "there are new masters downstairs. It's a change. And it will be for him when he gets better,"

" – If he ever does," added the child, unable to restrain her tears.

"Oh, he'll do that," said Kit. "I'm sure he will. You mustn't be cast down, Miss Nell!"

These few words of encouragement affected the child, and for the moment she wept the more.

"They tell me I must not even mention your name to him for a long, long time," rejoined the child. "We shall be very poor. We shall scarcely have bread to eat."

"If he would just believe that I've been faithful to him, perhaps he mightn't – "

Here Kit faltered so long that the child entreated him to speak out, and quickly, for it was time to shut the window.

"Perhaps he mightn't think it over venturesome of me to say – well, to say this," cried Kit with sudden boldness. "Your home is gone. Mother and I have a poor one, but better than this; and why not come there, till he's had time to look, and find better!"

The child did not speak. Kit, in the relief of having made his proposition, found his tongue loosened. "It might be small, but it's clean. Mother says it would be just the thing for you, and so it would, and you'd have her to wait upon you both, and me to run errands. We don't mean money, bless you; you're not to think of that! Will you try him, Miss Nell? Do try to make him come, and ask him what I have done. Will you only promise that, Miss Nell?"

40

Before the child could reply, the street-door opened, and Mr Brass thrusting out his night-capped head called in a surly voice, "Who's there!"

Kit immediately glided away, and Nell, closing the window softly, drew back into the room.

Moments later, Mr Quilp, also embellished with a night-cap, emerged from the same door and looked carefully up and down the street. Finding nobody in sight, he returned into the house. The child listened from the staircase and heard him say that he would delay no longer but take immediate steps for disposing of the property and returning to his own peaceful roof.

CHAPTER 11

At length, the crisis passed, and the old man began to mend. By slow degrees his consciousness returned; but his mind was weakened and the functions impaired. He was patient, and quiet; often sat brooding for a long space; was easily amused, even by a sun-beam on the wall, and appeared indeed to have lost all count of time. He would sit, for hours, with Nell's small hand in his, playing with the fingers and stopping sometimes to smooth her hair or kiss her brow. When he saw that tears were glistening in her eyes, he would look, amazed, about him for the cause, and forget his wonder even while he looked.

He sat in his easy chair one day, and Nell upon a stool beside him, when Quilp arrived at the door and inquired if he might enter.

"I'm glad to see you well again at last, neighbour," said the dwarf, sitting down. "You're quite strong now?"

"Yes," said the old man feebly, "yes."

"I don't want to hurry you, you know, neighbour," said the dwarf, "but, as soon as you can make arrangements, the better."

"Surely," said the old man. "The better for all parties."

"You see," pursued Quilp after a short pause. "Once the goods are gone, this house will be uninhabitable. I have sold the things. When shall they be moved? There's no hurry – shall we say this afternoon?"

"Say Friday morning," returned the old man.

"Very good," said the dwarf. "So be it – with the understanding that I can't go beyond that day, neighbour, on any account."

"Good," returned the old man. "I shall remember it."

All that day, and all the next, the old man wandered up and down the house and into and out of the various rooms, as if to bid them adieu, but he never referred to the interview of the morning or the necessity of finding some other shelter. He had a vague idea that the child was desolate and needed help; for he often drew her to him, bidding her be of good cheer; but he seemed unable to contemplate their real position more distinctly, and was still the listless creature that suffering of mind and body had left him.

Thursday arrived, and there was no change. That evening he and the child sat silently together. In a small dull yard below his window, there was a tree, and as the air stirred among its leaves, it threw a rippling shadow on the wall. The old man watched the shadows. The child thought more than once that he was moved, and now he shed tears and besought her to forgive him.

"Forgive you – what?" said Nell. "Oh grandfather, what should I forgive?"

"All that is past, Nell, all that was done in that uneasy dream," returned the old man.

"Do not talk so," said the child. "Let us speak of something else."

"Yes, yes, we will," he rejoined. "And it shall be of what we talked of long ago, or is it weeks, or days? Which is it Nell?"

"I do not understand you," said the child.

"It has come back upon me today, since we have been sitting here. I bless thee for it, Nell! Let us speak softly. Hush! For if they knew our purpose downstairs, they would cry that I was mad and take thee from me. We will not stop here another day. We will go far away from here."

"Yes, let us go," said the child earnestly. "Let us be gone from this place, and never turn back or think of it again. Let us wander barefoot through the world, rather than linger here."

"We will," answered the old man, "we will travel afoot through the fields and woods, and by the side of rivers, and trust ourselves to God. Let us steal away tomorrow morning – early – and leave no trace or track for them to follow by. Poor Nell! Thy cheek is pale, and thy eyes are heavy with watching and weeping for me, but thou wilt be well again, and merry too, when we are far away. Tomorrow morning, dear, we'll turn our faces from this scene of sorrow, and be as free and happy as the birds."

The child's heart beat high with hope and confidence. She had no thought of hunger, or cold, or thirst, or suffering. All she saw was a return of the simple pleasures they had once enjoyed, an escape from the heartless people by whom she had been surrounded in her late time of trial, the restoration of the old man's health and peace, and a life of tranquil happiness. There was no dark tint in the sparkling picture.

The old man had slept, for some hours, soundly in his bed, and she was yet busily engaged in preparing for their flight. There were a few articles of clothing to carry; a staff to support his feeble steps. But now she must visit the old rooms for the last time.

Her own little room, where she had so often knelt down and prayed at night, where she had slept so peacefully, and dreamed such pleasant dreams.

From dreams of rambling through light and sunny places, but with some vague object unattained that ran indistinctly through them all, she awoke to find that it was yet night.

The old man was yet asleep, and as she was unwilling to disturb him, she left him to slumber on, until the sun rose. He was anxious that they should leave without a minute's loss of time, and was soon ready.

The child then took him by the hand, and they trod lightly and cautiously down the stairs, trembling whenever a board creaked, and often stopping to listen.

At last they reached the passage on the ground floor, where the snoring of Mr Quilp and his legal friend sounded more terrible in their ears than the roars of lions. The bolts of the door were rusty, and difficult to unfasten without noise. But the door was locked, and worst of all, the key was gone. Then the child remembered Quilp always locked both the house-doors at night, and kept the keys in his bedroom.

Little Nell slipped off her shoes and gliding through the passageway, passed into her own little chamber.

Here she stood, for a few moments, terrified at the sight of Mr Quilp, who was hanging so far out of bed that he almost seemed to be standing on his head, and who was gasping and growling with his mouth wide open. Possessing herself of the key after one hasty glance about the room, she rejoined the old man in safety. They opened the door without noise, and stood in the street.

"Which way?" said the child.

The old man looked, irresolutely and helplessly, first at her, then right and left, then at her again, and shook his head. It was plain that she was thenceforth his guide. The child felt it, but had no misgivings, and putting her hand in his, led him gently away.

The streets were, as yet, almost free from people, the houses and shops were closed, and the healthy air of morning fell like breath from angels, on the sleeping town.

The old man and the child passed on through the glad silence in bright sunlight, full of hope. They were alone together, once again.

Forth from the sleeping city went the two poor adventurers, wandering they knew not whither.

CHAPTER 12

Daniel Quilp of Tower Hill, and Sampson Brass of Bevis Marks in the city of London, slumbered on, unaware of any mischance, until a knocking on the street door, often repeated and gradually mounting to a perfect battery of knocks, caused the said Daniel Quilp to struggle into a horizontal position, wondering at the noise.

As the knocking increased in vigour, Daniel Quilp realised that there might be somebody at the door. He slowly remembered that it was Friday morning, and he had ordered Mrs Quilp to be there early.

Mr Brass was by this time awake also. Seeing that Mr Quilp dressed, he hastened to do the same. While the attorney was thus engaged, the dwarf was groping under the table.

"The key," said the dwarf, looking viciously about him, "the door-key. D'ye know anything of it?"

"How should I know anything of it, sir?" returned Mr Brass.

"How should you?" repeated Quilp with a sneer. "You're a nice lawyer, an't you? Ugh, you idiot!"

Mr Brass humbly suggested that it must have been forgotten over night, and was, doubtless, at that moment in the keyhole. Mr Quilp, knowing that he had carefully taken it out, was reluctant to admit that this was possible, and therefore went grumbling to the door where, sure enough, he found it.

Now, just as Mr Quilp laid his hand upon the lock, and saw with great astonishment that the fastenings were undone, the knocking came again with the most irritating violence. The dwarf drew back the lock very silently and softly, and throwing open the door, pounced out upon the person on the other side, who had at that moment raised the knocker for another application, and at whom the dwarf ran head first.

Mr Quilp was no sooner in the arms of the individual whom he had taken for his wife than he found himself given two staggering blows on the head, and two more, of the same quality, in the chest. He found himself, all flushed and dishevelled, in the middle of the street, with Mr Richard Swiveller.

"I thought it was somebody else," said Quilp, "why didn't you say who you were? It was you that knocked?"

"Yes," replied Dick. "That lady had begun when I came, but she knocked too soft, so I relieved her." He pointed towards Mrs Quilp, who stood trembling at a little distance.

"Humph!" muttered the dwarf, darting an angry look at his wife, "I thought it was your fault! You came for some purpose, I suppose," said Quilp. "What do you want?"

"I want to know how the old gentleman is," rejoined Mr Swiveller, "and to hear from Nell herself, with whom I should like to have a little talk. I'm a friend of the family, sir."

"You'd better walk in then," said the dwarf. "Go on, sir. Now, Mrs Quilp, after you, ma'am. Please go upstairs, to Nelly's room, and tell her that she's wanted."

"You seem to make yourself at home here," said Dick, who was unacquainted with Mr Quilp's authority.

"I *am* at home, young gentleman," returned the dwarf.

Dick was pondering these words, when Mrs Quilp came hurrying downstairs, declaring that the rooms above were empty.

"Empty, you fool!" said the dwarf.

"I give you my word, Quilp," answered his trembling wife.

"And that," said Mr Brass, clapping his hands, "explains the mystery of the key!"

Quilp frowned at him, at his wife, and at Richard Swiveller; and then hurried upstairs, whence he soon hurried down again, confirming the report already made.

"It's strange," he said, glancing at Swiveller, "not to communicate with me who am such a close and intimate friend! He'll write to me no doubt, or he'll bid Nelly write. Nelly's very fond of me. We knew that they'd go today, but not that they'd go so early. But they have their reasons."

"Where in the devil's name are they gone?" wondered Dick.

Quilp shook his head, and pursed up his lips, almost implying that he knew very well, but was not at liberty to say.

Having only heard from Frederick Trent, late the previous night, of the old man's illness, Dick had come upon a visit of condolence and inquiry to Nell. And here, when he had been thinking of all kinds of graceful and insinuating approaches – here were Nell, the old man, and all the money gone, decamped he knew not whither, as if with fore-knowledge of the scheme and a resolution to defeat it at the very start.

In his secret heart, Daniel Quilp was both surprised and troubled by the flight that had been made. It had not escaped his keen eye that certain articles of clothing were also gone. He was not overly concerned about the two fugitives – his uneasiness arose from a misgiving that the old man had some secret store of money which he had not suspected; and the idea of its escaping his clutches, overwhelmed him with mortification.

It was some consolation to him to find that Richard Swiveller was, for different reasons, evidently irritated and disappointed by the same cause. It was plain, thought the dwarf, that he had come there, on behalf of his friend, to cajole or frighten the old man out of some of his so-called wealth.

"Well," said Dick, with a blank look, "there's no point my staying here."

"Not the least in the world," rejoined the dwarf.

"You'll mention that I called, perhaps?" said Dick. "And please say, that I came to remove, with the rake of friendship, the seeds of mutual violence, and to sow in their place, the germs of social harmony."

Quilp nodded.

"Will you be kind enough to add, sir," said Dick, producing a very small limp card, "that *that* is my address, and that I am to be found at home every morning. Good morning."

Quilp bade him good day.

By this time, vans had arrived to remove the goods, and divers strong men in caps were balancing chests of drawers and other trifles of that nature upon their heads. Quilp also went to work with surprising vigour; hustling people like an evil spirit. His presence diffused such alacrity among the persons employed that, in a few hours, the house was empty.

Seated, like an African chief on a piece of old matting, the dwarf spotted a boy prying in at the outer door. Assured that it was Kit, Mr Quilp called to him. Kit came in, demanding what he wanted.

"Come here, you sir," said the dwarf. "Well, so your old master and young mistress have gone?"

"Where?" rejoined Kit, looking round.

"You mean you don't know where?" answered Quilp sharply.

"I don't know," said Kit.

"Come," retorted Quilp, "no more of this! You don't know they went by stealth, as soon as it was light this morning?"

"No," said the boy, in evident surprise.

"You don't know that?" cried Quilp. "I know you were hanging about the house the other night, like a thief. Weren't you told, then?"

"No," replied the boy.

"What were you talking about?" said Quilp.

Kit, who knew no particular reason why he should keep the matter secret now, told the dwarf the proposal he had made.

"Oh!" said the dwarf after a little consideration. "Then, I think they'll come to you yet. And when they do, tell me; d'ye hear? Tell me, and I'll give you something. I want to do 'em a kindness, and I can't do that unless I know where they are."

Kit might have given a disagreeable answer, but instead took himself home. There he sat and considered ways to earn a shilling.

CHAPTER 13

Kit persuaded himself that the old house was in his way, and that he needed to pass it.

There was no need for caution this time. The place was entirely deserted. A rusty padlock was fastened on the door, and the crooked holes cut in the closed shutters below, were black with the darkness of the inside. Some of the glass in the window he had so often watched had been broken in the rough hurry of the morning. A group of urchins had taken possession of the doorsteps; some plied the knocker and listened with delighted dread to the hollow sounds it made. Standing alone in the midst of the business and bustle of the street, the house looked a picture of cold desolation. Kit, remembering the cheerful fire that burned there on a winter's night and the no less cheerful laugh that made the small room ring, turned quite mournfully away.

He instead turned his thoughts to making his family more comfortable if he could.

So many gentlemen on horseback were riding up and down, but how few of them wanted their horses held! Kit walked about, lingering as some rider slackened his horse's pace and looked about him. But on they all went, one after another, and there was not a penny stirring. "I wonder," thought the boy, "if one of these gentlemen knew there was nothing in the cupboard at home, whether he'd stop on purpose, and make believe that he wanted to call somewhere, that I might earn a trifle?"

He was quite tired out with pacing the streets, to say nothing of repeated disappointments, and was sitting down upon a step to rest, when there approached a little clattering four-wheeled chaise drawn by a little obstinate-looking rough-coated pony, driven by a little fat placid-faced old gentleman. Beside the little old gentleman sat a little old lady, plump and placid like himself. If the old gentleman remonstrated by shaking the reins, the pony replied by shaking his head.

As they passed where he sat, Kit looked so wistfully at the trio that the old gentleman looked at him. Kit rose and put his hand to his hat. The old gentleman intimated to the pony that he wished to stop, to which proposal the pony graciously acceded.

"I'm sorry you stopped, sir," said Kit. "I only meant did you want your horse minded."

"I'm getting down in the next street," returned the old gentleman. "If you would like to follow, you may have the job."

Kit thanked him, and joyfully obeyed. The pony ran off at a sharp angle to inspect a lamp post opposite, and then went off at a tangent to another lamp post on the other side. He then stopped, apparently absorbed in meditation.

"Will you go on, sir," said the old gentleman, gravely, "or are we to wait till it's too late for our appointment?"

48

The pony remained immoveable.

"Oh you naughty Whisker," said the old lady. "Fie upon you! I'm ashamed of such conduct."

The pony was touched by this appeal to his feelings, for he trotted on directly, and didn't stop until he came to a door whereon was a brass-plate with the words "Witherden – Notary". Here the old gentleman got out and helped out the old lady.

They went, as it was easy to tell from the sound of their voices, into the front parlour, which seemed to be a kind of office. The day being warm, the windows were wide open. It was easy to hear through the Venetian blinds all that passed inside.

"I have had many a gentleman articled to me, ma'am," said Mr Witherden, the Notary. "Some are now rolling in riches, unmindful of their old companion, ma'am, but there was never one among the number, ma'am, of whom I augured such bright things as I do of your only son."

"Oh dear!" said the old lady. "How happy you make us when you tell us that, to be sure!"

"Anything that Mr Witherden can say of me," observed a small quiet voice, "I can say, with interest, of him, I am sure."

"It's a happy circumstance," said the Notary, "to happen too upon his eight-and-twentieth birthday, and I hope I know how to appreciate it. I trust, Mr Garland, my dear sir, that we may mutually congratulate each other upon this auspicious occasion."

To this the old gentleman replied that he felt assured they might.

"Marrying as his mother and I did, late in life, sir, after waiting for a great many years, and then being blessed with one child who has always been dutiful and affectionate – why, it's a source of great happiness to us both, sir."

"Of course it is, I have no doubt of it," returned the Notary. "It's the contemplation of this sort of thing, that makes me deplore my fate in being a bachelor."

They came out a short time later; Mr Witherden, who was short, chubby, fresh-coloured, leading the old lady with extreme politeness, and the father and son following them, arm in arm. Mr Abel bore a wonderful resemblance to his father in face and figure. In the neatness of the dress, and even in the clubfoot, he and the old gentleman were alike.

49

Having seen the old lady safely in her seat, and assisted in the arrangement of her cloak, Mr Abel got into a little box behind, and smiled at everybody present. The old gentleman, taking his seat and the reins, put his hand in his pocket to find a sixpence for Kit.

He had no sixpence, neither had the old lady, nor anyone else. The old gentleman thought a shilling too much, but there was no shop nearby to get change at, so he gave it to the boy.

"There," he said jokingly, "I'm coming here again next Monday at the same time, and mind you're here, my lad, to work it out."

"Thank you, sir," said Kit. "I'll be sure to be here."

He was quite serious, but they all laughed heartily at his saying so. As the pony, convinced that he was going home, trotted away pretty nimbly, Kit had no time to justify himself, and went his way also. Having expended his treasure in such purchases as he knew would be most acceptable at home, he hastened back as fast as he could, so elated with his success and great good fortune, that he more than half expected Nell and the old man to have arrived before him.

CHAPTER 14

The two pilgrims, often pressing each other's hands, or exchanging a smile, pursued their way in silence. Bright and happy as it was, there was something solemn in the long, deserted streets. All was still at that early hour.

Before long straggling carts and coaches began rumbling by. The wonder was, at first, to see a tradesman's window open, but it was a rare thing soon to see one closed. Smoke rose slowly from the chimneys, and sashes were thrown up to let in air, and doors were opened, and servant girls scattered brown clouds of dust into the eyes of shrinking passengers.

They then came upon the haunts of commerce, where business was already rife. The old man looked about him, for these were places that he hoped to shun. Finger on his lip, he drew the child along by narrow and winding ways.

This quarter passed, they came upon a straggling neighbourhood, where the mean houses parcelled off in rooms, and windows patched with rags and paper, told of poverty. The shops sold goods that only poverty could buy, and sellers and buyers were pinched and griped alike.

Damp rotten houses, many to let, many yet building, many half-built and mouldering away – lodgings, where it would be hard to tell which needed pity most, those who let or those who came to take – children, scantily fed and clothed, spread over every street, and sprawling in the dust – scolding mothers, stamping their slipshod feet with noisy threats upon the pavement, mangling-women, washer-women, cobblers, tailors, chandlers, driving their trades in parlours and kitchens and back room and garrets.

At length these streets dwindled away, until there were only small garden patches bordering the road, with many a summerhouse innocent of paint and built of old timber. To these succeeded pert cottages, two and two with plots of ground in front, laid out in angular beds with stiff box borders and narrow paths between. Then came the public houses. Then fields, and then, some houses, one by one, of goodly size with lawns, some even with a lodge where dwelt a porter and his wife. Then came a turnpike; then, a hill, where the traveller might stop, and – looking back at old Saint Paul's looming through the smoke, its cross peeping above the cloud (if the day were clear), and glittering in the sun – he might feel at last that he was clear of London.

Near such a spot as this, the old man and his little guide sat down to rest. She had wisely brought some slices of bread and meat, and here they made their frugal breakfast.

The freshness of the day, the singing of the birds, the beauty of the waving grass, the deep green leaves, the wild flowers, and the thousand exquisite scents and sounds that floated in the air made them very glad.

"Never to return – never to return," muttered the old man, waving his hand towards the city. "Thou and I are free of it now, Nell. They shall never lure us back."

"Are you tired?" said the child, "you don't feel ill from this long walk?"

"I shall never feel ill again, now that we are away," was his reply. "Let us be stirring, Nell. We are too near to stop, and be at rest. Come!"

There was a pool of clear water in the field, in which the child laved her hands and face. She made the old man sit upon the grass, cast the water on him with her hands, and dried it with her dress.

51

"I can do nothing for myself, my darling," said the grandfather; "the time's gone. Don't leave me, Nell. Say that thou'lt not leave me. If I lose thee too, my dear, I must die!"

He laid his head upon her shoulder and moaned piteously. The time had been, and not many days before, when the child would have wept with him. But now she soothed him. He was soon calmed and fell asleep, singing to himself in a low voice, like a little child.

He awoke refreshed, and they continued their journey. The road was pleasant, lying between beautiful pastures and fields of corn. The air came laden with the fragrance it caught upon its way, and the bees hummed their drowsy satisfaction as they floated by.

They were now in the open country; the houses were very few and often miles apart. Occasionally they came upon a cluster of poor cottages, some with a chair or low board put across the open door to keep the scrambling children from the road, others shut up close while all the family were working in the fields. After an interval came a wheelwright's shed; then a thriving farm with sleepy cows lying about the yard, and horses peering over the low wall. There were dull pigs too, turning up the ground in search of dainty food. The farmyard passed, then came the little inn; and the village tradesman's; then the parson's; the church then peeped out modestly from a clump of trees. Then came the trim-hedged fields either side of the open road again.

They slept that night at a small cottage where beds were let to travellers. Next morning they were afoot again, and though jaded at first, and very tired, recovered before long and proceeded briskly forward.

They often stopped to rest, but only for a short space at a time, and still kept on, having had but slight refreshment since the morning.

They trudged forward, more slowly and painfully than they had done yet, for another mile or thereabouts, when they heard the sound of wheels behind them. On looking round they observed an empty cart approaching pretty briskly. The driver stopped his horse and looked at Nell and her grandfather.

"Jump up, master, I'm going your way," he said.

This was a great relief, and to them the jolting cart was a luxurious carriage. Nell had scarcely settled herself on a little heap of straw in one corner, when she fell asleep, for the first time that day.

She woke when the cart stopped, as it was about to turn up a bye-lane.

The driver kindly got down to help her out, and pointing to some trees, said that a town lay there, and that they had better take the path leading through the churchyard. Accordingly, towards this spot, they directed their weary steps.

CHAPTER 15

The sun was setting when they reached the wicket-gate at which the path began. The church was old and grey, with ivy clinging to the walls.

The old man and the child left the gravel path, straying among the tombs; for there the ground was soft, and easy to their tired feet. As they passed behind the church, they heard voices close by.

Two men were seated upon the grass, so busily engaged as to be unconscious of intruders. They were itinerant showmen – exhibitors of the freaks of Punch – for, perched cross-legged upon a tombstone behind them, was the hero himself, his nose and chin as hooked and his face as beaming as usual. His body was dangling in a most uncomfortable position, all limp and shapeless.

Scattered upon the ground at the feet of the two men, and jumbled together in a long flat box, were the other persons of the Drama. The hero's wife and child, the hobby-horse, the doctor, the executioner, and the devil, were all here. Their owners had evidently come to that spot to make some needful repairs, for one of them was binding together a small gallows with thread, while the other was intent upon fixing a new black wig.

They raised their eyes when they realized the old man and his young companion were close, and pausing in their work, returned their looks of curiosity. One of them, a little merry-faced man with a twinkling eye and a red nose, seemed to have unconsciously imbibed something of his hero's character. The other, Mr Codlin who took the money, had rather a cautious look.

The merry man greeted the strangers with a nod; and following the old man's eyes, he observed that perhaps that was the first time he had ever seen Punch off the stage.

"Why do you come here to do this?" said the old man, sitting down beside them, and looking at the figures with delight.

"Why you see," rejoined the little man, "we're at that public-house yonder tonight, and it wouldn't do to let 'em see the present company undergoing repair."

"No!" cried the old man, making signs to Nell to listen, "why not?"

"Because it would take away all the interest, wouldn't it?" replied the little man.

"Are you going to show 'em tonight?" said the old man, venturing to touch one of the puppets.

"That is the intention, governor," replied the other.

Mr Codlin drew a doll forth to show his friend: "Look here; here's all Judy's clothes falling to pieces again. You haven't a needle and thread, I suppose?"

The little man shook his head. Seeing that they were at a loss, the child said timidly: "I have a needle, sir, in my basket, and thread too. Shall I try to mend it for you? I think I could do it neatly."

Nelly, kneeling down beside the box, was soon busily engaged in her task. The merry little man looked at her with an interest that did not appear to be diminished when he glanced at her helpless companion. When she had finished her work he thanked her, and inquired whither they were travelling.

"N-no further tonight," said the child, looking at her grandfather.

"If you want a place to stop," the man remarked, "I should advise you to take up at the same house as us. That long, low, white house. It's very cheap."

They all rose and walked away together; the old man keeping close to the box of puppets in which he was quite absorbed, the merry little man carrying it slung over his arm by a strap, Nelly holding her grandfather's hand, and Mr Codlin sauntering behind.

The public house was kept by a fat old landlord and landlady who made no objection to receiving their new guests, but praised Nelly's beauty. There was no other company in the kitchen but the two showmen, and the child felt very thankful that they had fallen upon such good quarters. The landlady was astonished to learn that they had come all the way from London. The child parried her further inquiries as well as she could, and with no great trouble, for finding that they appeared to give her pain, the old lady desisted.

"These two gentlemen have ordered supper in an hour's time," she said. "Best you sup with them."

Presently the whole house hurried to an empty stable where the show stood, and where, by the light of a few flaring candles it was to be forthwith exhibited.

The whole performance was applauded to the echo, and voluntary contributions were showered in. Among the laughter none was louder than the old man's. Nell had fallen asleep, and slept too soundly to be roused by any of his efforts to awaken her to share in his glee.

The supper was very good, but she was too tired to eat. The old man, happily insensible to every worry, sat listening with a vacant smile to all that his new friends said; and it was not until they retired yawning to their room, that he followed the child upstairs.

There was a little window in her room, and when she left the old man, she opened it, amazed at the silence. The sight of the old church, and the graves about it in the moonlight, and the dark trees whispering, made her more thoughtful than before. She closed the window and sat upon the bed, thinking of the life before them.

She had a little money, but when that was gone, they must begin to beg. She had one piece of gold, and an emergency might come when it would be worth a great deal.

She therefore sewed this into her dress to hide it, and going to bed with a lighter heart sunk into a deep slumber.

CHAPTER 16

Another bright day shining in through the small window woke the child.

It was yet early, and the old man being still asleep, she walked out into the churchyard, brushing the dew from the long grass with her feet, and often turning aside into places where it grew longer than in others, that she might not tread upon the graves.

It was a very quiet place, save for the cawing of the rooks in the tall trees.

The child wandered from grave to grave, then peeped through a low latticed window into the church. There were the seats for the poor old people, worn spare, and yellow; the rugged font where children had their names, the homely altar where they knelt in after life, the plain black trestles to bear their weight on their last visit to the old shady church. Everything told of long use and slow decay.

The old man was by this time up and dressed. Mr Codlin was packing the candle ends saved from the previous night's performance; while his companion received the compliments of all the loungers in the stable-yard. When he had acknowledged his popularity he came in to breakfast.

"And where are you going today?" the little man asked Nell.

"Indeed I hardly know," replied the child.

"We're going on to the races," said the little man. "If that's your way, let us travel together. If you prefer going alone, only say the word and we shan't trouble you."

"We'll go with you," said the old man. "Nell – with them."

The child considered for a moment, and reflecting that she must shortly beg, decided there could be no better place than where crowds of rich ladies and gentlemen were assembled together for enjoyment and festivity. She therefore thanked the little man, and said, glancing timidly towards his friend, that if there was no objection to their accompanying them as far as the race town –

"Objection!" said the little man. "Now be gracious for once, Tommy, and say that you'd rather they went with us."

"Trotters," said Mr Codlin, "you're too free."

"Why, what harm can it do?" urged the other.

"No harm at all in this particular case, perhaps," replied Mr Codlin; "but still, the principle's dangerous."

"Well, do they go with us or not?"

"Yes," said Mr Codlin. "But you might have made a favour of it, mightn't you?"

The real name of the little man was Harris, but it had gradually merged into Trotters. The gentleman was known among his intimates either as "Short", due to the small size of his legs, or "Trotters", and was only called Short Trotters in formal conversations and on occasions of ceremony.

Breakfast being at length over, Mr Codlin called the bill, and charging the ale to the company generally, divided the sum-total into two fair and equal parts. These being duly discharged and all things ready for their

56

departure, they took farewell of the landlord and landlady and resumed their journey.

Short led the way; with the flat box, the private luggage (which was not extensive) tied up in a bundle, and a brazen trumpet slung from his shoulder. Nell and her grandfather walked next him on either hand, and Thomas Codlin brought up the rear.

When they came to any town or village, or even to a detached house of good appearance, Short blew a blast upon the trumpet and carolled a fragment of a song. If people hurried to the windows, Mr Codlin pitched the booth, and hastily unfurling the drapery and concealing Short therewith, flourished hysterically on the pipes and performed an air. Then the entertainment began as soon as might be.

Sometimes they played out the toll across a bridge or ferry, and once exhibited by particular desire at a turnpike, where the collector, being drunk in his solitude, paid a shilling to have it to himself. They were generally well received, and seldom left a town without a troop of ragged children at their heels.

They made a long day's journey, despite these interruptions, and were yet upon the road when the moon was shining in the sky. Short beguiled the time with songs and jests, making the best of everything. Mr Codlin on the other hand, cursed his fate, and limped along with the theatre on his back. Having rested a few minutes beneath a fingerpost, Short, bidding Nell to be of good cheer as they would soon be at the end of their journey for that night, and stimulating the old man with a similar assurance, led them at a pretty swift pace towards their destination, as the skies were beginning to threaten rain.

CHAPTER 17

The Jolly Sandboys was a small, ancient roadside inn. The travellers knew by the number of gipsy camps, carts laden with gambling booths, itinerant showmen of various kinds, and beggars of every degree, all wending their way in the same direction, that the race town was close by. Mr Codlin was afraid the inn would be full. He therefore quickened his pace, and even with the burden he carried, maintained a round trot until he reached the threshold. Here he found the landlord leaning against the doorpost looking at the rain, which by this time fell heavily.

"All alone?" said Mr Codlin, putting down his load.

"As yet," rejoined the landlord, glancing at the sky, "but we shall have more company tonight I expect. Here one of you boys, carry that show into the barn. Make haste in out of the wet, Tom. There's a glorious blaze in the kitchen, I can tell you."

Mr Codlin followed and soon found that the landlord had not boasted without good reason. A mighty fire roared up the chimney with a cheerful sound, and a large iron cauldron, bubbling and simmering in the heat, added to the comfort. There was a deep ruddy blush upon the room, and the landlord stirred the fire, sending the flames skipping and leaping up. When he took off the lid of the iron pot there rushed out a savoury smell, and Mr Codlin's heart was touched. He sat down in the chimney corner and smiled.

Mr Codlin eyed the landlord as he held the cover in his hand, and suffered the delightful steam to tickle his guest's nostrils. Mr Codlin drew his sleeve across his lips, and said in a murmuring voice, "What is it?"

"It's a stew of tripe," said the landlord smacking his lips, "and cow-heel," smacking them again, "and bacon, and steak," smacking them for the third time, "and peas, cauliflowers, new potatoes, and sparrow-grass, all working up together in one delicious gravy." He then smacked his lips a great many times, and taking a long hearty sniff of the fragrance, replaced the cover.

"When will it be ready?" asked Mr Codlin faintly.

"It'll be done to a turn," said the landlord looking up to the clock – "it'll be done to a turn at twenty-two minutes before eleven."

"Then," said Mr Codlin, "fetch me a pint of warm ale, and don't bring into the room even so much as a biscuit till the time arrives."

Nodding his approval at this manly decision, the landlord retired to draw the beer, and presently returned with it. He handed it over to Mr Codlin with creamy froth upon the surface.

Greatly softened by this soothing beverage, Mr Codlin now remembered his companions, and acquainted mine host that they would shortly arrive. Rain rattled against the windows, and such was Mr

Codlin's extreme amiability of mind, that he more than once expressed his earnest hope that they would not be so foolish as to get wet.

At length they arrived, drenched with the rain. Short had sheltered the child as well as he could under his own coat, and they were nearly breathless from the haste they had made. But the landlord, who had been at the outer door anxiously watching for them, rushed into the kitchen and took the cover off the pot.

The effect was electrical. They all came in with smiling faces though water dripped from their clothes upon the floor. Short's first remark was, "What a delicious smell!"

It is not very difficult to forget rain by the side of a cheerful fire. They were furnished with such dry garments as the house or their own bundles afforded, and ensconcing themselves, as Mr Codlin had already done, in the warm chimney corner, soon forgot their drenching. Overcome by the comfort and the fatigue they had undergone, Nelly and the old man had not long taken their seats, when they fell asleep.

"Who are they?" whispered the landlord. Short shook his head, and wished he knew himself. "Don't you know?" asked the host, turning to Mr Codlin.

"Not I," he replied. "They're no good, I suppose."

"They're no harm," said Short. "Depend upon that. It's plain that the old man an't in his right mind – "

"If you haven't got anything newer than that to say," growled Mr Codlin, glancing at the clock, "you'd better let us fix our minds upon the supper, and not disturb us."

"Hear me out, won't you?" retorted his friend. "It's very plain to me, that they're not used to this way of life. Don't tell me that child has been in the habit of prowling about the way she has these last two or three days. I know better."

Mr Codlin glanced again at the clock and from it to the cauldron. "Can't you think of anything more suitable to present circumstances than saying things and then contradicting 'em?"

"I wish somebody would give you your supper," returned Short, "for there'll be no peace till you've got it. Have you seen how anxious the old man is to get on, to be furder away, furder away. Have you seen that?"

"Ah! What then?" muttered Thomas Codlin.

"This, then," said Short. "He has given his friends the slip and persuaded this delicate young creetur to be his guide and travelling companion – where to, he knows no more than the man in the moon. Now I'm not a going to stand that."

"*You're* not a going to stand that!" cried Mr Codlin, glancing at the clock again and pulling his hair in a kind of frenzy, but whether occasioned by his companion's observation or the tardy pace of Time, it was difficult to determine.

"I," repeated Short, slowly, "am not a-going to see this fair young child a falling into bad hands. Therefore when they dewelope an intention of parting company from us, I shall take measures for detaining of 'em, and restoring 'em to their friends, who I dare say have had their disconsolation pasted up on every wall in London by this time."

"Short," said Mr Codlin, with his head upon his hands, and his elbows on his knees, "it's possible that there may be uncommon good sense in what you've said. If there is, and there should be a reward, Short, remember that we're partners in everything!"

His companion had only time to nod a brief assent to this position, for the child awoke. They had drawn close together during the previous whispering, and now hastily separated and were rather awkwardly endeavouring to exchange some casual remarks in their usual tone.

The landlord busied himself in laying the cloth, in which process Mr Codlin obligingly assisted by setting his own knife and fork in the most convenient place and establishing himself behind them. When everything was ready, the landlord took off the cover for the last time, and then indeed there burst forth such a goodly promise of supper, that if he had hinted at postponement, he would certainly have been sacrificed on his own hearth.

Instead he assisted a stout servant girl in turning the contents of the cauldron into a large tureen. The dish was lifted on the table, and mugs of ale having been previously set round, little Nell ventured to say grace, and supper began.

CHAPTER 18

After the meal and bidding the old man good night, Nell retired to her poor garret, but had scarcely closed the door, when it was gently tapped at. She was a little startled to see Mr Thomas Codlin, whom she had left, to all appearance, fast asleep down stairs.

"What is the matter?" said the child.

"Nothing, my dear," returned her visitor. "I'm your friend. Perhaps you haven't thought so, but it's me that's your friend – not him,"

"Not who?" the child inquired.

"Short, my dear. I tell you what," said Codlin, "for all his having a kind of way with him, I'm the real, openhearted man. I mayn't look it, but I am indeed."

The child began to be alarmed, considering that the ale had taken effect upon Mr Codlin.

"Short seems kind," resumed the misanthrope, "but he overdoes it. Now I don't."

Now it was certainly true that Mr Codlin underdid his kindness to those about him, rather than overdid it. But the child was puzzled.

"Take my advice," said Codlin. "As long as you travel with us, keep as near me as you can. Don't offer to leave but always stick to me and say that I'm your friend. Will you bear that in mind my dear, and always say that it was me that was your friend?"

"Say so where – and when?" inquired the child innocently.

"Oh, nowhere in particular," replied Codlin, a little put out it seemed by the question. "I'm only anxious that you should think me so, and do me justice. Why didn't you tell me your little history – about you and the poor old gentleman? I'm the best adviser that ever was, and so much more interested than Short. I think they're breaking up downstairs. You needn't tell Short, you know, that we've had this little talk together. God bless you. Recollect the friend. Codlin's the friend, not Short."

Thomas Codlin then stole away on tiptoe, leaving the child puzzling over his curious behaviour, when the floor of the crazy stairs and landing cracked beneath the tread of other travellers finding their beds. When the sound of their footsteps had died away, one of them returned, and after a hesitation, knocked at her door.

"Yes?" said the child from within.

"It's me – Short," a voice called through the keyhole. "Just to say that we must be off early tomorrow morning, my dear. You'll be sure to be stirring early and go with us? I'll call you."

The child answered in the affirmative, and returning his "good night" heard him creep away. She felt uneasy at the anxiety of these men, increased by the recollection of their whispering together downstairs, nor was she quite free from a misgiving that they were not the fittest companions she could have stumbled on. Her uneasiness, however, was nothing, weighed against her fatigue; and she soon forgot it in sleep.

Very early next morning Short fulfilled his promise, and knocking softly at her door, entreated that she would get up directly. She started from her bed without delay, and roused the old man with so much expedition that they were both ready as soon as Short himself, to that gentleman's unspeakable gratification and relief.

After a scrambled breakfast, they took leave of the landlord and left the Jolly Sandboys. The morning was fine, the ground cool to the feet after the late rain, the hedges more green, the air clear, and everything fresh and healthful.

They had not gone very far, when the child was again struck by the altered behaviour of Mr Thomas Codlin who, instead of plodding on sulkily as he had before, kept close to her, and when he had an opportunity of looking at her unseen by his companion, warned her by certain wry faces and jerks of the head not to put any trust in Short, but to reserve all confidences for Codlin.

All these proceedings naturally made the child more watchful and suspicious, and she soon observed that whenever they halted to perform outside a village alehouse or other place, Mr Codlin kept his eye steadily upon her and the old man, or with a show of great friendship invited the latter to lean upon his arm, and so held him tight until the entertainment was over and they again went forward. Even Short seemed to want to keep them in safe custody. This increased the child's misgivings, making her more anxious.

Meanwhile, they drew near the town where the races were to begin next day; for, they gradually fell into a stream of people, some walking beside covered carts, others with horses, others toiling on with heavy loads upon their backs, but all tending to the same point. The public houses now sent out boisterous shouts and clouds of smoke. The crowd grew thicker and more noisy; gilt gingerbread in blanket-stalls exposed its glories to the dust; and often a four-horse carriage, dashing by, obscured all objects in the gritty cloud it raised, and left them, blinded, far behind.

It was dark before they reached the town itself. Here all was tumult and confusion; the streets were filled with throngs of people, and church-bells rang out. In the large inn yards waiters flitted to and fro, horses clattered on the uneven stones, carriage steps fell rattling down, and sickening smells from many dinners came in a heavy lukewarm breath upon the sense.

Through this delirious scene, the child, frightened and repelled by all she saw, led on her bewildered charge, clinging close to her conductor, and trembling lest she should be separated from him and left to find her way alone. Quickening their steps, they passed through the town, making for the race-course upon an open heath, a mile beyond its furthest bounds.

Although there were many people here, busily erecting tents and driving stakes in the ground, and hurrying to and fro with dusty feet and many a grumbled oath, the child felt it preferable to the town and drew her breath more freely. After a scanty supper, the purchase of which reduced her little stock so low, that she had only a few halfpence with which to buy a breakfast on the morrow, she and the old man lay down to rest in a corner of a tent, and slept, despite the busy preparations.

Soon after sunrise she stole from the tent, and rambling into some nearby fields, plucked a few wild roses and such humble flowers, to make into nosegays to offer to the ladies in the carriages when the company arrived. Her thoughts were not idle and when she returned and was seated beside the old man, tying her flowers together, while the two men lay dozing, she plucked him by the sleeve, and slightly glancing towards them, said, in a low voice – "Grandfather, don't look at those I talk of. What did you say before we left the old house? That if they knew what we were going to do, they would say that you were mad, and part us?"

The old man turned to her with a look of terror; but she checked him by a glance, and bidding him hold some flowers while she tied them up, said, "It was not likely that I should forget your words. Grandfather, these men suspect that we have secretly left our friends, and mean to have us taken care of and sent back. If you let your hand tremble so, we can never get away from them, but if you're only quiet now, we shall do so, easily."

"How?" muttered the old man. "Dear Nelly, how? They will shut me up in a stone room, chained to the wall, Nell – flog me with whips, and never let me see thee more!"

"You're trembling again," said the child. "Keep close to me all day. I shall find a time when we can steal away. When I do, mind you come with me. Do not stop or speak a word. Hush! That's all."

"Halloa! What are you up to, my dear?" said Mr Codlin, raising his head, and yawning. Then observing that his companion was fast asleep, he added, "Codlin's the friend, remember – not Short."

"Making some nosegays," the child replied. "I shall try and sell some, at the races. Will you have one – as a present I mean?"

Mr Codlin stuck one in his buttonhole.

As the morning wore on, the tents assumed a gayer and more brilliant appearance, and long lines of carriages came rolling softly on the turf. Men who had lounged about all night in smock-frocks and leather leggings, came out in silken vests and hats and plumes, as jugglers or mountebanks. Black-eyed gipsy girls, hooded in showy handkerchiefs, sallied forth to tell fortunes, and pale slender women with consumptive faces lingered upon the footsteps of ventriloquists and conjurors, and counted the sixpences with anxious eyes long before they were gained.

The child bore upon her arm the little basket with her flowers, and sometimes stopped, with timid and modest looks, to offer them at some gay carriage; but although some ladies smiled gently as they shook their heads, and others cried to the gentlemen beside them "See, what a pretty face!" they let the pretty face pass on, and never thought that it looked tired or hungry.

There was but one lady who seemed to understand the child, and she sat alone in a handsome carriage, while two young men in dashing clothes, who had just dismounted from it, talked and laughed loudly at a little distance. She called the child towards her, and taking her flowers put money into her trembling hand, and bade her go home and stay there for God's sake.

Many a time they went up and down those long lines, and the eye of Thomas Codlin was upon them, and to escape was impossible.

At length, late in the day, Mr Codlin pitched the show in a convenient spot, and the spectators were soon in the very triumph of the scene. The child was sitting down with the old man close behind it when Mr Codlin's laugh roused her from her meditation and caused her to look around.

If they were ever to get away unseen, that was the moment. Short was plying the quarter staves vigorously, the people were laughing, and Mr Codlin had relaxed as his roving eye detected hands going into waistcoat pockets for sixpences. It was now or never.

They made a path through booths and carriages and throngs of people, and never once stopped to look behind. The bell was ringing and the course was cleared by the time they reached the ropes, but they dashed across it insensible to the shouts and screeching that assailed them for breaking in upon its sanctity, and creeping under the brow of the hill at a quick pace, made for the open fields.

CHAPTER 19

Day after day as he bent his steps homeward, returning from some new effort to procure employment, Kit raised his eyes to the window of the little room he had so much commended to the child, hoping to see some indication of her presence. His own earnest wish, coupled with the assurance he had received from Quilp, filled him with the belief that she would claim the humble shelter he had offered.

"I think they must certainly come tomorrow, eh mother?" said Kit, laying aside his hat. "They have been gone a week. They surely couldn't stop away more than a week, could they now?"

The mother shook her head, and reminded him how often he had been disappointed already.

His thoughts then went to the little old gentleman who had given him the shilling, and he suddenly recollected that that was the very day – almost the hour – at which the little old gentleman had said he should be at the Notary's house again. He hastily explained the nature of his errand, and went off at full speed.

He was some two minutes late when he reached the spot, but by great good luck the little old gentleman had not yet arrived. Kit leant against a lamp post to take breath, and waited.

Before long the pony came trotting round the corner, picking his steps as if looking for the cleanest places. Behind the pony sat the little old gentleman, and by his side sat the little old lady.

The old gentleman, the old lady, the pony, and the chaise, came up the street in perfect unanimity, until they were some half a dozen doors before the Notary's house. Then the pony, deceived by a brass-plate beneath a tailor's knocker, stopped, and maintained by a sturdy silence, that that was the house they wanted.

"Now, sir, will you ha' the goodness to go on; this is not the place," said the old gentleman.

"Oh dear, naughty Whisker," cried the old lady. "After being so good! I am quite ashamed of him. What should we do with him."

The old gentleman alighted to lead him, and perhaps because he spotted the other brass-plate, or perhaps because he was in a spiteful mood, the pony darted off with the old lady and halted at the right house, leaving the old gentleman to come panting on behind.

Kit presented himself at the pony's head at that moment, and touched his hat with a smile.

"Why, bless me," cried the old gentleman, "the lad is here! My dear, do you see?"

"I said I'd be here, sir," said Kit, patting Whisker's neck. "I hope you've had a pleasant ride, sir. He's a very nice little pony."

"My dear," said the old gentleman. "This is an uncommon lad; a good lad, I'm sure."

"I'm sure he is," rejoined the old lady. "A very good lad, and I am sure he is a good son."

Kit acknowledged these words by touching his hat again and blushing very much. The old gentleman then handed the old lady out, and after looking at him with an approving smile, they went into the house. Presently Mr Witherden came to the window and looked at him, and after that Mr Abel came to look, and after that they all came and looked at him together, which Kit, feeling very much embarrassed, pretended not to notice. He patted the pony and this the pony most handsomely permitted.

Moments later the clerk appeared, telling him he was wanted inside. Kit entered the office in a great tremor, not used to going among strange ladies and gentlemen. Mr Witherden bustled, talking loud and fast, and all eyes were upon him.

"Well, boy," said Mr Witherden, "you came to work out that shilling – not to get another, hey?"

"No indeed, sir," replied Kit, looking up. "I never thought of such a thing."

"Father alive?" said the Notary.

"Dead, sir."

"Mother?"

"Yes, sir."

"Married again – eh?"

Kit replied, not without some indignation, that she was a widow with three children, and that as to her marrying again, if the gentleman knew her he wouldn't think such a thing. At this Mr Witherden whispered to the old gentleman that he believed the lad was as honest a lad as need be.

"Now," said Mr Garland, "I am not giving you anything – "

"Thank you, sir," Kit replied.

" – But," resumed the old gentleman, "perhaps I may want to know something more about you, so tell me where you live, and I'll put it down in my pocket-book."

Kit told him. He was dismissed moments later. As he walked down the street, Mr Garland, the old lady and Mr Abel left the Notary's, more than once turning to nod kindly to Kit as he watched.

CHAPTER 20

Kit very soon forgot the pony, and the little old couple, and the young gentleman, in wondering what could have become of his late master and his lovely grandchild. Persuading himself that they must soon return, he bent his steps towards home.

When he came to the corner of the court in which he lived, there was the pony again, looking more obstinate than ever. Alone in the chaise, keeping a steady watch, sat Mr Abel, who, lifting up his eyes by chance and seeing Kit pass by, nodded to him.

Kit was even more surprised to find the old lady and gentleman deep in conversation with his mother when he entered the house. He pulled off his hat and made his best bow in some confusion.

"We are here before you, you see, Christopher," said Mr Garland smiling.

"Yes, sir," said Kit, looking towards his mother for an explanation.

"The gentleman's been kind enough, my dear," said she, in reply to this silent query, "to ask me whether you were employed, and when I told him no, you were not, he was so good as to say that – "

" – That we need a good lad in our house," said the old gentleman.

As this plainly meant engaging Kit, he immediately fell into a great flutter. The little old couple were very methodical and cautious, and asked so many questions that he began to be afraid there was no chance of his success.

"You see," said Mrs Garland to Kit's mother, "we need to be careful, for we're quiet regular folks, and it would be sad if we made a mistake."

Kit's mother replied, that certainly it was quite true, and quite right and proper. The old lady said that she was quite sure she was a very honest and very respectable person and that certainly the appearance of the children and the cleanliness of the house deserved great praise and did her the utmost credit.

Mr Garland put some questions to Kit respecting his qualifications and general acquirements, while Mrs Garland noticed the children. Lastly, inquiry was made into the nature and extent of Kit's wardrobe, and a small advance was made to improve the same.

He was then formally hired at an annual income of Six Pounds, over and above his board and lodging, by Mr and Mrs Garland, of Abel Cottage, Finchley.

It would be difficult to say which party appeared most pleased with this arrangement, the conclusion of which was hailed with nothing but cheerful smiles on both sides. It was settled that Kit should repair to his new abode on the next day but one, in the morning; and finally, the little old couple, after bestowing a bright half-crown on little Jacob and another on the baby, took their leaves; being escorted as far as the street by their new attendant, who saw them drive away with a lightened heart.

"Well, mother," said Kit, hurrying back into the house, "I think my fortune's about made now."

"I should think it was indeed, Kit," rejoined his mother. "Six pound a year! Only think!"

"Ah!" said Kit, grinning with delight in spite of himself. "There's a property!"

He drew a long breath when he had said this, and putting his hands deep into his pockets as if there were one year's wages at least in each, looked at his mother, as though he saw through her, and down an immense perspective of sovereigns beyond.

"Please God we'll make such a lady of you for Sundays, mother! Such a scholar of Jacob, such a child of the baby, such a room of the one up stairs! Six pound a year!"

"Hem!" croaked a strange voice. "What's that about six pound a year?"

And as the voice made this inquiry, Daniel Quilp walked in with Richard Swiveller at his heels.

"Who said he was to have six pound a year?" said Quilp, looking sharply round. "Did the old man say it? And what's he to have it for, and where are they, eh!"

The good woman was so alarmed that she grabbed the baby and retreated into the furthest corner. Little Jacob, sitting upon his stool, looked full at him in fascination. Richard Swiveller looked at the family over Mr Quilp's head, and Quilp himself, with his hands in his pockets, smiled in enjoyment at the commotion he occasioned.

"Don't be frightened, mistress," said Quilp, after a pause. "Your son knows me. Now you sir, why haven't you been to me as promised?"

"What should I come for?" retorted Kit. "I hadn't any business with you, no more than you had with me."

"Here, mistress," said Quilp, turning quickly, and appealing from Kit to his mother. "When did his old master come or send here last? Is he here now? If not, where's he gone?"

"He has not been here," she replied. "I wish we knew where they were, for it would ease my son's mind, and mine too."

"Humph!" muttered Quilp, evidently disappointed to believe that this was true. "That's what you tell this gentleman too, is it?"

"If the gentleman comes to ask the same question, I can't tell him anything else, sir," was the reply.

Quilp glanced at Richard Swiveller, and observed that having met him on the threshold, he assumed that he had come in search of some intelligence of the fugitives. He supposed he was right?

"Yes," said Dick, "I fancied it possible."

"You seem disappointed," observed Quilp.

"A baffler, sir, a baffler, that's all," returned Dick. "I have entered upon a speculation which has proved a baffler."

The dwarf eyed Richard with a sarcastic smile, but Richard, who had been taking a rather strong lunch with a friend, observed him not. Quilp plainly discerned that there was some secret reason for this visit and his uncommon disappointment, and resolved to worm it out. He instantly conveyed as much honesty into his face as it was capable of expressing, and sympathised with Mr Swiveller.

"I am disappointed myself," said Quilp, "out of mere friendly feeling for them. But you have real, private reasons for your disappointment, and therefore it comes heavier than mine."

"Why, of course it does," Dick observed, testily.

"Upon my word, I'm very sorry. I'm rather cast down myself. If you had no particular business, now," urged Quilp, plucking his sleeve, "there is a little summerhouse overlooking the river, where we might take a glass of a delicious liquor with a whiff of the best tobacco – or does another engagement take you another way, Mr Swiveller, eh?"

Dick's face relaxed into a compliant smile. By the time he had finished, Dick was looking down at Quilp in the same sly manner as Quilp was looking up at him, so they set out straightway.

The summerhouse was a wooden box, rotten and bare to see, which overhung the river's mud, and threatened to slide down into it. The tavern stood on waste ground, blighted with the smoke of factory chimneys. The rooms were low and damp, the clammy walls pierced with holes.

To this inviting spot Mr Quilp led Richard Swiveller, and on the table of the summerhouse there soon appeared a wooden keg.

Richard Swiveller began imperceptibly to become more friendly and confiding, so that, being led on by Mr Quilp, he grew at last very confiding indeed. Having got him into this mood, Daniel Quilp's task was comparatively easy, and he was soon in possession of the whole details of the scheme contrived between the easy Dick and his more designing friend.

"Stop!" said Quilp. "It can be brought about, it shall be brought about. There's my hand upon it. I am your friend from this minute."

"What! Do you think there's still a chance?" inquired Dick, in surprise.

"A chance!" echoed the dwarf, "a certainty! Oh you lucky dog! He's richer than any Jew alive; you're a made man. I see in you now nothing but Nelly's husband, rolling in gold and silver. I'll help you. It shall be done, mind my words."

"But how?" said Dick.

"There's plenty of time," rejoined the dwarf. "We'll talk it over again all the way through. Fill your glass while I'm gone. I shall be back directly." With these hasty words, Daniel Quilp withdrew into a dismantled skittle-ground behind the public house, and, throwing himself upon the ground, actually screamed and rolled about in uncontrollable delight.

"Here's sport!" he cried, "He shall marry Nell. He shall have her, and I'll be the first man, when the knot's tied hard and fast, to tell 'em what they've gained and what I've helped 'em to! Young Trent shall not look on my Mrs Quilp!"

Having composed himself, he returned to his unsuspicious companion, whom he found looking at the tide with gravity, and thinking of the gold and silver that Mr Quilp had mentioned.

CHAPTER 21

The next two days were busy for the Nubbles family. The box containing his wardrobe and necessaries was frequently opened and shut within four-and-twenty hours, with its three shirts and proportionate allowance of stockings and pocket-handkerchiefs. At last it was conveyed to the carrier's, at whose house, at Finchley, Kit was to find it next day. Once the box was gone, there remained the question whether Kit's mother perfectly understood how to take care of herself in the absence of her son.

"*You* know you must keep up your spirits, mother, and not be lonesome because I'm not at home. I shall look in when I come into town, and I shall send you a letter sometimes, and when the quarter comes round, I can get a holiday of course."

With more kisses, and hugs, and tears, Kit left the house early the next morning, and set out to walk to Finchley. He was dressed in a coat of pepper-and-salt with waistcoat of canary colour, and nether garments of iron-grey; besides these glories, he shone in the lustre of a new pair of boots and an extremely stiff and shiny hat.

Without encountering any remarkable adventure on the road, Kit arrived in course of time at the carrier's house, where he found his box in safety. Receiving directions to Mr Garland's, he took the box upon his shoulder.

To be sure, it was a beautiful little cottage with a thatched roof and little spires at the gable-ends, and pieces of stained glass in some of the windows. On one side of the house was a little stable, just the size for the pony, with a little room over it, just the size for Kit. White curtains fluttered, and plants were arranged on either side of the path, and clustered about the door; and the garden was bright with flowers in full bloom. Everything seemed to be the perfection of neatness and order. In the garden there was not a weed to be seen, and to judge from some dapper gardening-tools, a basket, and a pair of gloves lying in one of the walks, old Mr Garland had been at work in it that very morning.

Kit looked about him, and admired, before he rang the bell. There was plenty of time to look about him again because nobody came, so after ringing it twice or thrice he sat down upon his box to wait.

He rang the bell a great many times, and yet nobody came. But at last, as he sat upon the box, the door opened, and a little servant-girl, very tidy, modest, and demure, but very pretty too, appeared. "I suppose you're Christopher, sir," she said.

Kit stood and said yes, he was.

"You've probably rung a good many times," she rejoined, "but we couldn't hear you, because we've been catching the pony."

Kit rather wondered what this meant, but as he couldn't stop there, asking questions, he shouldered the box again and followed the girl into the hall, where through a back-door he descried Mr Garland leading Whisker in triumph up the garden. The self-willed pony had (as he afterwards learned) dodged the family round a small paddock in the rear, for one hour and three-quarters.

The old gentleman received him very kindly and so did the old lady, whose previous good opinion of him was greatly enhanced by his wiping his boots on the mat. He was then inspected in his new clothes; and then was taken into the stable to reacquaint himself with the pony and thence into the neat and comfortable little chamber he had already observed. He then went into the garden, where the old gentleman told him he would be taught to employ himself. All these kindnesses, Kit acknowledged with various expressions of gratitude. Next he was handed over again to the old lady, who, summoning the little servant-girl (whose name was Barbara) instructed her to take and give him something to eat and drink.

Downstairs Kit went; and at the bottom of the stairs there was such a kitchen with everything in it as bright and glowing, and as precisely ordered too, as Barbara herself. And in this kitchen, Kit sat himself down at a table as white as a tablecloth, to eat cold meat, and drink small ale, and use his knife and fork the more awkwardly, because there was an unknown Barbara looking on and observing him.

It did not appear, however, that there was anything remarkably tremendous about this strange Barbara, who having lived a very quiet life, blushed very much and was quite as embarrassed as Kit was. When he had sat for some little time, attentive to the ticking of the clock, he glanced curiously at the dresser, and there, among the plates and dishes, were Barbara's little workbox, and Barbara's prayer-book, and Barbara's hymn-book, and Barbara's Bible. Barbara's bonnet was on a nail behind the door. He then naturally glanced at Barbara herself, who sat silently, shelling peas into a dish. Just when Kit was looking at her eyelashes and wondering, quite in the simplicity of his heart, what colour her eyes might be, Barbara raised her head a little to look at him. Both pairs of eyes were hastily withdrawn, and Kit leant over his plate, and Barbara over her pea-shells, each in extreme confusion at having been detected by the other.

CHAPTER 22

It was not without great reluctance and misgiving that Mr Swiveller, next morning, his head racked by alcohol, repaired to the lodging of his friend Trent and recounted very slowly what had taken place. It was with great surprise and much speculation on Quilp's probable motives, and many bitter comments on Swiveller's folly, that his friend received the tale.

"I don't defend myself, Fred," said the penitent Richard; "but the fellow has such a queer way with him, that firstly he set me upon thinking whether there was any harm in telling him, and while I was thinking, screwed it out of me."

Frederick Trent threw himself into a chair, burying his head in his hands, and endeavoured to fathom the motives that had led Quilp to befriend Richard Swiveller, for he had sought the information — it had not been spontaneously revealed by Dick. This was obvious from Quilp's seeking Richard's company and enticing him away.

The dwarf had twice encountered him while trying to obtain intelligence of the fugitives. This, perhaps, as he had not previously been anxious about them, was enough to awaken suspicion. But knowing the scheme they had planned, why should he offer to help? This was a question more difficult to solve; but the idea immediately presented itself that irritation between Quilp and the old man, arising out of their secret transactions and not unconnected perhaps with his sudden disappearance, now meant Quilp wanted to revenge himself by seeking to entrap the sole object of the old man's love and anxiety into a connection of which he knew he had a dread and hatred. As Frederick Trent himself, utterly regardless of his sister, had this object at heart, only second to the hope of gain, it seemed to him the more likely to be Quilp's main aim. Once investing the dwarf with a design of his own in abetting them, it was easy to believe him sincere and hearty in the cause. As there could be no doubt he would be a powerful and useful ally, Trent determined to go to his house that night. If what he said and did confirmed the impression he had formed, he would let him share the labour of their plan, but not the profit. Having arrived at this conclusion, he communicated to Mr Swiveller as much of his meditations as he thought proper, and giving him the day to recover, accompanied him that evening to Mr Quilp's house.

Mighty glad Mr Quilp seemed to see them; and fearfully polite was he to Mrs Quilp and Mrs Jiniwin. Very sharp was the look he cast on his wife to see how affected she was by the sight of young Trent. Mrs Quilp was innocent of any emotion, painful or pleasant, which the sight of him awakened, but as her husband's glance made her confused, Mr Quilp did not fail to assign her embarrassment to the cause he had in mind, and while he chuckled was secretly exasperated by his jealousy.

Nothing of this appeared, however. On the contrary, Mr Quilp was all suavity, and presided over the rum with extraordinary open-heartedness.

"Why," said Quilp. "It must be nearly two years since we were first acquainted."

"Nearer three, I think," said Trent.

"Nearer three!" cried Quilp. "How fast time flies. Does it seem as long as that to you, Mrs Quilp?"

"Yes, I think it seems full three years, Quilp," was the unfortunate reply.

"Oh indeed, ma'am," thought Quilp, "you have been pining, have you? Very good, ma'am."

"It seems to me but yesterday that you went out to Demerara in the Mary Anne," said Quilp. "Well, I like a little wildness. I was wild myself once."

Quilp set down his glass. "I thought you'd come back directly, Fred. And when the Mary Anne returned with you on board, instead of a letter to say how happy you were, I was exceedingly amused. Ha ha ha!"

The young man smiled, but not as though he was enjoying the topic of conversation, and for that reason Quilp pursued it.

"I always will say," he resumed, "that when a rich relation having two young people – sisters or brothers, or brother and sister – dependent on him, attaches himself exclusively to one, and casts off the other, he does wrong. Your grandfather urged repeated forgiveness, ingratitude, riot, and extravagance, and all that; but as I told him 'these are common faults', 'But he's a scoundrel,' said he. 'Granting that,' said I, 'a great many young noblemen and gentlemen are scoundrels too!' But he wouldn't be convinced."

"I wonder at that, Mr Quilp," said the young man sarcastically.

"Well, so did I at the time," returned Quilp, "but he was always obstinate. Little Nell is a nice girl, a charming girl, but you're her brother, Frederick. As you told him the last time you met, he can't alter that."

"He would if he could," said the young man impatiently. "But nothing can come of this subject now, and let us have done with it."

"Agreed," returned Quilp, "why have I alluded to it? Just to show you, Frederick, that I am always your friend. You little knew who was your friend, and who your foe; now did you? You thought I was against you, and so there has been a coolness between us; but it was all on your side. Let's shake hands again, Fred."

With his head sunk down between his shoulders, and a hideous grin over-spreading his face, the dwarf stood up and stretched his short arm across the table. After a moment's hesitation, the young man stretched out his to meet it. Quilp clutched his fingers, and pressing his other hand upon his lip and frowning towards the unsuspecting Richard, released them and sat down.

This action was not lost upon Trent, who, knowing that Richard Swiveller was a mere tool in his hands and knew no more of his designs than he thought proper to communicate, saw that the dwarf perfectly understood their relative position. It is something to be appreciated, even in knavery. This silent homage to his superior abilities, inclined the young man towards that ugly worthy, and determined him to profit by his aid.

It being now Mr Quilp's cue to change the subject with all convenient expedition, lest Richard Swiveller in his heedlessness should reveal anything that it was inexpedient for the women to know, he proposed a game at four-handed cribbage. Partners being cut for, Mrs Quilp fell to Frederick Trent, and Dick himself to Quilp. Mrs Jiniwin, being very fond of cards, was excluded by her son-in-law from any participation in the game.

Among his various eccentric habits Quilp always cheated at cards, which rendered necessary on his part, not only a close observance of the game, and a sleight-of-hand in counting and scoring, but also involved the constant correction, by looks, and frowns, and kicks under the table, of Richard Swiveller, who being bewildered by the rapidity with which his cards were told, and the rate at which the pegs travelled down the board, could not be prevented from sometimes expressing his surprise. Mrs Quilp being the partner of young Trent, for every look that passed between them, and every word they spoke, and every card they played, the dwarf had eyes and ears.

At length, when they had played a great many rubbers and drawn pretty freely upon the case-bottle, Mr Quilp warned his lady to retire to rest, and being followed by her indignant mother, Mr Swiveller fell asleep. The dwarf, beckoning his remaining companion to the other end of the room, held a short conference with him in whispers.

"It's as well not to say more than one can help before our worthy friend," said Quilp, making a grimace towards the slumbering Dick. "Is it a bargain between us, Fred? Shall he marry little rosy Nell by-and-by?"

"You have your own end, of course," returned the other.

"Of course I have, dear Fred," said Quilp, grinning to think how little he suspected what the real end was. "It's retaliation perhaps; perhaps whim. I have influence, Fred, to help or oppose. Which way shall I use it? There are a pair of scales, and it goes into one."

"Throw it into mine then," said Trent.

"It's done, Fred," rejoined Quilp, stretching out his clenched hand and opening it as if to let some weight fall out. "It's in the scale from this time, and turns it, Fred. Mind that."

"Where have they gone?" asked Trent.

Quilp shook his head, and said that point remained to be discovered. When it was, they would begin their preliminary advances. He would visit the old man, or even Richard Swiveller might visit him, and by pretending deep concern and imploring him to settle in some worthy home, the child would remember him with gratitude and favour. After this it would be easy, he said, to win her in a year or two, for she supposed the old man to be poor, as it was a part of his jealous policy (in common with many other misers) to feign to be so, to those about him.

"He has feigned it often enough to me, of late," said Trent.

"Oh! And to me too!" replied the dwarf. "Which is quite extraordinary, as I know how rich he really is."

"I suppose you should," said Trent.

"I think I should indeed," rejoined the dwarf, finally speaking the truth.

After a few more whispered words, they returned to the table, and the young man rousing Richard Swiveller informed him that he was waiting to depart. After a few words, they bade the grinning Quilp good night.

Quilp crept to the window as they passed in the street below, and listened. Both men were wondering by what enchantment Mrs Quilp had been brought to marry such a misshapen wretch as he. The dwarf after watching their retreating shadows with a wider grin than his face had yet displayed, stole softly in the dark to bed.

In this hatching of their scheme, neither Trent nor Quilp had had one thought about the happiness or misery of poor innocent Nell.

CHAPTER 23

It was not until they were quite exhausted and could no longer keep up the pace at which they had fled the race-ground, that the old man and the child stopped to rest upon the borders of a little wood. Here, though the course couldn't be seen, they could still make out distant shouts, the hum of voices, and the beating of drums. Climbing the slope that lay between them and the spot they had left, the child could even discern fluttering flags, but no person was approaching them.

Some time elapsed before she could reassure her companion. He could only imagine a crowd stealing towards them beneath the cover of the bushes, lurking in every ditch, and peeping from the boughs of every rustling tree. He was haunted by the fear of being led captive to some gloomy place where Nell could never come to see him, save through iron bars and gratings in the wall. His terrors affected the child. Separation from her grandfather was the greatest evil she could dread; and feeling as though, go where they would, they would be hunted down, and could never be safe but in hiding, her heart failed her.

In one so young, and so unused to the scenes in which she had lately moved, this sinking of the spirit was not surprising. But, when the child, casting her tearful eyes upon the old man, remembered how weak he was, and how helpless he would be if she failed him, her heart swelled within her, giving her new strength and fortitude.

"We have nothing to fear now, dear grandfather," she said.

"How," said the old man, looking fearfully round, "can you bear to think that we are safe, when they search for me everywhere?"

"Because I'm sure we have not been followed," said the child. "Look round – see how quiet and still it is. We are alone, and may ramble where we like."

"True, too," he answered, pressing her hand, but still looking anxiously about. "What noise was that?"

"A bird," said the child, "flying and leading the way for us to follow. You remember that we said we would walk in woods and fields, and how happy we would be? But here, while the sun shines above our heads, we are sitting and losing time. See what a pleasant path; and there's the bird flying onwards. Come!"

She bounded on before, printing her tiny footsteps in the moss, and thus she lured the old man on, with many a backward look, now pointing to some lone bird as it perched and twittered on a branch, now stopping to listen to the songs that broke the happy silence. As they passed onward, the old man cast no more fearful looks behind, but felt at ease, for the further they passed into the deep green shade, the more tranquil they felt.

At length the path brought them to the end of the wood, and into a public road. They spent that night at the house of a kindly schoolmaster. Early the next morning they were back on the road.

But this highway led them on and still stretched out, far in the distance, the same tedious, winding course. As they had no choice, they still kept on, though at a much slower pace, being very weary.

The afternoon had worn away when they arrived at a point where the road made a sharp turn and struck across a common. Here a caravan was drawn up to rest.

It was a smart little house upon wheels, with white dimity curtains, and window-shutters of green picked out with panels of red. A pair of horses were grazing on the frouzy grass. At the open door (graced with a bright brass knocker) sat a Christian lady, stout and comfortable to look upon, who wore a large bonnet trembling with bows. The lady was taking tea. The tea things, including a cold knuckle of ham, were set forth upon a drum covered with a white napkin.

At that moment the lady of the caravan had her cup to her lips. It was not until she was setting down the cup, that she beheld an old man and a young child walking slowly by, glancing at her proceedings with eyes of modest but hungry admiration.

"Hey!" cried the lady. "Yes, to be sure – Who won the Helter-Skelter Plate at the races, child?"

"I don't know, ma'am."

"Don't know!" repeated the lady. "Why, you were there. I saw you with my own eyes."

Nell was not a little alarmed to hear this, thinking the lady might be intimately acquainted with the firm of Short and Codlin; but what followed tended to reassure her.

"And very sorry I was," said the lady, "to see you in company with a Punch; a low, practical, wulgar wretch."

"I was not there by choice," returned the child. "We didn't know our

79

way, and the two men were very kind to us, letting us travel with them. Do you know them, ma'am?"

"Know 'em, child!" cried the lady in a sort of shriek. "Know them! But you're young and inexperienced. Do I look as if I know'd 'em, does the caravan look as if it know'd 'em?"

"No, ma'am, no," said the child, fearing she had committed some grievous fault. "I beg your pardon."

It was granted immediately, though the lady still appeared much ruffled by the degrading supposition. The child then explained that they had left the races and were travelling to the next town on that road, and she ventured to inquire how far it was. The reply was, that the town was eight miles off.

This discouraging information dashed the child, who could scarcely repress a tear as she glanced along the darkening road. Her grandfather made no complaint, but he sighed heavily as he leaned upon his staff.

The lady noted the child's anxious manner. The child curtseyed, thanked her for her information, and giving her hand to the old man had already got some fifty yards, when the lady called to her.

"Come nearer," said she. "Are you hungry, child?"

"Not very, but we are tired, and it's – a – a long way."

"Well, hungry or not, you had better have some tea," rejoined her new acquaintance. "I suppose you are agreeable to that, old gentleman?"

The grandfather humbly pulled off his hat and thanked her. The lady handed down to them the tea-tray, the bread, butter and ham.

"Set 'em out near the hind wheels, child, that's the best place," said their friend, superintending the arrangements from above. "Now, both of you eat and drink as much as you can."

While they were thus engaged, the lady alighted on the earth, and hands clasped behind her, walked up and down, surveying the caravan from time to time with an air of calm delight. She then sat down upon the steps and called "George"; whereupon a man in a carter's frock parted the twigs in the hedge that concealed him.

"Yes, Missus," said George.

"How did you find the cold pie? And the beer," said the lady, "is it passable, George?"

"It's more flatterer than it might be," George returned, "but it an't so bad for all that."

80

He then took a sip from the stone bottle, and smacked his lips, winked his eye, and nodded his head.

The lady looked on approvingly, and then said, "we are not a heavy load, George? Would these two travellers make much difference to the horses?" pointing to Nell and the old man, who were preparing to resume their journey.

"They'd make a difference in course," said George doggedly.

"Would they make much difference?" repeated his mistress.

"The weight o' the pair, mum," said George, eyeing them with the look of a man who was calculating within half an ounce or so, "would be a trifle under that of Oliver Cromwell."

Nell was overjoyed to hear that they were to go forward in the caravan, for which she thanked its lady. She helped to put away the tea things, and, the horses being by that time harnessed, mounted into the vehicle, followed by her delighted grandfather. Their patroness then shut the door and sat herself at an open window; and, the steps being struck by George and stowed under the carriage, away they went, with a great noise of flapping and creaking and straining, and the bright brass knocker, which nobody ever knocked at, knocking one perpetual double knock of its own accord as they jolted heavily along.

CHAPTER 24

When they had travelled for some short distance, Nell ventured to look round the caravan and observe it more closely. One half was carpeted, to accommodate a sleeping-place, constructed after the fashion of a berth on board ship. The other half served for a kitchen, and was fitted up with a stove whose small chimney passed through the roof. It held also a larder, several chests, a great pitcher of water, and a few cooking-utensils and articles of crockery.

The lady of the caravan sat at one window, and little Nell and her grandfather sat at the other. The old man eventually fell asleep and the lady invited Nell to come and sit beside her.

"Well, child," she said, "how do you like this way of travelling?"

Nell replied that she thought it was very pleasant indeed. The lady sat looking at the child for a long time in silence, and then getting up, brought out from a corner a large roll of canvas about a yard in width, which she laid upon the floor and spread open with her foot.

"There, child," she said, 'read that,"

Nell walked down it, and read aloud, in enormous black letters, the inscription, "Jarley's *waxwork*."

"That's me," said the lady. "I am Mrs Jarley."

Giving the child an encouraging look, intended to reassure her, the lady unfolded another scroll, whereon was the inscription, "One hundred figures the full size of life," and then another scroll, "The only stupendous collection of real waxwork in the world," and then several smaller scrolls with such inscriptions as "Now exhibiting within", "The genuine and only Jarley", "Jarley is the delight of the Nobility and Gentry", "The Royal Family are the patrons of Jarley". When she had shown these to her young companion, Mrs Jarley rolled them up, put them carefully away, and sat down, looking at the child in triumph.

"Never go into the company of a filthy Punch any more," said Mrs Jarley, "after this."

"I never saw any waxwork, ma'am," said Nell. "Is it funnier than Punch?"

"Funnier!" said Mrs Jarley in a shrill voice. "It is not funny at all."

"Oh!" said Nell, with all possible humility.

"It isn't funny at all," repeated Mrs Jarley. "It's calm and – what's that word again – critical? – no – classical, that's it – it's calm and classical. No low beatings and knockings about, but always the same, with a constantly unchanging air of coldness and gentility; and so like life, that if waxwork only spoke and walked about, you'd hardly know the difference."

"Is it here, ma'am?" asked Nell, whose curiosity was awakened.

"Is what here, child?"

"The waxwork, ma'am."

"Why, bless you, child, what are you thinking of? How could such a collection be here? It's gone on in the other wans to the assembly rooms, and there it'll be exhibited the day after tomorrow. You are going to the same town, and you'll see it I dare say."

"I shall not be in the town, I think, ma'am," said the child.

"Not there!" cried Mrs Jarley. "Then where will you be?"

"I – I'm not quite certain."

"You don't mean to say that you're travelling about the country without knowing where you're going?" said the lady of the caravan. "What curious people you are! What line are you in? You looked to me at the races, child, quite out of your element."

"We were there quite by accident," returned Nell, confused by this abrupt questioning. "We are poor people, ma'am, wandering about. We have nothing to do – I wish we had."

"You amaze me even more," said Mrs Jarley, after a pause. "I never heard of such a thing!"

She remained silent after this exclamation, but at length said, "And yet you can read. And write too, I expect?"

"Yes, ma'am," said the child, fearful of giving new offence by the confession.

"Well, and what a thing that is," returned Mrs Jarley. "I can't!"

Mrs Jarley then relapsed into a thoughtful silence, and remained in that state so long that Nell withdrew to the other window and rejoined her grandfather, who was now awake.

At length the lady summoned the driver to her window, and held a long conversation with him in a low voice, as if she were asking his advice on an important point. This conference at length concluded, she drew in her head again, and beckoned Nell to approach.

"And the old gentleman too," said Mrs Jarley, "for I want to speak with him. Do you want a good situation for your granddaughter, master?"

"I can't leave her," answered the old man. "We can't separate. What would become of me without her?"

"I should have thought you were old enough to take care of yourself," retorted Mrs Jarley sharply.

"But I fear he never will be again," said the child in an earnest whisper. "Pray do not speak harshly to him. We are very thankful to you," she added aloud, "but we could not part if all the wealth of the world were halved between us."

Mrs Jarley was a little disconcerted by this answer, and looked at the old man, who tenderly took Nell's hand. After an awkward pause, she had another conference with the driver upon some point on which they did not seem to agree quite so readily; but they concluded at last, and she addressed the grandfather again.

"If you're really disposed to employ yourself," said Mrs Jarley, "you could help to dust the figures, and so forth. What I want your granddaughter for, is to point 'em out to the company. They would be soon learnt, and she has a way with her that people wouldn't think unpleasant. It's not a common offer, bear in mind," said the lady, rising into the tone and manner in which she was accustomed to address her audiences. "It's Jarley's waxwork, remember. The duty's very light and genteel, the company particularly select, the exhibition takes place in assembly rooms, town halls, large rooms at inns, or auction galleries. The whole forms an effect of imposing brilliancy hitherto unrivalled in this kingdom. Remember that the price of admission is only sixpence, and that this is an opportunity which may never occur again!"

Mrs Jarley then remarked that with reference to salary she could pledge herself to no specific sum until she had sufficiently tested Nell's abilities, and narrowly watched her in the performance of her duties. But board and lodging, both for her and her grandfather, she would provide.

Nell and her grandfather consulted together, and while they were so engaged, Mrs Jarley with her hands behind her walked up and down the caravan.

"Now, child?" cried Mrs Jarley, coming to a halt as Nell turned towards her.

"We are very much obliged to you, ma'am," said Nell, "and thankfully accept your offer."

"And you'll never be sorry for it," returned Mrs Jarley. "I'm pretty sure of that. So as that's all settled, let us have a bit of supper."

In the meanwhile, the caravan came at last upon the quiet paved streets of a town which were clear of passengers, for it was by this time near midnight. They turned aside into waste ground that lay just within the old town-gate, and drew up for the night, near to another caravan, bearing the great name of Jarley.

This machine being empty (for it had deposited its burden at the place of exhibition) was assigned to the old man as his sleeping-place for the night; and within its wooden walls, Nell made him up the best bed she could, from the materials at hand. For herself, she was to sleep in Mrs Jarley's own travelling-carriage, as a signal mark of that lady's favour and confidence.

CHAPTER 25

When the child awoke, Mrs Jarley was already decorated with her large bonnet, and preparing breakfast. She received Nell's apology for being so late with perfect good humour, and said that she should not have roused her if she had slept on until noon.

"Because it does you good," said the lady, "when you're tired, to sleep as long as ever you can, and get the fatigue quite off."

The meal finished, Mrs Jarley then arrayed herself in an exceedingly bright shawl ready to make a progress through the streets of the town.

"The wan will come on to bring the boxes," said Mrs Jarley, "and you had better come in it, child. I am obliged to walk; the people expect it of me. How do I look, child?"

Nell returned a satisfactory reply, and Mrs Jarley went forth majestically.

The caravan followed at no great distance. As it jolted through the streets, Nell peeped from the window, curious to see what kind of place it was. It was a pretty large town, with an open square that they were crawling slowly across, and in the middle of which was the Town Hall, with a clock tower. There were houses of stone, red brick, yellow brick, houses of lath and plaster; and houses of wood, many of them very old. The streets were very clean, very sunny, very empty, and very dull. A few idle men lounged about the two inns and some old people were dozing in chairs outside an alms-house wall.

Rumbling along, the caravan stopped at last, and Nell dismounted amidst an admiring group of children, who evidently supposed her to be an important item of the curiosities, and were fully impressed with the belief that her grandfather was a cunning device in wax. The chests were taken out, to be unlocked by Mrs Jarley who, attended by George and another man in velveteen, disposed their contents to the best advantage in the decoration of the room.

They all swiftly got to work. As the stupendous collection was still concealed by cloths, lest the envious dust should injure their complexions, Nell helped in the embellishment of the room. The two men being well used to it, did a great deal in a short time.

When the festoons were all put up as tastily as they might be, the stupendous collection was uncovered, and there were displayed, on a raised platform some two feet from the floor, running round the room and parted from the rude public by a crimson rope breast high, divers effigies of celebrated characters, singly and in groups, clad in glittering dresses of various climes and times, with their eyes very wide open, and their nostrils very much inflated, and the muscles of their legs and arms very strongly developed, and all their countenances expressing great surprise. All the gentlemen were very pigeon-breasted and very blue about the beards; and all the ladies were miraculous figures.

When Nell had exhausted her first raptures at this glorious sight, Mrs Jarley ordered the room to be cleared of all but herself and the child, and, sitting herself down in an armchair in the centre, formally invested Nell with a willow wand, long used by herself for pointing out the characters, and began to instruct her.

"That," said Mrs Jarley in her exhibition tone, as Nell touched a figure at the beginning of the platform, "is an unfortunate Maid of Honour in the Time of Queen Elizabeth, who died from pricking her finger in consequence of working upon a Sunday. Observe the blood which is trickling from her finger; also the gold-eyed needle of the period, with which she is at work."

All this, Nell repeated twice or thrice, pointing to the finger and the needle at the right times, and then passed on to the next.

"That, ladies and gentlemen," said Mrs Jarley, "is Jasper Packlemerton who courted and married fourteen wives, and destroyed them all, by tickling the soles of their feet when they slept. On the scaffold, asked if he was sorry for what he had done, he replied yes, he was sorry for having let 'em off so easy, and hoped all Christian husbands would pardon him the offence. Let this be a warning to all young ladies to be particular in the character of the gentlemen of their choice. Observe that his fingers are curled as if in the act of tickling, and that his eye is winking, as he appeared when committing his barbarous murders."

When Nell knew all about Mr Packlemerton, and could say it without faltering, Mrs Jarley passed on to the fat man, and then the thin man, the tall man, the short man, the lady who died of dancing at a hundred and thirty-two, the wild boy of the woods and other characters and interesting but misguided individuals. After a couple of hours, Nell was in full possession of all their histories, and perfectly able to enlighten visitors.

CHAPTER 26

Although her duties were sufficiently laborious, Nell found Mrs Jarley to be a very kind and considerate person, who made sure everybody about her was comfortable. As Nell's popularity procured her various little fees from the visitors on which her patroness never demanded any toll, and as her grandfather too was well treated and useful, she had no cause of anxiety.

She slept, for their better security, in the room where the waxwork figures were. She would often sit at the open window and feel a companionship in the bright stars. At these times, she would recall the old house, and then she would think of poor Kit and all his kindness, until the tears came, and she would weep and smile together.

Often at this silent hour, her thoughts reverted to her grandfather, and she wondered how much he remembered of their former life. He was very patient, and glad to be of use, but he was in the same listless state, a harmless fond old man, alive to nothing more.

But, cause for deeper and heavier sorrow was yet to come.

One evening, Nell and her grandfather went out to walk. They had been rather closely confined for some days, and the weather being warm, they strolled a long distance. Clear of the town, they took a path through some pleasant fields, judging that it would return to the road they had left. It made, however, a much wider circuit.

It had been gradually getting overcast, and now the sky was dark. The wind began to moan in hollow murmurs, as the sun went down and a train of dull clouds coming up against it, menaced thunder and lightning. Large drops of rain soon began to fall, and, as the storm clouds came sailing onward, there was heard the low rumbling of distant thunder.

They hurried along the road, hoping to find some house where they could shelter from the storm, which every moment increased in violence. Drenched with pelting rain, confused by the deafening thunder, they would have passed a solitary house unawares, had not a man, standing at the door, called to them.

"Why were you going past, eh?" he said, as he led the way along a passage to a room behind.

"We didn't see the house, sir, till we heard you calling," Nell replied.

"No wonder," said the man, "with this lightning. You had better stand by the fire and dry yourselves. Call for what you like if you want anything. If you don't want anything, you are not obliged to give an order. This is a public house, that's all. The Valiant Soldier is pretty well known hereabouts. Run by James Groves – Jem Groves – honest Jem Groves."

The night being warm, there was a large screen drawn across the room, for a barrier against the heat of the fire. There were men's voices coming from the other side.

"Nell, they're – they're playing cards," whispered the old man, suddenly interested. "Don't you hear them?"

"Look sharp with that candle," said a voice. "It's as much as I can do to see the pips on the cards as it is. Game! Seven-and-sixpence to me. Hand over."

"Do you hear, Nell, do you hear them?" whispered the old man again, as the money chinked upon the table.

The child saw with alarm that his whole appearance had changed completely. His face was flushed and eager, his eyes were strained, his breath came short, and the hand he laid upon her arm trembled.

"Bear witness," he muttered, looking upward, "that I always said it; that I knew it, dreamed of it, felt it was the truth! What money have we, Nell? I saw you with money yesterday. Give it to me."

"No, no, let me keep it, grandfather," said the frightened child. "Let us leave. Forget the rain. Pray let us go."

"Give it to me, I say," returned the old man fiercely. "Hush, don't cry, Nell. If I spoke sharply, dear, I didn't mean it. It's for thy good. I have wronged thee, Nell, but I will right thee yet. Where is the money?"

"Do not take it," said the child. "For both our sakes let me keep it, or better let me throw it away, than you take it now. Let us go."

"Give me the money," returned the old man, "I must have it. There – that's my dear Nell. I'll right thee one day, child, never fear!"

She took from her pocket a little purse. He seized it, and hastily made his way to the other side of the screen. The trembling child followed close behind.

The landlord had placed a light upon the table, and was drawing the curtain. The speakers were two men, with a pack of cards and some money between them.

The old man shook the little purse in his eager hand, and then threw it

88

down upon the table, and gathered his cards as a miser would clutch at gold.

"We'll make a four-handed game of it, and take in Groves," said the stout man. "Come, Jemmy."

The landlord approached the table and took his seat. The child, in a perfect agony, drew her grandfather aside, and implored him, even then, to come away.

"Come, and we may be so happy," said the child.

"We *will* be happy," replied the old man hastily. "Let me go, Nell. The means of happiness are on the cards. We must rise from little winnings to great. I shall but win back my own."

"God help us!" she cried. "What hard fortune brought us here?"

"Hush!" rejoined the old man laying his hand upon her mouth, "Fortune will not bear chiding."

"Now, mister," said the stout man. "If you're not playing, give us the cards, will you?"

"I am," cried the old man. "Sit thee down, Nell, and look on. Be of good heart, it's all for thee, every penny."

The child sat by, and watched the progress with a troubled mind. Mindful only of the desperate passion that had taken hold upon her grandfather, losses and gains were to her alike. Exulting in some brief triumph, or cast down by a defeat, there he sat so wild and restless, so feverishly and intensely anxious, that she could have almost preferred to see him dead. And yet she was the innocent cause of all this torture, and he, gambling with such a savage thirst for gain as the most insatiable gambler never felt, had not one selfish thought!

On the contrary, the other three were yet as cool as if every virtue had been centered in their breasts. They sat, with a calm indifference to everything but their cards.

The storm had raged for full three hours; the lightning had grown fainter and less frequent; the thunder had gradually died away – still the game went on, and the anxious child was quite forgotten.

CHAPTER 27

At length play came to an end, with but one winner.

Although Nell's purse lay empty by his side, and the other players had now left the table, the old man sat poring over the cards, dealing as they had been dealt before, and turning up the different hands to see what each man would have held if they had still been playing. The child drew near, telling him it was near midnight.

"See the curse of poverty, Nell," he said, pointing to the packs on the table. "If I could have gone on just a little longer, luck would have turned on my side. See here – and there – and here again."

"Put them away," urged the child. "Try to forget them."

"Forget them!" he rejoined incredulously, raising his haggard face to hers. "How are we ever to grow rich if I forget them?"

The child could only shake her head.

"No, Nell," said the old man, patting her cheek. "They must not be forgotten. Patience, and we'll right thee yet, I promise thee. Lose today, win tomorrow. Come, I am ready."

"Do you know what the time is?" said Mr Groves, who was smoking with his friends. "Past twelve o'clock – "

"It's very late," said the uneasy child. "I wish we had gone before. What will they think! It will be two o'clock by the time we get back. What would it cost, sir, if we stopped here?"

"Two good beds, one-and-sixpence; supper and beer one shilling; total two shillings and sixpence," replied the Valiant Soldier.

Now, Nell had still the piece of gold sewn in her dress; and when she reflected that if they remained where they were, and rose early in the morning, they might get back before Mrs Jarley awoke, and could plead the violence of the storm as a good apology for their absence – she decided, after some hesitation, to remain. She therefore took her grandfather aside, and telling him that she had still enough left for the cost of their lodging, proposed that they should stay there for the night.

"If I had only known that just now!" muttered the old man.

"We will stop here if you please," said Nell, turning to the landlord.

"I think that's prudent," returned Mr Groves. "You shall have your suppers directly."

Accordingly, he brought in the bread and cheese, and beer, and bade his guests fall to, and make themselves at home. Nell and her grandfather ate sparingly, both occupied with their own reflections.

As they would leave the house very early, the child was anxious to pay before they retired to bed. But she felt she must conceal her little hoard from her grandfather, and needing change from her piece of gold, she removed it from its hiding place, and followed the landlord when he left the room.

"Will you give me the change here, please?" said the child.

Mr Groves was evidently surprised, and checked it. The coin being genuine, he counted out her change. The child returned to the room, but she fancied she saw a figure gliding in at the door. She had been watched!

But by whom? When she re-entered the room, she found its inmates as she had left them. She was puzzled for a moment. Then she asked her grandfather in a whisper whether anybody had left the room while she was absent. "No," he said, "nobody."

It must have been her fancy then. She was still thinking of it, when a girl came to light her to bed.

The old man took leave of the company at the same time, and they went upstairs together. It was a great, rambling house and she left her grandfather in his chamber, and followed her guide to another at the end of a passage.

The child could not help thinking of the figure downstairs.

Then came the anxieties to which the adventures of the night gave rise. Here was the old passion awakened again in her grandfather's breast. What fears their absence might have occasioned already! Persons might be seeking for them even then. Would they be forgiven in the morning, or turned adrift again! Oh! Why had they stopped in that strange place?

At last, sleep gradually stole upon her – a broken, fitful sleep, troubled by dreams. A deeper slumber followed this – and then – What! That figure in the room.

A figure was there. It slunk along, groping its way with noiseless hands, and stealing round the bed. She had no voice to cry for help, no power to move, but lay still, watching it.

She saw the turning of the head, and knew how the eyes looked and the ears listened. There it remained, motionless as she. At length, it busied its hands, and she heard the chink of money.

91

Then, replacing the garments it had taken from the bedside, it dropped upon its hands and knees, and crawled away. How slowly it seemed to move, creeping along the floor! It reached the door at last, and stood up. The steps creaked, and it was gone.

The child's first impulse was to fly from the terror of being alone in that room. With no consciousness of having moved, she gained the door. There was the dreadful shadow, pausing at the bottom of the steps. It stood quite still, and so did she.

The rain beat fast and furiously without. The figure moved again. The child involuntarily did the same. Once in her grandfather's room, she would be safe.

It crept along the passage until it came to the very door she longed to reach. The child, in the agony of being so near, had almost darted forward meaning to burst into the room when the figure stopped again.

The idea flashed suddenly upon her – what if it entered there! She felt faint and sick. It went in. There was a light inside. The figure was now in the room, and she, still dumb, stood looking on.

The door was partly open. Not knowing what she meant to do, she staggered forward and looked in.

What sight was that which met her view!

The bed had not been lain on. And at a table sat the old man himself, his white face pinched and sharpened and his eyes unnaturally bright – counting the money of which his hands had robbed her.

CHAPTER 28

With faltering steps, the child withdrew, groping her way back. No strange robber, no treacherous host, no nightly prowler could have awakened in her bosom half the dread which the recognition of her silent visitor inspired. The grey-headed old man gliding into her room and acting the thief while he supposed her asleep, then bearing off his prize and hanging over it with the ghastly exultation she had witnessed, was worse than her wildest dreams.

She had no fear of the dear old grandfather, in whose love for her this disease of the brain had been engendered; but the man she had seen that night, caught up in the game of chance, lurking in her room, and counting the money by the glimmering light, seemed like a monstrous distortion of his image, something to recoil from, because of the likeness to him. She had wept to see him dull and quiet. How much more she wept now!

She stole down the stairs and passage again. The door was still ajar, and the candle burning as before. Looking into the room, she saw him lying calmly on his bed.

Fast asleep. No passion in the face, no avarice, no wild desire; all gentle, tranquil, and at peace. This was her dear old friend, her good, kind grandfather.

She had no fear as she looked upon his slumbering features, but she had a deep and weighty sorrow, and it found its relief in tears.

"God bless him!" said the child, stooping softly to kiss his placid cheek. "I know now, that they would indeed part us if they found us, and shut him up. He has only me to help him."

She regained her own room and sat up the remainder of that long miserable night.

At last she fell asleep. She was roused early by the girl who had shown her to her bed. But first she searched her pocket and found that her money was all gone – not a sixpence remained.

The old man was ready, and in a few seconds they were on their road. The child thought he avoided her eye, as if expecting that she would tell him of her loss. She felt she must do that, or he might suspect the truth.

"Grandfather," she said, after they had walked about a mile in silence, "do you think they are honest people at the house yonder?"

"Why?" returned the old man, trembling. "Do I think them honest – they played honestly."

"I lost some money last night," rejoined Nell, "from my bedroom. Unless it was taken by somebody in jest, dear grandfather, which would make me laugh heartily if I could but know it – "

"Who would take money in jest?" returned the old man in a hurried manner. "Those who take money, take it to keep. Don't talk of jest."

"Then it was stolen from my room, dear," said the child, whose last hope was destroyed by the manner of this reply.

"But is there no more, Nell?" said the old man. "Was it all taken – was there nothing left?"

"Nothing," replied the child.

"We must get more," said the old man, "we must earn it, Nell, hoard it up, scrape it together. Never mind this loss. Tell nobody of it, and perhaps we may regain it. Don't ask how – we may regain it, but tell nobody, or trouble may come of it."

The child hung down her head and wept.

"Not a word about it to anyone but me," said the old man, "no, not even to me. All the losses that ever were, are not worth thy tears, darling. Why should they be, when we will win them back?"

"Let them go," said the child looking up. "Let them go, once and for ever, and I would never shed another tear if every penny had been a thousand pounds."

"Well, well," returned the old man, checking himself as some impetuous answer rose to his lips, "She knows no better. I ought to be thankful for it."

"Have we been worse off," asked the child, "since you forgot these cares, and we have been travelling on together? Have we not been happier without a home to shelter us, than we were in that unhappy house?"

"She speaks the truth," murmured the old man. "It must not turn me, but it is the truth."

"Only remember what we have been since that bright morning when we turned our backs upon it for the last time – what peaceful days and quiet nights we have had – what pleasant times we have known. If we have been tired or hungry, we have been soon refreshed, and slept the sounder for it. Think what beautiful things we have seen, and how contented we have felt. And why was this blessed change?"

He stopped her with a motion of his hand, and bade her talk to him no more just then, for he was busy. After a time he kissed her cheek, still motioning her to silence, and walked on, looking far before him, as if he were painfully trying to collect his disordered thoughts. Once she saw tears in his eyes. When he had gone on thus for some time, he took her hand as he was accustomed to do, with nothing of the violence or animation of his late manner; and so, by fine degrees, he settled down into his usual quiet way, and suffered her to lead him where she would.

When they presented themselves back at the stupendous collection, they found, as Nell had anticipated, that Mrs Jarley was not yet out of bed. Although she had suffered some uneasiness and had indeed sat up for them until past eleven o'clock, she had retired convinced that they had sought the nearest shelter, and would not return before morning.

That same evening, as she had dreaded, her grandfather stole away, and did not come back until the night was far spent. Worn out as she was, and fatigued in mind and body, she sat up alone, counting the minutes, until he returned – penniless, broken-spirited, and wretched, but still hotly bent upon his infatuation.

"Get me money," he said wildly, as they parted for the night. "I must have money, Nell. It shall be paid thee back with gallant interest one day, but all the money that comes into thy hands, must be mine – not for myself, but to use for thee. Remember that, Nell!"

What could the child do, but give him every penny that came into her hands, lest he should be tempted to rob their benefactress? She thought if she told the truth he would be treated as a madman. If she did not supply him with money, he would supply himself – but supplying him, she fed the fire that burnt him up, putting him perhaps beyond recovery. Distracted by these thoughts, tortured by anxiety whenever the old man was absent, and dreading alike his return, the colour left her cheek, her eye grew dim, and her heart was heavy. All her old sorrows returned, augmented by new fears and doubts; by day they were ever present to her mind; by night they hovered round her pillow, and haunted her dreams.

CHAPTER 29

We should now become acquainted with a few particulars connected with the domestic economy of Mr Sampson Brass, so we travel swiftly to Bevis Marks. We arrive before a small dark house, once the residence of Mr Sampson Brass.

In the parlour window of this little habitation, while occupied by Sampson Brass, there hung, all awry, and faded by the sun, a curtain of faded green. Inside there was not much to look at. A rickety table, with bundles of papers, yellow and ragged from long carriage in the pocket, a couple of stools set on opposite sides of this piece of furniture, a treacherous old chair by the fire-place, a second-hand wig box, used as a depository for blank writs and declarations, two or three common books of practice, a jar of ink, a stunted hearth-broom, a carpet trodden to shreds – these were among the most prominent decorations of the office of Mr Sampson Brass.

The office commonly held two examples of animated nature, important in this history.

Of these, one was Mr Brass himself. The other was his clerk, assistant, housekeeper, secretary, confidential plotter, adviser, intriguer, and bill of cost increaser, Miss Brass – a kind of Amazon at common law, of whom it may be desirable to offer a brief description.

Miss Sally Brass, then, was a lady of about thirty-five, a gaunt and bony figure. She bore a striking resemblance to her brother. In complexion Miss Brass was sallow, her voice deep and rich in quality, and, once heard, not easily forgotten. Her usual dress was a green gown, tight to the figure, and terminating at the throat, fastened by a peculiarly massive button.

In mind, she was of a strong and vigorous turn, having from her earliest youth devoted herself to the study of law. Nor had she, like many persons of great intellect, confined herself to theory, or stopped short where practical usefulness begins; inasmuch as she could fair-copy, fill up printed forms with perfect accuracy, and, in short, transact any ordinary duty of the office down to preparing a skin of parchment or mending a pen.

One morning Mr Sampson Brass sat upon his stool copying some legal process; and Miss Sally Brass sat upon her stool preparing a little bill, which was her favourite occupation. So they sat in silence for a long time.

"Have we got any other client like him?" said Brass. "Have we – will you answer me that?"

"Do you mean in the face?" said his sister.

"Do I mean in the face!" sneered Sampson Brass, reaching over to take up the bill-book. "Look here – Daniel Quilp, Esquire – Daniel Quilp, Esquire – Daniel Quilp, Esquire – all through. Do I take a clerk that he recommends, and says, 'this is the man for you,' or lose all this, eh?"

Miss Sally made no reply, but smiled, and went on with her work.

"But I know what it is," resumed Brass after a short silence. "You're afraid you won't have as long a finger in the business as you've been used to have. Do you think I don't see through that?"

"The business wouldn't go on very long, I expect, without me," returned his sister. "Don't be a fool and provoke me, Sammy."

Sampson Brass, who feared his sister, sulkily bent over his writing again, and listened as she said: "If I decided that the clerk ought not to come, of course he wouldn't be allowed to come. You know that well enough, so don't talk nonsense."

They both plied their pens at a great pace, the discussion ended.

While they were thus employed, the window was suddenly darkened. As Mr Brass and Miss Sally looked up, the top sash was lowered from without, and Quilp thrust in his head.

"Hallo!" he said, standing on tip-toe on the window-sill. "Is there anybody at home? Is Brass at a premium, eh?"

"Ha, ha, ha!" laughed the lawyer in an affected ecstasy. "Oh, very good, sir! Dear me, what humour he has!"

"Is that my Sally?" croaked the dwarf, ogling the fair Miss Brass. "Is it Justice with the bandage off her eyes, and without the sword and scales? Open the door, I've got him here. Such a clerk for you, Brass, such a prize. Be quick and open the door."

Pretending great alacrity, Mr Brass opened the door, and returned, introducing his client, who led by the hand none other than Mr Richard Swiveller.

"There she is," said Quilp, stopping at the door, as he looked towards Miss Sally. "There is the woman I ought to have married – there is the beautiful Sarah – there is the female who has all the charms of her sex and none of their weaknesses. Oh Sally, Sally!"

To this amorous address Miss Brass briefly responded "Bother!"

"Hard-hearted as the metal from which she takes her name," said Quilp. "Why don't she change it – melt down the brass, and take another name?"

"Hold your nonsense, Mr Quilp, do," returned Miss Sally, with a grim smile. "I wonder you're not ashamed of yourself before a strange young man."

"The strange young man," said Quilp, handing Dick Swiveller forward, "is too susceptible himself not to understand me well. This is Mr Swiveller, my intimate friend – a gentleman of good family and great expectations, but who is content for a time to fill the humble station of a clerk. To be out of harm's way he prudently thinks is something too, and therefore he accepts your brother's offer. Brass, Mr Swiveller is yours."

"I am very glad, sir," said Mr Brass, "Mr Swiveller, sir, is fortunate enough to have your friendship. You may be very proud, sir, to have the friendship of Mr Quilp."

Dick murmured something but he appeared to be absorbed in the contemplation of Miss Sally Brass, at whom he stared with blank and rueful looks, which delighted the watchful dwarf beyond measure. As to the divine Miss Sally herself, she rubbed her hands as men of business do, and took a few turns of the office with her pen behind her ear.

"I suppose," said the dwarf, turning briskly to his legal friend, "that Mr Swiveller enters upon his duties at once? It's Monday morning."

"At once, if you please, sir, by all means," returned Brass.

"Miss Sally will teach him law, the delightful study of the law," said Quilp; "she'll be his guide, his friend, his Young Lawyer's Best Companion. With Miss Sally, and the beautiful fictions of the law, his days will pass like minutes."

"He is exceedingly eloquent," said Brass, looking at the roofs of the opposite houses. "He has an extraordinary flow of language. Beautiful, really."

"Where will Mr Swiveller sit?" said Quilp, looking round.

"Why, we'll buy another stool, sir," returned Brass. "We hadn't any thoughts of having a gentleman with us, sir, until you were kind enough to suggest it, and our accommodation's not extensive. In the meantime, if Mr Swiveller will take my seat, and try his hand at a fair copy of this ejectment, as I shall be out pretty well all the morning – "

"Walk with me," said Quilp. "I have a word or two to say to you on points of business. Can you spare the time?"

"You're joking, sir," replied the lawyer, putting on his hat. "I'm ready, Sir, quite ready. It's not everybody, sir, who has an opportunity of improving himself by the conversation of Mr Quilp."

The dwarf glanced sarcastically at his brazen friend, and turned upon his heel to bid adieu to Miss Sally. He then nodded to Dick Swiveller, and withdrew with the attorney.

Dick stood at the desk, staring with all his might at the beauteous Sally. When the dwarf reached the street, he mounted again upon the windowsill, and looked into the office for a moment with a grinning face. Dick glanced upward at him, but without recognizing him; and long after he had disappeared, still stood gazing upon Miss Sally Brass, seeing or thinking of nothing else.

Miss Brass being by this time deep in the bill of costs, took no notice whatever of Dick, but went scratching on, with a noisy pen. There stood Dick, gazing now at the green gown, now at the brown headdress, now at the face, and now at the rapid pen, in a state of stupid perplexity, wondering how he got into her company, and whether it was a dream. At last he heaved a deep sigh, and began slowly pulling off his coat.

Keeping his eye upon her, he dropped down silently upon Mr Brass's stool. Then becoming powerless again, rested his chin upon his hand, and opened his eyes wide.

When he had looked so long that he could see nothing, Dick turned over the leaves of the draft he was to copy, dipped his pen into the inkstand, and at last began to write. But he had not written half-a-dozen words when, reaching over to the inkstand to take a fresh dip, he happened to raise his eyes. There was Miss Sally Brass, in all her charms, and more tremendous than ever.

The unconscious maiden worked away, and never raised her eyes.

CHAPTER 30

After a couple of hours or so of diligent application, Miss Brass concluded her task, and recorded the fact by wiping her pen upon the green gown. She then arose from her stool, tied her papers into a formal packet with red tape, and taking them under her arm, marched out of the office.

"I am going out," said Miss Brass.

"Very good, ma'am," returned Dick. "And don't hurry yourself on my account to come back, ma'am," he added inwardly.

"If anybody comes on office business, take their messages, and say that the gentleman who attends to that matter isn't in at present, will you?" said Miss Brass.

"I will, ma'am," replied Dick.

"I shan't be very long," said Miss Brass, retiring.

"I'm sorry to hear it, ma'am," rejoined Dick when she had shut the door. "I hope you may be unexpectedly detained, ma'am. If you could manage to be run over, ma'am, but not seriously, so much the better."

Uttering these expressions of good will with extreme gravity, Mr Swiveller sat down in the client's chair and pondered.

"So I'm Brass's clerk, am I?" said Dick. "Brass's clerk, eh? And the clerk of Brass's sister – clerk to a female Dragon. Very good!"

As he was entirely alone, Mr Swiveller was directing his observations to the ceiling.

"Quilp offers me this place, which he says he can ensure me," resumed Dick after a thoughtful silence, and telling off the circumstances, one by one, upon his fingers. "Fred, who, I would have sworn would not have heard of such a thing, backs Quilp to my astonishment, and urges me to take it also – staggerer number one! My aunt in the country writes an affectionate note to say that she has made a new will, and left me out of it – staggerer number two. No money; no credit; no support from Fred; notice to quit the old lodgings – staggerers, three, four, five, and six!"

Dismissing his downfall with these reflections, Mr Swiveller shook off his despondency and assumed the cheerful ease of an irresponsible clerk.

He looked into the wig-box, the books, and ink-bottle; untied and inspected all the papers; carved a few devices on the table with a sharp blade; and wrote his name on the inside of the wooden coal-scuttle. Having, as it were, taken formal possession of his clerkship, he opened the window and leaned negligently out of it until a beer-boy happened to pass, whom he commanded to serve him with a pint of mild porter. Then, three or four little boys dropped in, on legal errands from three or four attorneys of the Brass grade. Then he tried his hand at drawing caricatures of Miss Brass with pen and ink, whistling very cheerfully all the time.

He was occupied in this diversion when a coach stopped near the door, and presently afterwards there was a loud double-knock. As the person did not ring the office bell, he pursued his diversion with perfect composure, even though no one else was in the house.

In this, he was mistaken; for, after the knock had been repeated, the door was opened, and somebody with a heavy tread went up the stairs and into the room above. There came a rapping of knuckles at the office door.

"Come in!" said Dick. "Don't stand upon ceremony. Come in!"

"Oh, please," said a little voice very low down in the doorway, "will you come and show the lodgings?"

Dick leant over the table, to see a small slipshod girl in a dirty apron and bib, which left nothing visible but her face and feet.

"Why, who are you?" said Dick.

To which the only reply was, "Oh, please will you come and show the lodgings?"

There never was such an old-fashioned child in her looks and manner. She seemed as much afraid of Dick, as Dick was amazed at her.

"I haven't got anything to do with the lodgings," said Dick. "Tell 'em to call again."

"Oh, but please will you come and show the lodgings," returned the girl. "It's eighteen shillings a week and us finding plate and linen. Boots and clothes is extra, and fires in winter-time is eightpence a day."

"Why don't you show 'em yourself? You seem to know all about 'em," said Dick.

"Miss Sally said I wasn't to, because people wouldn't believe the attendance was good if they saw how small I was first."

"This is strange," muttered Dick, rising. "Do you mean to say you are – the cook?"

"Yes, I do plain cooking," replied the child. "I'm housemaid too; I do all the work of the house."

The girl again urged her request, and certain mysterious bumping sounds on the staircase seemed to give note of the applicant's impatience. Richard Swiveller, therefore, sticking a pen behind each ear, hurried out to meet the single gentleman.

He was a little surprised to realise that the bumping sounds were the progress upstairs of the single gentleman's trunk. Mr Swiveller followed slowly behind.

The single gentleman said not a word, but when the trunk was at last in the bedroom, he sat down on it and wiped his face with his handkerchief. He was very warm, and well he might be; for, not to mention the exertion of getting the trunk upstairs, he was closely muffled in winter garments, though the thermometer had stood all day at eighty-one in the shade.

"I believe, sir," said Richard Swiveller, "that you desire to look at these apartments. They are very charming apartments, sir. They command an uninterrupted view of – of over the way, and they are within one minute's walk of – of the corner of the street."

"What's the rent?" said the single gentleman.

"One pound per week," replied Dick, improving on the terms.

"I'll take 'em."

"The boots and clothes are extras," said Dick; "and the fires in winter time are – "

"Are all agreed to," answered the single gentleman.

"Two weeks certain," said Dick, "are the – "

"Two weeks!" cried the single gentleman gruffly, eyeing him from top to toe. "Two years. I shall live here for two years. Here. Ten pounds down. The bargain's made." He turned to the other man.

"Coachman, you may go. So may you, sir,"

Mr Swiveller was so much confounded by the single gentleman riding roughshod over him, that he stood looking at him. The single gentleman, however, proceeded with perfect composure to unwind the shawl tied round his neck, and then to pull off his boots. Freed of these encumbrances, he went on to divest himself of his other clothing, which he folded up, piece by piece, and ranged in order on the trunk. Then, he pulled down the window-blinds, drew the curtains, wound up his watch, and, quite leisurely, got into bed.

"Take down the bill," were his parting words, as he looked out from between the curtains. "Let nobody call me till I ring the bell."

With that the curtains closed, and he seemed to snore immediately.

"This is a most remarkable sort of house!" said Mr Swiveller, as he walked into the office with the bill in his hand. "She-dragons conducting themselves like professional gentlemen; plain cooks of three feet high appearing mysteriously from underground; strangers walking in and going to bed without leave in the middle of the day! Well, it's no business of mine!"

CHAPTER 31

Mr Brass received the report of his clerk with much satisfaction, and as the ten-pound note proved to be a good and lawful note of the Bank of England, his good humour increased considerably. He even invited Mr Swiveller to partake of a bowl of punch with him at that indefinite period, "one of these days".

However, Miss Sally showed little emotion since she was not a little disappointed that the single gentleman had obtained the lodgings at such an easy rate, arguing that as he had set his mind upon them, he should have been charged double the usual terms. But neither the good opinion of Mr Brass, nor the dissatisfaction of Miss Sally, wrought any impression upon the young gentleman.

"Good morning, Mr Richard," said Brass, on the second day of Mr Swiveller's clerkship. "Sally found you a second-hand stool, sir, yesterday evening, in Whitechapel. You'll find that a first-rate stool, sir, take my word for it."

They had been writing for a long time in silence, in such a dull silence that Mr Swiveller (who required excitement) had several times fallen asleep, and written divers strange words with his eyes shut, when Miss Sally at length broke in upon the monotony of the office by expressing that Mr Richard Swiveller had "done it".

"Done what, ma'am?" said Richard.

"Do you know," returned Miss Brass, "that nothing has been seen or heard of the lodger since he went to bed yesterday afternoon?"

"Well, ma'am," said Dick, "I suppose he may sleep his ten pound out, in peace and quietness, if he likes."

"Ah! I begin to think he'll never wake," observed Miss Sally.

"Did he say, for instance," asked Brass, in a kind of comfortable tone – "I only ask you, to refresh your memory – did he say, for instance, that he was a stranger in London?"

"He said nothing," replied Dick.

The paper work continued until Mr Swiveller's dinner-time. At the first stroke of three, the new clerk disappeared. At the last stroke of five, he reappeared, and the office magically became fragrant with the smell of gin and water and lemon-peel.

"Mr Richard," said Brass, "this man's not up yet. Nothing will wake him, sir. What's to be done?"

"I should let him have his sleep out," returned Dick.

"Sleep out!" cried Brass. "He has been asleep now, six-and-twenty hours. We have been moving chests of drawers over his head, we have knocked double knocks at the street-door, but nothing wakes him."

"Perhaps a ladder," suggested Dick, "at the first-floor window – "

Mr Brass proposed that they should go upstairs together, and make a last effort to awaken the sleeper. Mr Swiveller, assenting, armed himself with his stool and the large ruler. Miss Brass was already ringing a hand-bell with all her might, and yet without producing the smallest effect upon their mysterious lodger.

"I can't see anything but the bed curtain," said Brass, his eye to the keyhole. "Is he strong, Mr Richard?"

"Very," answered Dick.

"It would be an extremely unpleasant circumstance if he was to bounce out suddenly," said Brass. "Keep the stairs clear. I should be more than a match for him, but I'm the master of the house, and the laws of hospitality must be respected. – Hallo there! Hallo, hallo!"

While Mr Brass, with his eye curiously twisted into the keyhole, tried to attract the lodger's attention, and while Miss Brass plied the hand-bell, Mr Swiveller stood on his stool close against the wall beside the door, and began a violent battery upon the upper panels. He rained down such a shower of blows that the noise of the bell was drowned; and the small servant, who lingered on the stairs below, was obliged to hold her ears lest she should be rendered deaf for life.

Suddenly the door was unlocked on the inside, and flung violently open. The small servant flew to the coal-cellar; Miss Sally dived into her own bedroom; Mr Brass, who was not remarkable for personal courage, ran into the next street.

Meanwhile, Mr Swiveller, on the top of the stool, drew himself into as flat a shape as possible against the wall, and looked, not unconcernedly, down upon the single gentleman, who appeared at the door growling and cursing in a very awful manner. He was turning into his room again, still growling vengefully, when his eyes met those of the watchful Richard.

"Have *you* been making that horrible noise?" said the single gentleman.

"I have been helping, sir," returned Dick, keeping his eye upon him, and waving the ruler gently in his right hand, as an indication of what the single gentleman had to expect if he attempted any violence.

"How dare you then," said the lodger.

"We had fears that you were dead, sir," said Dick, gently sliding to the ground.

The lodger lapsed into a broad grin and looked at Mr Swiveller with twinkling eyes. He was a brown-faced sunburnt man. Mr Swiveller was relieved to find him in such good humour, and, to encourage him, smiled himself.

"Come here, you impudent rascal!" was the lodger's answer as he re-entered his room.

Mr Swiveller followed him in, leaving the stool outside. The single gentleman, without notice or explanation of any kind, double-locked the door.

"Can you drink anything?" was his next inquiry.

Mr Swiveller replied that he was open to "a modest quencher" if the materials were at hand. Without another word, the lodger took from his great trunk a kind of temple, shining as of polished silver, and placed it carefully on the table.

Greatly interested, Mr Swiveller observed him closely. Into one little chamber of this temple, he dropped an egg, into another some coffee, into a third a compact piece of raw steak from a neat tin case, into a fourth, he poured some water. Then, with the aid of a phosphorus-box and some matches, he lit a spirit-lamp below the temple, then shut down the lids of all the little chambers. When he opened them, the steak was done, the egg was boiled, the coffee was accurately prepared, and his breakfast was ready.

"Hot water – " said the lodger, handing it to Mr Swiveller, "extraordinary rum, sugar, and a travelling glass. Mix for yourself. And make haste."

Dick complied, while the lodger took his breakfast.

"The man of the house is a lawyer, is he not?" said the lodger.

Dick nodded. The rum was amazing.

"The woman of the house – what's she?"

"A dragon," said Dick.

The single gentleman, perhaps because he had met with such things in his travels, merely inquired "Wife or Sister?"

"Sister," said Dick.

"So much the better," said the single gentleman, "he can get rid of her when he likes."

"I want to do as I like, young man," he added after a short silence; "to go to bed when I like, get up when I like, come in when I like, and to be asked no questions. The place will suit me, will it?"

"Yes," said Dick.

"Let them know my humour," said the single gentleman, rising. "If they disturb me, they lose a good tenant. If they try to know more, it's a notice to quit. It's better to understand these things at once. Good day."

"I beg your pardon," said Dick, halting at the door, which the lodger prepared to open. " The name – in case of letters – "

"I never have any," returned the lodger.

"Or if anybody should call."

"Nobody ever calls on me."

"If any mistake should arise from not having the name, don't say it was my fault, sir," added Dick, still lingering.

"I'll blame nobody," said the lodger, and in a moment Dick found himself on the staircase, and the door locked.

CHAPTER 32

As the single gentleman after some weeks' occupation of his lodgings invariably chose Richard Swiveller as his channel of communication; and as he proved himself a highly desirable inmate, paying for everything beforehand, giving very little trouble, making no noise; Mr Richard imperceptibly rose to an important position in the family.

He also found favour in the eyes of Miss Sally Brass.

It is obvious that Miss Brass knew but little of the world, other than in connection with the law; and that she would have little proficiency in those gentler and softer arts in which women usually excel. Miss Sally's accomplishments were all of a masculine and strictly legal kind.

It was on this lady, then, that Mr Swiveller burst in full freshness as something new and hitherto undreamed of, lighting up the office with scraps of song and merriment, conjuring with inkstands and boxes of wafers, and catching three oranges in one hand. A sort of friendship sprung up between them. Mr Swiveller gradually came to look upon her as her brother Sampson did. He would often persuade her to undertake his share of writing in addition to her own; nay, he would sometimes reward her with a hearty slap on the back, and protest that she was a devilish good fellow, a jolly dog, and so forth; all of which compliments Miss Sally would receive with perfect satisfaction.

One circumstance troubled Mr Swiveller's mind very much, and that was that the small servant always remained somewhere in the bowels of the earth under Bevis Marks, and never came to the surface unless the single gentleman rang his bell. She never went out, or came into the office, or had a clean face, or took off the coarse apron, or looked out of any one of the windows, or stood at the street-door for a breath of air, or had any rest or enjoyment whatever. Nobody ever came to see her, nobody spoke of her.

"It's of no use asking the dragon," thought Dick one day, as he sat contemplating Miss Sally Brass. "I suspect if I asked any questions on that head, our alliance would be at an end."

"Where are you going, old fellow?" said Dick aloud, as Miss Sally wiped her pen as usual on the green dress, and stood up.

"To dinner," answered the dragon.

"To dinner!" thought Dick, "that's another thing. I don't believe that small servant ever has anything to eat."

"Sammy won't be home," said Miss Brass. "Stop till I come back. I shan't be long."

Dick nodded, and followed Miss Brass with his eyes to the door, and with his ears to a little back parlour, where she and her brother took their meals.

"Now," said Dick, walking up and down with his hands in his pockets, "I'd give something, if I had it, to know how they use that child, and where they keep her."

Mr Swiveller softly opened the office door, intenting to dart across the street for a glass of porter. At that moment he caught a parting glimpse of Miss Brass flitting down the kitchen stairs. "By Jove!" thought Dick, "she's going to feed the small servant. Now or never!"

First peeping over the handrail and allowing her head-dress to disappear in the darkness below, he groped his way down, and arrived at the door of a back kitchen immediately after Miss Brass had entered the same, bearing in her hand a cold leg of mutton. It was a miserable place, the walls disfigured by a thousand rents and blotches. The water was trickling out of a leaky butt. The grate was wound and screwed up tight, so as to hold no more than a little thin sandwich of fire. Everything was locked up; the coal-cellar, the candle-box, the salt-box, the meat-safe, were all padlocked.

The small servant stood before Miss Sally, and hung her head.

"Are you there?" said Miss Sally.

"Yes, ma'am," was the answer in a weak voice.

"Go further away from the leg of mutton, or you'll be picking it, I know," said Miss Sally.

The girl withdrew, while Miss Brass took a key from her pocket, and opening the safe, brought from it a dreary waste of cold potatoes. This she placed before the small servant, ordering her to sit down, and then took up a great carving knife.

"Do you see this?" said Miss Brass, slicing off about two square inches of cold mutton, and holding it out on the point of the fork.

The small servant looked hard at it with her hungry eyes, and answered, "yes."

"Then don't you ever go and say," retorted Miss Sally, "that you hadn't meat here. Eat it up."

This was soon done. "Now, do you want any more?"

The hungry creature answered with a faint "No," They were evidently going through an established form.

"You've been helped once to meat," said Miss Brass, summing up the facts. "You have had as much as you can eat, you're asked if you want any more, and you answer, 'no!'

With those words, Miss Sally put the meat away and locked the safe, and then drawing near to the small servant, overlooked her while she finished the potatoes.

Then Miss Brass, without the smallest present cause, rapped the child with the blade of the knife, now on her hand, on her head, and on her back, as if she found it quite impossible to stand so close to her without administering a few slight knocks. But then Mr Swiveller saw his fellow-clerk dart suddenly forward, and give the servant-girl some hard blows with her clenched hand. The victim cried, but in a subdued manner as if she feared to raise her voice, and Miss Sally, comforting herself with a pinch of snuff, ascended the stairs, just as Richard had safely reached the office.

CHAPTER 33

The single gentleman among his other peculiarities took a most extraordinary interest in the exhibition of Punch. If ever the sound of a Punch's voice reached Bevis Marks, the single gentleman, though in bed and asleep, would start up, and, hurrying on his clothes, make for the spot with all speed. As soon as the performance was over, the manager of the puppets and his partner were summoned to the single gentleman's chamber, where they conversed. But the secret of these discussions was of little importance. Bevis Marks was revolutionised by these popular movements, and peace and quiet fled its precincts.

One afternoon Mr Brass stopped short, and listening for a moment, and recognising the well-known voice, rested his head upon his hand, raised his eyes to the ceiling, and muttered faintly, "There's another!"

Up went the single gentleman's window directly.

The distant squeak was heard again. The single gentleman's door burst open. He ran violently down the stairs, out into the street, towards the quarter whence the sound proceeded.

"I wish I only knew who his friends were," muttered Sampson, filling his pocket with papers. With which words, and knocking his hat over his eyes as if to shut out even a glimpse of the dreadful visitation, Mr Brass hurried from the house.

As Mr Swiveller enjoyed these performances, upon the grounds that looking at a Punch, or indeed looking at anything out of window, was better than working, both he and Miss Sally rose as with one accord and took up their positions at the window.

The glass being dim, Mr Swiveller, following the friendly custom that he had established between them, hitched off the brown head-dress from Miss Sally's head, and dusted it carefully therewith. By the time he had handed it back, the lodger returned with the show and showmen at his heels. The exhibitor disappeared with all speed behind the drapery; and his partner, stationed himself by the side of the Theatre.

The drama proceeded to its close, and held the spectators in the customary manner. The lodger, as usual, summoned the men upstairs.

"Both of you," he called from the window, for only the actual exhibitor, a little fat man, prepared to obey the summons. "I want to talk to you!"

"Come, Tommy," said the little man.

"I an't a talker," replied the other. "What should I go and talk for?"

"The gentleman's got a bottle and glass up there," returned the little man.

"So what are we waiting for?" retorted the other with sudden alacrity. "Are you going to keep the gentleman waiting all day? Haven't you no manners?"

With this remonstrance, the melancholy man, no other than Mr Thomas Codlin, pushed past his friend, Mr Harris, otherwise Short or Trotters, and hurried to the single gentleman's apartment.

"Now, my men," said the single gentleman; "you have done very well. What will you take?"

The gentleman pointed to a couple of chairs, expecting them to be seated. Messrs Codlin and Short sat down, and held their hats very tight, while the single gentleman filled a couple of glasses from a bottle on the table beside him, and presented them in due form.

"You're pretty well browned by the sun, both of you," said their entertainer. "Have you been travelling?"

Mr Short replied in the affirmative with a nod and a smile.

"To fairs, markets, races, and so forth, I suppose?" pursued the single gentleman.

"Yes, sir," returned Short, "pretty nigh all over the West of England."

"I have talked to men of your craft from North, East, and South," returned their host; "but I never lighted on any from the West before."

"It's our reg'lar summer circuit is the West, master," said Short.

"Let me fill your glass again."

"Much obleeged to you sir, I think I will," said Mr Codlin, suddenly thrusting in his own and turning Short's aside. "In town or country, wet or dry, hot or cold, Tom Codlin suffers. But Tom Codlin isn't to complain. Oh, no! Short may complain, but if Codlin says a word – oh dear, down with him."

"Codlin an't without his usefulness," observed Short with an arch look, "but he don't always keep his eyes open. He falls asleep sometimes, you know. Remember them last races, Tommy."

"Will you never leave off?" said Codlin. "I couldn't have my eyes in twenty places at once. If I an't a match for an old man and a young child, you an't neither, so don't throw that out against me."

"You may as well drop the subject, Tom," said Short. "It isn't particular agreeable to the gentleman, I dare say."

"Then you shouldn't have brought it up," returned Mr Codlin.

Their entertainer had sat perfectly quiet in the beginning of this dispute, but, from the point where Mr Codlin was charged with sleepiness, he showed an increasing interest in the discussion.

"You are the two men I want," he said, "the two I have been searching after! Where are the old man and child you speak of?"

"Sir?" said Short, hesitating, and looking towards his friend.

"The old man and his grandchild who travelled with you – where are they? It will be worth your while to speak out, I assure you. They left you, you say – at those races, as I understand. They have been traced to that place, and there lost sight of. Have you no clue to their recovery?"

"Did I always say, Thomas," cried Short, turning with a look of amazement to his friend, "that there was sure to be an inquiry after them two travellers?"

"*You* said!" returned Mr Codlin. "Did I always say that that 'ere blessed child was the most interesting I ever see?"

"Good Heaven!" said the single gentleman, pacing up and down the room. "Have I found these men at last, only to discover that they can not help me! It would have been better never to have lighted on them, than to have my expectations scattered thus."

"Stay a minute. A man of the name of Jerry, sir," said Short, turning to their new acquaintance, "wot keeps a company of dancing dogs, told me, that he had seen the old gentleman in connection with a travelling waxwork."

"Is this man in town?" said the impatient single gentleman.

"Not now, but he will be tomorrow, for he lodges in our house," replied Mr Short rapidly.

"Then bring him here," said the single gentleman. "Here's a sovereign a-piece. If I can find these people through your means, it is but a prelude to twenty more. Return to me tomorrow, and keep your own counsel on this subject."

The address was given, the two men departed, the crowd went with them, and the single gentleman for two mortal hours walked in uncommon agitation up and down his room, over the wondering heads of Mr Swiveller and Miss Sally Brass.

CHAPTER 34

Kit, meanwhile, was gradually familiarising himself with Mr and Mrs Garland, Mr Abel, the pony, and Barbara, and gradually coming to consider them one and all as his particular private friends, and Abel Cottage, Finchley, as his own proper home.

Kit knew that his old home was a very poor place, and that his new one was very unlike it, and yet he was constantly looking back with grateful satisfaction and affectionate anxiety, and often sent square-folded letters to his mother, enclosing a shilling or such other small remittance, which Mr Abel's liberality enabled him to make. Sometimes being in the neighbourhood, he had leisure to call upon her, and then great was the joy and pride of Kit's mother.

Although Kit was in the very highest favour with the old lady and gentleman, and Mr Abel, and Barbara, it is certain that no member of the family liked him quite as much as the self-willed pony, who, from being the most obstinate and opinionated pony on the face of the earth, was, in his hands, the meekest and most tractable of animals.

Besides becoming in a short time a perfect marvel in all stable matters, Kit soon made himself a very tolerable gardener, a handy fellow within doors, and an indispensable attendant on Mr Abel. Mr Witherden the Notary, too, regarded him with a friendly eye.

One morning Kit drove Mr Abel to the Notary's office, and was about to drive off to a livery stable hard by, when the clerk emerged from the office.

"Pull up, Snobby," he cried to Kit. "You're wanted inside here."

"Has Mr Abel forgotten anything, I wonder?" said Kit as he dismounted. He scraped his shoes very carefully and tapped at the office door, which was opened by the Notary himself.

"Oh! Come in, Christopher," he said.

"Is that the lad?" asked an elderly gentleman in the room.

"That's the lad," said Mr Witherden. "He fell in with my client, Mr Garland, sir, at this very door. I have reason to think he is a good lad, sir, and that you may believe what he says. Let me introduce Mr Abel Garland, sir – his young master, my articled pupil, sir, and most particular friend, sir."

"Your servant, sir," said the stranger gentleman.

"Yours, sir, I'm sure," replied Mr Abel mildly. "You were wishing to speak to Christopher, sir?"

"Yes, I was. Have I your permission?"

"By all means."

"My business need be no secret here," said the stranger, observing that Mr Abel and the Notary were preparing to retire. "It relates to a dealer in curiosities with whom he lived, and in whom I am earnestly and warmly interested. I have been a stranger to this country, gentlemen, for very many years."

The Notary and Mr Abel remained.

"I have been making inquiries in the neighbourhood in which his old master lived," said the stranger, "and I learn that he was served by this lad. I have found out his mother's house, and have been directed by her to this place."

He turned to Kit and said: "If you think, my lad, that I am pursuing these inquiries with any other view than that of serving and reclaiming those I am in search of, you do me a very great wrong. Don't be deceived, I beg of you, but rely upon my assurance. The fact is, gentlemen," he added, turning again to the Notary and his pupil, "that I am in a very painful and wholly unexpected position. I came to this city with a darling object at my heart, expecting to find no obstacle. Instead I find myself checked and stopped short, in the execution of my design, by a mystery that I cannot penetrate. Every effort I have made has only served to render it darker and more obscure. I am afraid to stir openly in the matter, lest those whom I anxiously pursue, should fly still farther from me. I assure you that if you could give me any assistance, you would not be sorry to do so, if you knew how greatly I stand in need of it, and what a load it would relieve me from."

There was a simplicity in this confidence and the good-natured Notary replied, in the same spirit, that the stranger had not mistaken his desire, and that if he could be of service to him, he would, most readily.

Kit was then closely questioned by the gentleman on his old master and the child, their lonely way of life, and strict seclusion. The nightly absence of the old man, the solitary existence of the child at those times, his illness and recovery, Quilp's possession of the house, and their sudden disappearance, were all the subjects of much questioning and answer.

113

Finally, Kit informed the gentleman that the premises were now to let, and that a board upon the door referred all inquirers to Mr Sampson Brass, Solicitor, of Bevis Marks, from whom he might perhaps learn some further particulars.

"Not by inquiry," said the gentleman shaking his head. "I live there."

"Live at Brass's the attorney's!" cried Mr Witherden.

"Aye," was the reply. "I entered on his lodgings t'other day. It matters little where I live, and I hoped that some intelligence might be cast my way there, which would not reach me elsewhere. Yes, I live at Brass's, more shame for me, I suppose?"

"That's a mere matter of opinion," said the Notary, shrugging his shoulders. "He is looked upon as rather a doubtful character."

"Doubtful?" echoed the other. "I am glad to hear there's any doubt about it. I supposed that had been thoroughly settled, long ago. But may I speak a word or two with you in private?"

They walked into Mr Witherden's private closet, and remained there, in close conversation, for some quarter of an hour. The stranger seemed to have established himself in this short interval on quite a friendly footing.

"I'll not detain you any longer now," he said, putting a crown into Kit's hand, and looking towards the Notary. "You shall hear from me again. Not a word of this, you know, except to your master and mistress."

"Mother, sir, would be glad to know – " said Kit, faltering.

"Glad to know what?"

"Anything about Miss Nell."

"Would she? Well then, you may tell her if she can keep a secret. But mind, not a word of this to anybody else."

"I'll take care, sir," said Kit. "Thankee, sir, and good morning."

Now, it happened that the gentleman, in his anxiety to impress upon Kit that he was not to tell anybody, followed him out to the door to repeat his caution, and it further happened that at that moment Mr Richard Swiveller, in the area on an errand, turned in that direction, and beheld his mysterious friend and Kit together.

"Humph!" said Mr Swiveller pondering, "this is queer. Nothing but mysteries in connection with Brass's house. I'll keep my own counsel, however. Queer – very queer!"

CHAPTER 35

All that day, though he waited for Mr Abel until evening, Kit kept clear of his mother's house, determined not to anticipate the pleasures of the morrow, for tomorrow was the end of his first quarter – the day of receiving, for the first time, one fourth part of his annual income of Six Pounds in one vast sum of Thirty Shillings. It was to be a half-holiday devoted to a whirl of entertainments, including a play.

Not only were Mr and Mrs Garland intending to pay him the full amount; but the unknown gentleman had increased the stock by the sum of five shillings, which was in itself a fortune. But it was Barbara's quarter too and Barbara had a half-holiday as well. Barbara's mother was going to make one of the party, and to take tea with Kit's mother, and cultivate her acquaintance.

They were both up very early, with small appetites for breakfast and less for dinner. Barbara's mother arrived with news of glorious weather.

Time came for them to receive their gold and silver, and wasn't Mr Garland kind when he said, "Christopher, here's your money, and you have earned it well"; and wasn't Mrs Garland kind when she said, "Barbara, here's yours, and I'm much pleased with you."

Kit's mother was quite ready with a display of tea things that might have warmed the heart of a china-shop. Didn't she say within five minutes that Barbara's mother was exactly the sort of lady she expected, and didn't Barbara's mother say that Kit's mother was the very picture of what she had expected?

Soon it was high time to be thinking of the play. Kit's mother carried the baby, who was wide awake, and Kit held little Jacob in one hand, and escorted Barbara with the other, a state of things which occasioned the two mothers, who walked behind, to declare that they looked quite family folks, and caused Barbara to blush and say, "Now don't, mother!"

Dear, dear, what a place the theatre looked, with all the paint, gilding, and looking-glass; the vague smell of horses suggestive of coming wonders; the curtain that hid such gorgeous mysteries; the clean white sawdust down in the circus; the company coming in and taking their places; the fiddlers looking carelessly up at them while they tuned their instruments! What a glow was that, which burst upon them all, when that

115

long, clear, brilliant row of lights came slowly up; and what the feverish excitement when the little bell rang and the music began in good earnest!

Then the play itself! The horses which little Jacob believed from the first to be alive, and the ladies and gentlemen of whose reality he could be by no means persuaded, having never seen or heard anything at all like them – everything was delightful, splendid, and surprising! Little Jacob applauded till his hands were sore; Kit cried "an-kor" at the end of everything.

Supper was at an oyster shop, and they fell to work upon the supper in earnest. The greatest miracle of the night was little Jacob, who ate oysters as if he had been born and bred to the business – sprinkling the pepper and the vinegar with a discretion beyond his years. There never was a more successful supper; and when Kit ordered in a glass of something hot to finish with, and proposed Mr and Mrs Garland before sending it round, there were not six happier people in all the world.

But it was now growing late, and they agreed it was time to turn their faces homewards. So, after going a little out of their way to see Barbara and Barbara's mother safe to a friend's house, Kit and his mother left them at the door, with an early appointment for returning to Finchley next morning, and a great many plans for next quarter's enjoyment. Then, Kit took little Jacob on his back, and giving his arm to his mother, and a kiss to the baby, they all trudged merrily home together.

CHAPTER 36

Kit turned out at sunrise, and went to meet Barbara and her mother at the appointed place. Being careful not to awaken any of the little household, Kit left his money on the chimney-piece, with an inscription in chalk informing her that it came from her dutiful son; and went his way.

Kit and Barbara reached the cottage in Finchley in such good time that Kit had rubbed down the pony and made him as spruce as a race-horse, before Mr Garland came down to breakfast. At his usual hour Mr Abel walked out, to be overtaken by the London coach, and Kit and the old gentleman went to work in the garden.

This was not the least pleasant of Kit's employments. Today they were to trim the grape-vine, so Kit mounted half-way up a short ladder, and began to snip and hammer away, while the old gentleman handed up the nails and shreds of cloth as he wanted them. The old lady and Whisker looked on as usual.

"Well, Christopher," said Mr Garland, "and so you have made a new friend, eh?"

"I beg your pardon, sir?" returned Kit, looking down.

"You have made a new friend, I hear from Mr Abel," said the old gentleman, "at the office!"

"Oh! Yes sir, yes. He behaved very handsome, sir."

"I'm glad to hear it," returned the old gentlemen with a smile. "He is disposed to behave more handsomely still, though, Christopher."

"Indeed, sir! It's very kind in him, but I don't want him to, I'm sure," said Kit.

"He is rather anxious," pursued the old gentleman, "to have you in his own service."

"To have me in his service, sir?" cried Kit, stopping short in his work and facing about on the ladder. "Why, sir, I don't think he can be in earnest when he says that."

"Oh! He is indeed," said Mr Garland. "And he has told Mr Abel so."

"I never heard of such a thing!" muttered Kit, looking ruefully at his master and mistress.

"You see, Christopher," said Mr Garland, "this is important to you, and you should consider it in that light. This gentleman is able to give you more money than I – not, I hope, to carry through the various relations of master and servant, more kindness and confidence, but certainly, Christopher, to give you more money."

"Well," said Kit, "after that, sir – "

"Wait a moment," interposed Mr Garland. "That is not all. You were a very faithful servant to your old employers, as I understand, and should this gentleman recover them, as he is attempting to do by every means in his power, I have no doubt that you, being in his service, would meet with your reward. Besides," added the old gentleman with stronger emphasis, "besides meeting again those to whom you seem to be very strongly attached. You must consider, Christopher, and not be hasty in your choice."

117

Kit did suffer one twinge, one momentary pang, in keeping the resolution he had already formed. But it was gone in a minute, and he answered that the gentleman must look for somebody else.

"He cannot think that I'd be led away to go to him, sir," said Kit, turning after half a minute's hammering. "Does he think I'm a fool?"

"He may, perhaps, Christopher, if you refuse his offer," said Mr Garland gravely.

"Then let him, sir," retorted Kit; "what do I care, sir, what he thinks? Why should I care, sir, when I know that I should be a fool, to leave the kindest master and mistress that ever was or can be? If Miss Nell was to come back, ma'am," added Kit, turning suddenly to his mistress, "why that would be another thing, and perhaps if she wanted me, I might ask you now and then to let me work for her when all was done at home. But when she comes back, she'll be rich as old master always said she would, and being a rich young lady, what could she want of me? No, no," added Kit, shaking his head sorrowfully, "she'll never want me any more, and bless her, I hope she never may, though I'd like to see her too!"

Here Kit drove a nail into the wall, very hard – much harder than was necessary and having done so, faced about again.

"There's the pony, sir," said Kit. "Whisker, ma'am, would he let anybody come near him but me, ma'am? Here's the garden, sir, and Mr Abel, ma'am. Would Mr Abel part with me, sir, or is there anybody that could be fonder of the garden, ma'am? It would break mother's heart, sir, if she thought that Mr Abel could wish to part with me so soon, after having told me, only the other day, that he hoped we might be together for years to come – "

At that moment Barbara came running up to say that a messenger had brought a note, which, with an expression of some surprise at Kit's oratorical appearance, she put into her master's hand.

"Oh!" said the old gentleman after reading it, "ask the messenger to walk this way."

Barbara tripping off to do as she was bid, he turned to Kit and said that they would not pursue the subject any further, and that Kit could not be more unwilling to part with them, than they would be to part with Kit.

"At the same time, Christopher," added Mr Garland, glancing at the note in his hand, "if the gentleman should want to borrow you now and then for an hour or so, or even a day or so, at a time, we must consent to lend you, and you must consent to be lent. – Oh! Here is the young gentleman. How do you do, sir?"

This salutation was addressed to Mr Chuckster.

"Hope I see you well sir," returned that gentleman. "Hope I see *you* well, ma'am."

"You want to take Kit with you, I see?" observed Mr Garland.

"I have a cab waiting," replied the clerk.

When they reached the Notary's house, Kit followed into the office, and was desired by Mr Abel to sit down and wait, for the gentleman who wanted him had gone out, and perhaps might not return for some time. It was indeed some time before the gentleman whom he had seen before, returned.

He was closeted with Mr Witherden for some little time, and Mr Abel had been called in to assist at the conference, before Kit, wondering very much why he was wanted, was summoned to attend them.

"Christopher," said the gentleman, turning to him as he entered the room, "I have found your old master and young mistress."

"No, sir! Have you?" returned Kit, his eyes sparkling with delight. "Where are they, sir? How are they? Are they near here?"

"A long way from here," returned the gentleman, shaking his head. "But I am leaving tonight to bring them back, and I want you to go with me."

"Me, sir?" cried Kit, full of joy and surprise.

"The place," said the strange gentleman, turning to the Notary, "is – how far – sixty miles? If we travel post all night, we shall reach there early tomorrow morning. Now, as they will not know me, and the child, God bless her, would think that any stranger pursuing them had a design upon her grandfather's liberty – can I do better than take this lad, whom they both know and will readily remember, as an assurance to them of my friendly intentions?"

"Certainly not," replied the Notary. "Take Christopher by all means."

"I beg your pardon, sir," said Kit, whose face had lengthened while listening to the conversation, "but if that's the reason, I'm afraid I may do more harm than good. Miss Nell, sir, she knows me, and would trust in me, I am sure. But the old master – I don't know why, nobody does – he would not see me after he had been ill. Miss Nell herself told me that I must not let him see me again. I should spoil all that you were doing if

I went, I'm afraid. I'd give the world to go, but you had better not take me, sir."

"Another difficulty!" cried the impetuous gentleman. "Was ever man so beset as I? Is there nobody else that knew them, nobody else they trusted?"

"There's my mother," said Kit thoughtfully.

"Did they know her?" said the single gentleman.

"She was always coming backwards and forwards. Bless you, sir, she expected they'd come to her house."

"Then where the devil is the woman?" said the impatient gentleman, catching up his hat. "Why isn't she here?"

Kit, after weighing the matter in his mind and considering it carefully, promised, on behalf of his mother, that she should be ready within two hours from that time to undertake the expedition.

Having given this pledge, Kit lost no time in sallying forth.

CHAPTER 37

Kit made his way through the crowded streets, dividing the stream of people, dashing across the busy road-ways.

"Now, if she should be out," thought Kit, as he approached his mother's house, "and I not able to find her, this impatient gentleman would be in a pretty taking. And sure enough there's no light, and the door's fast," said Kit, knocking at the door.

A second knock brought no reply; but caused a woman over the way to look out and inquire who was wanting Mrs Nubbles.

"Me," said Kit. "She's at – at Little Bethel, I suppose?"

The neighbour nodded assent.

At the chapel, Kit paused at the door to take breath that he might enter with becoming decency.

A small gentleman was delivering in a by no means small voice, a by no means small sermon. Most of his audience were asleep, including Kit's mother.

"And now I'm here," thought Kit, gliding into the nearest empty pew which was opposite his mother's, and on the other side of the little aisle, "how am I ever to get at her? She'll never wake till it's all over! If they'd only sing!"

In his desperation and restlessness Kit cast his eyes about the chapel, and happening to glance upon a little seat in front of the clerk's desk, could scarcely believe he saw – Quilp!

He rubbed his eyes, but Quilp was there, sitting with his hands upon his knees, with the accustomed grin on his dirty face, and his eyes fixed upon the ceiling. He certainly did not glance at Kit or at his mother, and appeared utterly unconscious of their presence; still Kit could not help feeling, that the attention of the sly little fiend was fastened upon them, and upon nothing else.

But, astounded as he was by the apparition of the dwarf and certain that it was the forerunner of some trouble, he knew he had to withdraw his mother. Therefore, the next time little Jacob woke, Kit set himself to attract his attention – one sneeze did it, and he signed to him to rouse his mother.

Ill-luck would have it, however, that just then the preacher leaned over the pulpit and seemed to stare straight into little Jacob's eyes. Distracted by the sudden appearance of Kit, and fascinated by the eyes of the preacher, the miserable Jacob sat bolt upright, wholly incapable of motion.

With that Kit walked softly out of his pew and into his mother's.

"Mother!" whispered Kit. "Come with me, I've something to tell you."

"Where am I?" said Mrs Nubbles.

"In this blessed Little Bethel," returned her son, peevishly. "Come along, mother, everybody's looking at us. Don't make a noise – bring Jacob – that's right!"

"Stay, Satan, stay!" cried the preacher, as Kit moved off.

"This gentleman says to stay, Christopher," whispered his mother.

"Stay, Satan, stay!" roared the preacher again. "Tempt not the woman that doth incline her ear to thee, but harken to the voice of him that calleth. He hath a lamb from the fold!" cried the preacher, raising his voice still higher and pointing to the baby. "He beareth off a precious lamb!"

Somewhat excited by the circumstances, Kit turned round to the pulpit with the baby in his arms, and replied aloud, "No, I don't. He's my brother."

"He's *my* brother!" cried the preacher.

"He isn't," said Kit indignantly. "How can you say that? I shouldn't have come to take 'em away, unless I was obliged. I wanted to do it very quiet, but you wouldn't let me. Now, you have the goodness to let me alone, if you please."

So saying, Kit marched out of the chapel, followed by his mother and little Jacob, and found himself in the open air. Quilp, throughout the interruption, kept his eyes to the ceiling, seeming not to take the smallest notice.

"Oh, Kit!" said his mother, with her handkerchief to her eyes, "what have you done! I never can go there again!"

Kit led them briskly forward; and on the road home, he related what had passed at the Notary's house, and why he had intruded on the solemnities of Little Bethel.

His mother was not a little startled on learning what was required of her, and presently fell into a confusion of ideas, of which the most prominent were that it was a great honour to ride in a post-chaise, and that it was a moral impossibility to leave the children behind. But Kit was determined at the idea of recovering Nell.

"We've only ten minutes now, mother," said Kit when they reached home. "There's a bandbox. Throw in what you want, and we'll be off."

Kit hustled into the box all the things that might be wanted; he persuaded a neighbour to stop with the children; Kit's mother wouldn't leave off kissing them, but within a few minutes after the two hours had expired, Kit and his mother arrived at the Notary's door, where a post-chaise waited.

"With four horses I declare!" exclaimed Kit. "Here's my mother, sir. She's quite ready, sir."

"That's well," returned the gentleman. "Now, don't be in a flutter, ma'am. You'll be taken great care of. Come along." Thereupon he gave his arm to Kit's mother, handed her into the carriage as politely as you please, and took his seat beside her. Up went the steps, bang went the door, round whirled the wheels, and off they rattled.

Kit stood in the middle of the road, and looked after them with tears in his eyes – brought there by the return he anticipated. "They went away," he thought, "on foot with nobody to speak to them or say a kind word at parting, and they'll come back, drawn by four horses, with this rich gentleman for their friend, and all their troubles over! She'll forget that she taught me to write."

CHAPTER 38

We now return to follow the fortunes of little Nell; resuming the thread of the narrative at the point where it was left.

Between the old man and herself there had come a gradual separation. Every evening, and often in the daytime too, he was absent; and although she well knew where he went, and why – from the constant drain upon her scanty purse and from his haggard looks – he evaded all inquiry, even shunning her presence.

After wandering one evening she sat meditating sorrowfully upon this change, and mingling it, as it were, with everything about her, when the distant church-clock bell struck nine. Rising at the sound, she retraced her steps, and turned thoughtfully towards the town, aiming to return from her walk to Mrs Jarley's waxwork.

She had gained a little wooden bridge, when she came suddenly upon a ruddy light. As she drew closer she glanced towards the fire. There was a form between it and her, and the outline struck her as familiar. But she assured herself that it was not who she had supposed, and went on again.

But then the conversation by the fire resumed, and the tones of the voice that spoke sounded as familiar to her as her own.

It was her grandfather.

Her first impulse was to call to him. Instead she crept nearer to the place. Soon she stood among a few trees, and could both see and hear, without much danger of being observed.

She recognized the men as the card-players at the public house on the night of the storm. A lean gipsy stood close by.

"You keep me poor, and plunder me, and make a jest of me besides," said the old man, turning from one to the other.

The utter irresolution and feebleness of the grey-haired child, contrasted with the keen and cunning looks of those in whose hands he was, smote upon the little listener's heart. But she made herself listen to every word.

"What do you mean?" said the stout man. "You'd keep us poor if you could, wouldn't you? That's the way with you whining, puny, pitiful players. When you lose, you're martyrs; but when you win, do you look upon the other losers in that light?"

It was obvious that the speaker acted the bully, and his friend the peacemaker; or rather, it would have been clear to anyone but the weak old man. They exchanged glances quite openly, both with each other and with the gipsy, who grinned his approval.

The old man stood helplessly among them for a little time.

"I go on then," said one, "where I left off. If you feel that it's time for luck to turn but haven't means enough to try it, help yourself to what seems put in your way. Borrow it, and, when you're able, pay it back again."

"Certainly," the other added, "if this good lady as keeps the waxworks has money, and keeps it in a tin box when she goes to bed, and doesn't lock her door for fear of fire, it seems easy. Oh, imagine, the pleasures of winning! The delight of picking up the money and sweeping it into one's pocket! The – but you're not going, old gentleman?"

"I'll do it," said the old man, who had taken two or three steps away, and now returned as hurriedly. "I'll have it, every penny. He gives me my revenge, mind," he added, pointing to the other eagerly with his shrivelled hand.

"When does this match come off? Tonight?"

"I must have the money first," said the old man; "and that I'll have tomorrow – "

"Why not tonight?" urged one.

"It's late now, and I should be flurried," said the old man. "It must be softly done. No, tomorrow night."

"Then tomorrow be it. A drop of comfort here. Luck to the best man! Fill!" The gipsy produced tin cups, and filled them to the brim with brandy. The old man turned aside and muttered to himself before he drank.

"God be merciful to us!" cried the child within herself. "What shall I do to save him!"

They watched his stooping figure retreating slowly, and when he turned his head to look back, waved their hands, or shouted some brief encouragement. It was not until he was a mere speck that they turned to each other to laugh aloud.

"So," said one, warming his hands at the fire, "finally. He wanted more persuading than I expected. It's three weeks since we first put this in his head. What'll he bring, do you think?"

"Whatever he brings, it's split between us," returned the other.

The child crept away with cautious steps, keeping in the shadow of the hedges until she could emerge upon the road at a point beyond their range of vision. Then she fled homeward as quickly as she could.

The first idea that flashed upon her mind was instant flight; rather dying of want upon the roadside, than exposing him to such temptation. Then, she remembered that the crime was not to be committed until next night. There was time for thinking, and resolving what to do.

She tried to sleep. But who could lie passively down, distracted by such terrors? Half undressed, she flew to the old man's bedside, and roused him from his sleep.

"What's this!" he cried, starting up in bed.

"I have had a dreadful dream," cried the child. "A dreadful dream. I have had it before. It is a dream of grey-haired men like you, in darkened rooms by night, robbing sleepers of their gold. Up, up!"

The old man shook, and folded his hands like one who prays.

"I cannot sleep, I cannot stay here," she cried. "I cannot be under the roof where such dreams come. Up! We must fly,"

He looked at her as if she were a spirit and trembled.

"There is no time to lose," said the child. "Up! And away, with me!"

"Tonight?" murmured the old man.

"Yes, tonight," replied the child. "Tomorrow night will be too late. Nothing but flight can save us!"

The old man rose from his bed, his forehead bedewed with the cold sweat of fear. She took him by the hand and led him on. As they passed the door of the room he meant to rob, she shuddered and looked up at him. With what a look did he meet hers!

She took him to her own chamber, and, still holding him by the hand as if she feared to lose him for an instant, gathered together what she had, and hung her basket on her arm. The old man took his staff, and then she led him forth.

Through the streets, and narrow crooked outskirts, their trembling feet passed quickly. Up the steep hill too, crowned by the old grey castle, and not once did they look behind.

But as they drew nearer the ruined walls, the moon rose in all her gentle glory, and the child looked back upon the sleeping town, deep in the valley's shade; and as she did so, she clasped the hand she held less firmly, and bursting into tears, fell upon the old man's neck.

CHAPTER 39

Her momentary weakness past, the child urged her grandfather onward and looked back no more.

While he, subdued and abashed, seemed to crouch before her, the child herself was inspired with an energy and confidence she had never known. The whole burden of their two lives had fallen upon her, and henceforth she must think and act for both. At any other time, the thought of having deserted the friend who had shown them so much homely kindness, without a word of justification, would have filled her with sorrow and regret.

The night crept on, the moon went down, the stars grew pale and dim, and morning slowly approached. Then, from behind a distant hill, the noble sun rose up, driving the mists in phantom shapes before it. When it had climbed higher into the sky, they lay down to sleep, upon a bank, hard by some water.

But Nell retained her grasp upon the old man's arm, and long after he was slumbering soundly, watched him with untiring eyes. Fatigue stole over her at last; her grasp relaxed, tightened, relaxed again, and they slept side by side.

The next morning they walked on, keeping to quiet roads and tracks. The child walked with difficulty, for pain racked her joints. But she made no complaint; and the two travellers proceeded very slowly.

That evening she lay down with nothing between her and the sky; and with no fear for herself, for she was past it now. So very weak and spent, she felt, so very calm and unresisting, that she had no thought of any wants of her own. She tried to recall the way they had come.

A penny loaf was all they had had that day. It was very little, but even hunger was forgotten in the strange tranquillity that crept over her. She fell into a slumber. Morning came. Much weaker, diminished powers even of sight and hearing, and yet the child made no complaint. She felt a dull conviction that she was very ill, perhaps dying; but no fear or anxiety.

A loathing of food that she was not conscious of until they spent their last penny on another loaf prevented her joining in this meal. Her grandfather ate greedily, which she was glad to see.

With an undiminished resolution not to betray by any word or sigh her sinking state, the child, throughout that hard day, made herself proceed. Evening was drawing on, but had not closed in, when they came to a town.

They were dragging themselves along through the street, and the child felt that she could bear no more. There appeared before them, going in the same direction, a traveller on foot, reading from a book.

He walked fast, but at length stopped to look more attentively at some passage. The child shot on before her grandfather, and, going close to the stranger, began faintly, to implore his help.

He turned his head. The child clapped her hands together, cried out and fell senseless at his feet.

CHAPTER 40

It was none other than the schoolmaster they had so recently stayed with. Scarcely less surprised by the sight of the child, he stood for a moment, without even the presence of mind to lift her.

Quickly recovering his self-possession, he threw down his stick and book, and dropping on one knee beside her, endeavoured to restore her to herself. Her grandfather was standing by, wringing his hands, and imploring her to speak to him.

"She is quite exhausted," said the schoolmaster, glancing upward into his face. "You have taxed her powers too far, friend."

"I never thought how weak and ill she was," rejoined the old man.

Casting a look upon him, half-reproachful and half-compassionate, the schoolmaster took the child in his arms, and bid the old man follow.

There was a small inn within sight. Towards this place he hurried with his unconscious burden, and rushing into the kitchen, deposited it on a chair before the fire.

The landlady soon came running in, with a little hot brandy and water, which, being duly administered, recovered the child so far as to enable her to thank them in a faint voice, and to extend her hand to the poor schoolmaster. The women straightway carried her off to bed, and sent for the doctor.

While a light supper was being prepared, the child fell into a refreshing sleep, from which they were obliged to rouse her when it was ready. Her grandfather took his supper with her. They also made him up a bed in an inner room, to which he presently retired. The key of this chamber was on Nell's side of the door; she turned it when the landlady had withdrawn, and crept to bed again with a thankful heart.

The report in the morning was, that the child was better, but was extremely weak, and would require a day's rest, and careful nursing, before she could proceed. The schoolmaster observed that he had a day to spare, two days for that matter, and could afford to wait. He decided to visit her in her room that evening, and rambling out with his book, did not return until the hour arrived.

Nell could not help weeping when they were left alone. "It makes me unhappy even in the midst of all this kindness," said the child, "to think that we should be a burden upon you. How can I ever thank you? If I had not met you, I might have died, and he would have been left alone."

"We'll not talk about dying," said the schoolmaster; "and as to burdens, there have been some changes in my life since you stayed with me. I am to be clerk and schoolmaster to a village and I am on my way there now. They allowed me the stage-coach-hire, but as I had plenty of time, I determined to walk instead. How glad I am, to think I did so!"

"How glad should we be!"

"Yes, yes," said the schoolmaster, moving restlessly in his chair, "certainly, that's very true. But you – what have you been doing since you left me? Now, tell me."

The plain, frank kindness of the honest schoolmaster gave the child confidence in him and she told him all – that they had no friend or relative, that she had fled with the old man to save him from a madhouse and all the miseries he dreaded – that she was flying now, to save him from himself, and that she sought some remote place, where there would be no temptation, and her late sorrows and distresses could have no place.

The schoolmaster heard her tale with astonishment. "This child has heroically persevered under all doubts and dangers, struggled with poverty and suffering, upheld and sustained by strong affection and the consciousness of rectitude alone!"

It was concluded that Nell and her grandfather should accompany him to the village whither he was bound, and that he should try to find them some humble occupation by which they could subsist. "We shall be sure to succeed," said the schoolmaster, heartily. "The cause is too good to fail."

They arranged to continue their journey next evening, as a stage-waggon, which travelled for some distance on the same road, would stop at the inn to change horses, and the driver for a small gratuity would give Nell a place inside. A bargain was soon struck when the waggon came; and in due time it rolled away with the child comfortably bestowed among the softer packages, her grandfather and the schoolmaster walking on beside the driver.

What a soothing, luxurious, drowsy way of travelling, to lie inside that slowly-moving mountain, listening to the tinkling of the horses' bells, the occasional smacking of the carter's whip, the smooth rolling of the great broad wheels and the rattle of the harness! What a delicious journey was that journey in the waggon.

Sometimes walking for a mile or two while her grandfather rode inside, and sometimes even prevailing upon the schoolmaster to take her place and lie down to rest, Nell travelled on very happily until they came to a large town, where the waggon stopped, and where they spent a night. They passed a large church; and in the streets were a number of old houses, built of a kind of earth or plaster, crossed and re-crossed in a great many directions with black beams, which gave them a very ancient look. When they had passed through this town, they entered again upon the country, and began to draw near their place of destination.

It was not so near, however, but that they spent another night upon the road; for the schoolmaster was unwilling to make his entry in dusty shoes, and travel-disordered dress. It was a fine, clear, autumn morning, when they came upon the scene of his promotion, and stopped to contemplate its beauties.

"See – here's the church!" cried the delighted schoolmaster in a low voice; "and that old building close beside it, is the school-house, I'll be sworn. Five-and-thirty pounds a year in this beautiful place!"

They admired everything – the old grey porch, the mullioned windows, the venerable gravestones dotting the green churchyard, the ancient tower, the brown thatched roofs of cottage, barn, and homestead peeping from among the trees, and the distant blue Welsh mountains.

"I must leave you somewhere for a few minutes," said the

schoolmaster at length. "I have a letter to present, and inquiries to make, you know. Shall I take you to the little inn yonder?"

"Let us wait here," rejoined Nell. "We will sit in the church porch."

"A good place too," said the schoolmaster, leading the way, leaving his portmanteau on the stone seat. "Be sure that I come back with good news, and am not long gone!"

So the happy schoolmaster hurried off, full of ardour and excitement.

The child watched him from the porch until the intervening foliage hid him from her view, and then stepped softly out into the old churchyard. It was a very aged, ghostly place – the church had been built many hundreds of years ago, and ruined arches, remains of oriel windows, and fragments of blackened walls, were yet standing. Hard by the gravestones of dead years, and forming a part of the ruin, were two small dwellings with sunken windows and oaken doors, fast hastening to decay, empty and desolate.

The child could look at nothing else. She knew not why. The church, the ruin, the antiquated graves were fascinating enough, but from the moment she first saw the two dwellings, she could turn to nothing else. Even when she had walked around the enclosure, and, returning to the porch, sat waiting for their friend, she sat where she could see them, fascinated at the sight.

CHAPTER 41

Kit's mother and the single gentleman soon left the town behind them, and struck fire from the flints of the broad highway.

The good woman, being not a little embarrassed by the novelty of her situation, preserved an uneasy silence.

The single gentleman never sat in the same position for two minutes together, but was perpetually tossing his arms and legs about, or thrusting his head out of one window to draw it in again and thrust it out of another. Whenever they halted, there he was – out of the carriage without letting down the steps, bursting about the inn-yard like a lighted cracker, committing so many extravagances that Kit's mother was quite afraid of him. Then, when the horses were to, in he came like a Harlequin.

In this way they travelled on until near midnight, when they stopped to supper. Kit's mother didn't eat at once, and he took it into his head that she must be ill.

"You're faint," said the single gentleman, who did nothing but walk about. "That's the matter with you, ma'am. You're faint."

"Thank you, sir, I'm not indeed."

"I know you are. I'm sure of it. I drag you from the bosom of your family and you're getting fainter and fainter before my eyes. I'm a pretty fellow! How many children have you, ma'am?"

"Two, sir, besides Kit."

"Boys, ma'am?"

"Yes, sir."

"Are they christened?"

"Only half baptised as yet, sir."

"I'm godfather to both of 'em. Remember that, if you please, ma'am. You had better have some mulled wine."

He immediately flew to the bell, and called for mulled wine, then made Kit's mother swallow it at such a high temperature that the tears ran down her face, and then hustled her off to the chaise again, where she soon fell fast asleep. She did not awake until it was broad day, and they were clattering into a town.

"This is the place!" cried her companion, letting down all the glasses. "Drive to the waxwork!"

The four horses broke into a smart canter, and dashed through the streets with a noise that brought the good folks to their doors and windows. They drove up to a door round which a crowd of persons were collected, and there stopped.

"What's this?" said the single gentleman thrusting out his head. "Is anything the matter here?"

"A wedding sir, a wedding!" cried several voices. "Hurrah!"

The single gentleman, rather bewildered at finding himself the centre of the noisy throng, alighted and handed out Kit's mother, at which the crowd cried out, "Here's another wedding!" and roared and leaped for joy.

"The world has gone mad, I think," said the gentleman, pressing through the concourse with his supposed bride. "Stand back and let me knock."

131

"Now, sir, what do you want!" said a man with a large white bow at his buttonhole, opening the door.

"Who has been married here, my friend?" said the single gentleman. "Where is the child you have here? You call her Nell. Where is she?"

As he put this question, somebody in a room near at hand, shrieked, and a stout lady in a white dress came running.

"Where is she!" cried this lady. "What news have you brought?"

The single gentleman started back, and gazed upon the face of the late Mrs Jarley, with looks of conflicting disappointment, and incredulity. At length he stammered out, "I ask *you* where she is? What do you mean?"

"Oh sir!" cried the bride, "If you are here to do her any good, why weren't you here a week ago?"

"She is not – not dead?" said the single gentleman, turning pale.

"No, not so bad as that."

"I thank God!" cried the single gentleman feebly. "Let me come in."

They drew back and when he had entered, they closed the door.

"You see in me, good people," he said, turning to the newly married couple, "one to whom life itself is not dearer than the two persons whom I seek. My features are strange to them, but if they or either of them is here, take this good woman with you, and let them see her first, for her they both know."

"I always said it!" cried the bride, "I knew she was not a common child! Alas, sir! We cannot help you."

With that, they related to him, without disguise or concealment, all that they knew of Nell and her grandfather, from their first meeting with them, down to the time of their sudden disappearance; adding that they had made every effort to trace them, but without success. They dwelt upon the old man's simpleness of mind, upon the uneasiness of the child when he was absent, upon the company he had been supposed to keep, and upon the increased depression which had gradually crept over her. Whether she had missed the old man in the night, and knowing or conjecturing whither he had bent his steps, had gone in pursuit, or whether they had left the house together, they had no means of determining. To all this, the single gentleman listened with the air of a man quite borne down by grief and disappointment. He shed tears when they spoke of the grandfather, and appeared in deep affliction.

After a while, the happy couple jolted away in the caravan for their honeymoon; and the single gentleman and Kit's mother stood before their carriage-door.

"Where shall we drive you, sir?" said the post-boy.

To the inn they went.

Rumours were already abroad that the little girl was the child of great people who had been stolen from her parents in infancy, and had only just been traced. All agreed that the single gentleman was her father; and all bent forward to catch a glimpse, if only of the tip of his noble nose, as he rode back to London in his four-horse chaise.

What would he have given to know, that at that moment both child and grandfather were seated in the old church porch, patiently awaiting the schoolmaster's return!

CHAPTER 42

Urgent business had taken Mr Quilp away from Tower Hill for some two or three days. He smiled to himself when he considered how his sudden absence would have been taken.

"They'll probably think me dead!" he grinned to himself. He gazed up at the window of his own sitting-room, thinking he saw more light than is usual in a house of mourning. Drawing nearer, and listening attentively, he could hear several voices, not only those of his wife and mother-in-law, but the tongues of men.

"Ha!" cried the jealous dwarf. "What's this? Do they entertain while I'm away!"

He had forgotten his key. He had to knock at the door.

A very low and gentle rap received no answer from within. But after a second application to the knocker, the door was opened by the boy from the wharf. Quilp instantly dragged him into the street.

"Who's upstairs, you dog?" asked Quilp. "Tell me."

The boy could only point to the window, and giggle.

"Will you answer me?" said Quilp. "What's going on, above?"

"They – ha, ha, ha! – ," replied the boy. "They think you're – you're dead. Ha ha ha!"

"Dead!" cried Quilp, relaxing into a grim laugh himself. "Do they really, you dog?"

"They think you're – drowned," replied the boy. "You was last seen on the brink of the wharf, and they think you tumbled over. Ha ha!"

The prospect of playing the spy and disappointing them all by walking in alive, gave huge delight to Quilp. It also appealed to his assistant, and they both stood for some seconds, grinning.

"Not a word," said Quilp, making towards the door on tiptoe. "Not a sound. Drowned, eh, Mrs Quilp!"

So saying, he kicked off his shoes, and groped his way upstairs; leaving his delighted young friend on the pavement.

Mr Quilp slipped into the bedroom, and planted himself behind the door to the sitting-room, which standing ajar, enabled him not only to hear, but to see, what was passing.

Applying his eye to this convenient place, he descried Mr Brass seated at the table with pen, ink, and paper, and the case-bottle of rum convenient to his hand. Sampson had a mighty glass of punch, which he was stirring with a teaspoon, and contemplating with looks in which faint sentimental regret struggled weakly with a look of joy. Mrs Jiniwin sat taking deep draughts from a jorum of her own. Her daughter meanwhile, not exactly with ashes on her head but preserving a becoming appearance of sorrow, was reclining in an easy chair, and soothing her grief with a smaller glass. A couple of waterside men were also present.

"If I could poison that dear old lady's rum and water," murmured Quilp, "I'd die happy."

"Ah!" said Mr Brass, breaking the silence, and raising his eyes to the ceiling, "Who knows but he may be looking down upon us now!"

Here Mr Brass stopped to drink half his punch, and then resumed; looking at the other half with a dejected smile. "When shall we look upon his like again? Never! One minute we are here" – holding his tumbler before his eyes – "the next we are there" – gulping down its contents. "To think that I should be drinking his very rum! It seems like a dream."

Mr Brass pushed his tumbler towards Mrs Jiniwin to have it replenished, and turned towards the attendant mariners. "The search has been quite unsuccessful then?"

"Quite, master. But if he turns up anywhere, he'll come ashore somewhere about Grinidge tomorrow."

"Then we have nothing for it but resignation," said Mr Brass. "It would be a comfort to have his body."

"Oh, beyond a doubt," assented Mrs Jiniwin hastily. "If we had that, we should be quite sure."

"With regard to the descriptive advertisement," said Sampson Brass, taking up his pen. "It is a fact, but we must recall his traits. Respecting his legs now – ?"

"Crooked, certainly," said Mrs Jiniwin.

There followed a short discussion as to the crookedness of Quilp's legs.

"Let us not be hard on the weaknesses of the deceased. He is gone," said Brass finally, "to where his legs will never come in question. We will content ourselves with crooked."

"I thought you wanted the truth," said the old lady.

"Bless your eyes, how I love you," muttered Quilp.

"The question now arises, concerning his nose," said Mr Brass.

"Flat," said Mrs Jiniwin.

"Aquiline!" cried Quilp, thrusting in his head, and striking the feature with his fist. "Aquiline, you hag. Do you see it? Do you call this flat? Do you?"

"Oh capital!" shouted Brass, from force of habit. "Excellent! He's a most remarkable man! An amazing power for surprising people!"

Quilp paid no regard to these compliments, nor to the frightened look of the lawyer, nor to the shrieks of his wife and mother-in-law. Keeping his eye fixed on Sampson Brass, he walked up to the table, and drank off the contents of all the glasses and then seized the case-bottle, and hugging it under his arm, surveyed him with a most extraordinary leer.

"Not yet, Sampson," said Quilp. "Not just yet!"

"Oh very good indeed!" cried Brass, recovering his spirits a little. "Ha ha ha! Oh exceedingly good! There's not another man alive who could carry it off like that!"

"Good night," said the dwarf, nodding expressively.

"Good night, sir," cried the lawyer, retreating towards the door. "This is a joyful occasion indeed, extremely joyful!"

Quilp then advanced towards the two stunned men.

"Have you been dragging the river all day, gentlemen?" said the dwarf, holding the door open.

"And yesterday too, master."

"Dear me, you've had a deal of trouble. Pray consider everything yours that you find upon the – body. Good night!"

The men looked at each other, but had no inclination to argue the point just then, and left the room. Quilp then locked the doors; and still embracing the case-bottle, stood looking at his wife.

CHAPTER 43

"So you thought me dead and gone, did you?" said Quilp. "You thought you were a widow, eh? Ha, ha, ha, you jade."

"Indeed, Quilp," returned his wife. "I'm very sorry – "

"Who doubts it!" cried the dwarf. "To be sure you are. Who doubts that you're *very* sorry!"

"I don't mean sorry that you are home again alive and well," said his wife, "but sorry that I should have believed such a thing. I am glad to see you, Quilp."

In truth Mrs Quilp did seem a great deal more glad to behold her lord than might have been expected. This had no effect upon Quilp, however.

"How could you go away so long, without saying a word to me or letting me hear from you?" asked the poor little woman, sobbing. "How could you be so cruel, Quilp?"

"How could I be so cruel? Cruel!" cried the dwarf. "Because I was in the humour. I shall be cruel when I like. I'm going away again."

"Not again!"

"Yes, again. I'm going away now. I mean to go and live at the wharf, the counting house – and be a jolly bachelor. You were a widow in anticipation. Damme," screamed the dwarf, "I'll be a bachelor in earnest."

"You can't be serious, Quilp," sobbed his wife.

"I tell you," said the dwarf, exulting in his project, "that I'll be a bachelor, a devil-may-care bachelor with a bachelor's hall at the counting house. And mind too that I don't pounce in upon you at unseasonable hours again, for I'll be a spy upon you, and come and go like a mole or a weasel. Tom Scott – where's Tom Scott?"

"Here I am, master," cried the boy, as Quilp threw up the window.

"Wait there, you dog," returned the dwarf, "to carry a bachelor's portmanteau. Pack it up, Mrs Quilp."

The eccentric gentleman superintended the packing of his wardrobe, and having added to it a plate, knife and fork, spoon, teacup and saucer, and other small household matters of that nature, he strapped up the portmanteau, took it on his shoulders, and actually marched off without another word. Consigning the case to the care of Tom Scott when he reached the street, Quilp led the way to the wharf, and reached it at between three and four o'clock in the morning.

"Snug!" said Quilp, groping his way to the wooden counting house, and unlocking the door. "Beautifully snug! Call me at eight, you dog."

With no more formal leave-taking, he clutched the portmanteau, shut the door on his attendant, and climbing on the desk, and rolling himself up in an old boat-cloak, fell fast asleep.

Being roused in the morning, Quilp instructed Tom Scott to prepare breakfast. He then went to a place close by, to purchase a second-hand hammock, and had it slung in seamanlike fashion from the ceiling of the counting house.

"I have a country house like Robinson Crusoe," said the dwarf, ogling the accommodations, "a solitary, desolate-island sort of spot, where I can be quite alone when I have business on hand, and be secure from all spies and listeners."

The dwarf then sped away to reach Mr Swiveller's usual house of entertainment, just as that gentleman sat down to dinner.

"Dick," said the dwarf, thrusting his head in at the door, "my pet, my pupil, the apple of my eye!"

"Oh you're here, are you?" returned Mr Swiveller. "How are you?"

"How's Dick?" retorted Quilp. "How's the cream of clerkship, eh?"

"Rather sour, sir," replied Mr Swiveller. "Beginning to border upon cheesiness, in fact."

"What's the matter?" said the dwarf, advancing

"The law don't agree with me," returned Dick. "I have been thinking of running away."

"Bah!" said the dwarf. "Where would you run to, Dick?"

"I don't know," returned Mr Swiveller. "Towards Highgate, I suppose. Perhaps the bells might strike up 'Turn again Swiveller, Lord Mayor of London.'"

Quilp looked at his companion and patiently awaited his further explanation. But Mr Swiveller ate his very long dinner in profound silence, finally pushed away his plate, threw himself back into his chair, folded his arms, and stared ruefully at the fire.

"A thought has occurred to me, Dick; your friend over the way – "

"Which friend?"

"In the first floor. Fred may know him."

"No, he don't," said Mr Swiveller, shaking his head.

"No, because he has never seen him," rejoined Quilp. "But if we were to bring them together, who knows, Dick, but Fred, properly introduced – it might make the young fellow's fortune, and, through him, yours, eh?"

"Why, the fact is," said Swiveller. "They *have* been brought together."

"Have been!" cried the dwarf, looking suspiciously at his companion. "Through whose means?"

"Through mine," said Dick, slightly confused. "Didn't I mention it the last time you called?"

"You know you didn't," returned the dwarf.

"I believe you're right," said Dick. "No. I didn't, I recollect. It was Fred's suggestion. And instead of my friend's bursting into tears when he knew who Fred was, he flew into a tremendous passion; called him all manner of names; said it was mostly his fault that little Nell and the old gentleman had ever been brought to poverty."

"That's strange," said the dwarf, musing.

"So we remarked to each other," returned Dick coolly, "but quite true."

Quilp was plainly surprised, and he brooded for some time, often raising his eyes, and sharply scanning Mr Swiveller's expression. As he could read in it no additional information, the dwarf soon took his departure.

"Have been brought together, eh?" said the dwarf as he walked the streets alone. "My friend has stolen a march upon me. It led him to nothing, and therefore is no great matter. The blockhead mustn't leave the law at present. I'm sure of him where he is, whenever I want him for my own purposes, and, besides, he's a good unconscious spy on Brass, and tells, in his cups, all that he sees and hears. You're useful to me, Dick, and cost nothing but a little treating now and then. So for the present we'll remain the best friends in the world, with your good leave."

Pursuing these thoughts, Mr Quilp once more crossed the Thames, and shut himself up in his Bachelor's Hall.

CHAPTER 44

The proprietor of Bachelor's Hall slept on amidst the congenial accompaniments of rain, mud, dirt, and rats, until late in the day, then summoned Tom Scott to assist him to rise. He then took himself to Bevis Marks.

This visit was intended for Mr Sampson Brass. But he was from home, nor was Miss Sally at her post either.

"There's a servant, I suppose," said the dwarf, knocking at the house-door. "She'll do."

After a long interval, the door opened, and a small voice said, "Please will you leave a card or message?"

"Eh?" said the dwarf, looking down, (it was something quite new to him) upon the small servant.

To this, the child repeated, "Please will you leave a card or message?"

"I'll write a note," said the dwarf, pushing past her into the office; "and mind your master has it directly he comes home." So Mr Quilp climbed up to the top of a tall stool to write the note. The small servant looked on with her eyes wide open.

As Mr Quilp folded his note he met the gaze of the small servant. He looked at her, long and earnestly. "How are you?" he said.

The small servant, frightened by his looks, returned no audible reply.

"Do they use you ill here? Is your mistress a Tartar?" said Quilp with a chuckle.

In reply, the small servant, with a look of infinite cunning mingled with fear, screwed up her mouth very tight and round, and nodded violently. Mr Quilp was fascinated and he planted his elbows square and firmly on the desk, and squeezing up his cheeks with his hands, looked at her fixedly.

"Where do you come from?" he said after a long pause.

"I don't know."

"What's your name?"

"Nothing."

"Nonsense!" retorted Quilp. "What does your mistress call you when she wants you?"

"A little devil," said the child.

These unusual answers might naturally have provoked some more inquiries. Quilp, however, without uttering another word, stroked his chin, and then, bending over the note, looked at her from under his bushy eyebrows. He then tossed the letter to the child, and hastily withdrew.

Once in the street, moved by some secret impulse, he laughed, and held his sides, and laughed again, and tried to peer through the railings as if to catch another glimpse of the child, until he was quite tired out. At last, he travelled back to the Wilderness, which was close to his bachelor retreat, and ordered tea in the wooden summer-house that afternoon for three persons; an invitation to Miss Sally Brass and her brother to join him, having been the object both of his journey and his note.

In due course, he received Mr Sampson and his sister Sally.

"A word," said the dwarf, "before we go farther. Sally, hark'ee for a minute. There's a lad named Kit – "

Miss Sally nodded.

"I don't like Kit, Sally."

"Nor I," rejoined Miss Brass.

"Nor I," said Sampson.

"Why!" cried Quilp. "Half our work is done. This Kit is one of your honest people; one of your fair characters; a hypocrite; a double-faced, white-livered, sneaking spy."

"Fearfully eloquent!" cried Brass with a sneeze. "Quite appalling!"

"Come to the point," said Miss Sally, "and don't talk so much."

"Right again!" exclaimed Quilp, with a contemptuous look at Sampson. "I say, Sally, he is a yelping, insolent dog to all besides, and most of all, to me. In short, I owe him a grudge."

"That's enough, sir," said Sampson.

"No, it's not enough, sir," sneered Quilp; "will you hear me out? Besides that I owe him a grudge, he thwarts me at this minute, and stands between me and an end that might otherwise prove a golden one to us all. Apart from that, I repeat that he crosses my humour. Now, you know the lad. Devise your own means of putting him out of my way. Shall it be done?"

"It shall, sir," said Sampson.

"Then give me your hand," retorted Quilp. "Sally, girl, yours. I rely as much, or more, on you than him. Tom Scott comes back. Lantern, pipes, more grog, and a jolly night of it!"

No other word was spoken, no other look exchanged, which had the slightest reference to this, the real occasion of their meeting. The trio were well accustomed to act together, and were linked to each other by ties of mutual interest and advantage, and nothing more was needed. Quilp was in an instant the same uproarious, reckless little savage he had been a few seconds before. It was ten o'clock at night before the amiable Sally supported her beloved and loving brother from the Wilderness.

The dwarf lost no time in creeping to his dainty house, and was soon dreaming in his hammock.

CHAPTER 45

After a long time, the schoolmaster appeared at the wicket-gate and hurried towards them, tinkling in his hand, as he came along, a bundle of rusty keys. At first he could only point towards the old building the child had been contemplating.

"You see those two old houses," he said at last.

"Yes, surely," replied Nell. "I have been looking at them nearly all the time you have been away."

"And you would have looked at them more curiously yet, if you could have guessed what I have to tell you," said her friend. "One of those houses is mine."

Without saying any more, the schoolmaster took her hand, and led her to the place.

They stopped before its low arched door. After trying several of the keys, the schoolmaster found one to fit the huge lock.

The room was a vaulted chamber once nobly ornamented by cunning architects. The broken figures supporting the chimneypiece, though mutilated, were still distinguishable for what they had been.

In some old time, a wooden partition had been constructed in one part of the chamber to form a sleeping-closet. This screen, together with two seats in the broad chimney, had at some forgotten date been part of the church or convent.

An open door leading to a small room or cell, dim with the light that

141

came through leaves of ivy, completed the interior of this portion of the ruin. A few strange chairs; a table; a great old chest that had once held records in the church, with other quaintly fashioned domestic necessaries, and store of fire-wood for the winter, were scattered around.

They were all three hushed, and drew their breath softly, as if fearing to break the silence.

"It is a very beautiful place!" said the child, in a low voice.

"I almost feared you thought otherwise," said the schoolmaster. "You shivered when we first came in."

"It was not that," said Nell, glancing round with a slight shudder. "Indeed I cannot tell you why, but when I saw the outside, from the church porch, the same feeling came over me. Maybe it is because it is so old."

"A peaceful place to live in, don't you think so," said her friend.

"Oh yes," rejoined the child, clasping her hands earnestly. "A quiet, happy place – a place to live and learn to die in!"

"A place to live, and learn to live, and gather health of mind and body in," said the schoolmaster; "for this old house is yours."

"Ours!" cried the child.

"Ay," returned the schoolmaster gaily, "for many a merry year to come, I hope. I shall be a close neighbour – only next door – but this house is yours."

Having shared his great surprise, the schoolmaster drew Nell to his side, told her how the ancient house had been occupied by an old person who kept the keys of the church, opening it for the services, and showing it to strangers. She had died recently, and nobody had yet been found to fill the office. Learning all this from the sexton, who was confined to his bed by rheumatism – in a word, Nell and her grandfather were to meet the sexton the next day; and, his approval of their conduct and appearance reserved as a matter of form, they were already appointed to the vacant post.

"There's a small allowance of money," said the schoolmaster. "It is not much, but enough to live upon. By clubbing our funds together, we shall do bravely; no fear of that."

"Heaven bless and prosper you!" sobbed the child.

"Amen, my dear," returned her friend cheerfully. "But we must look at *my* house now. Come!"

They went to the other house, trying the rusty keys as before, and opened the worm-eaten door. It led into a chamber, vaulted and old, similar to the other, but not so spacious, and having only one other little room attached. It was then clear that the other house was of right the schoolmaster's, and that he had chosen for himself the least roomy, in his regard for them. It also held such old articles of furniture as were absolutely necessary, and had its stack of firewood.

To make these dwellings habitable and full of comfort was now their pleasant care. Each soon had its cheerful fire crackling on the hearth. Nell, busy with her needle, repaired the tattered window-hangings and made them whole. The schoolmaster swept the ground before the door, trimmed the long grass, and trained the ivy and creeping plants. The old man, sometimes by his side and sometimes with the child, lent his aid to both, and was happy. Neighbours, too, as they came from work, proffered their help; or sent children with such small presents or loans as the strangers needed most. It was a busy day; and night came on, and found them with still so much to do.

They took their supper together, in the house which may be henceforth called the child's; and, when they had finished, drew round the fire, and in whispers discussed their future plans. They then parted for the night.

At that silent hour, when her grandfather was sleeping peacefully in his bed, and every sound was hushed, the child lingered before the dying embers, and thought of her past fortunes as if they had been a dream. The glare of the flame, reflected in the oaken panels, where strange shadows came and went, filled her with deep and thoughtful feelings, but with none of terror or alarm. A change had been gradually stealing over her, in the time of her loneliness and sorrow. With failing strength and heightening resolution, there had sprung up a purified and altered mind. There were none to see the frail figure, as it glided to the open casement; none but the stars, to look into the upturned face and read its history. The old church bell rang out the hour with a mournful sound; the fallen leaves rustled; the grass stirred upon the graves; all else was still and sleeping.

With the brightness of morning, came the renewal of yesterday's labours, the restoration of its energies, cheerfulness, and hope. They worked gaily in ordering and arranging their houses, and then went to visit the clergyman.

He was a simple-hearted old gentleman, of a subdued spirit, accustomed to retirement. His wife had died in the house in which he still lived, and he had long since lost sight of any earthly cares or hopes beyond it.

He received them very kindly, and at once showed an interest in Nell; asking her name, and age, her birthplace, the circumstances that had led her there, and so forth. The schoolmaster had already told her story. They had no other friends or home to leave, he said, and had come to share his fortunes. He loved the child as though she were his own.

"Well, well," said the clergyman. "Let it be as you desire. She is very young."

"Old in adversity and trial, sir," replied the schoolmaster.

"God help her. Let her rest, and forget them," said the old gentleman. "But an old church is a dull and gloomy place for one so young as you, my child."

"Oh no, sir," returned Nell. "I have no such thoughts, indeed."

"I would rather see her dancing on the green at nights," said the old gentleman, smiling sadly, "than have her sitting in the shadow of our mouldering arches. You must see that her heart does not grow heavy among these solemn ruins. Your request is granted, friend."

After more kind words, they withdrew, and repaired to the child's house; they were discussing their happy fortune, when another friend appeared.

This was a little old gentleman, who lived in the parsonage-house, and had resided there ever since the death of the clergyman's wife, fifteen years before. He had been his college friend and always his close companion; in the first shock of his grief he had come to comfort him; and had never left. The little old gentleman was the active spirit of the place, the promoter of all merry-makings, the dispenser of his friend's bounty, and of no small charity of his own besides. None of the simple villagers knew his name. Due to his unmarried status, he had been called the bachelor. The name pleased him, and the Bachelor he had stayed.

The bachelor, then, lifted the latch, showed his little round mild face for a moment, and stepped into the room like one who was no stranger to it.

"You are Mr Marton, the new schoolmaster?" he said, greeting Nell's kind friend.

"I am, sir."

"You come well recommended, and I am glad to see you. This is our young church-keeper? You are not the less welcome, friend, for her sake,

144

or for this old man's; nor the worse teacher for having learnt humanity."

"She has been ill, sir, very lately," said the schoolmaster, in answer to the look with which their visitor regarded Nell when he had kissed her cheek.

"Yes, yes. I know she has," he rejoined. "There have been suffering and heartache here."

"Indeed there have, sir."

The little old gentleman glanced at the grandfather, and back again at the child, whose hand he took tenderly in his, and held.

"You will be happier here," he said; "we will try, at least, to make you so."

CHAPTER 46

Nell was stirring early in the morning, and having discharged her household tasks, took down, from its nail by the fireside, a little bundle of keys and went out alone to the old church. The sky was bright, the air clear, perfumed with the fresh scent of newly fallen leaves. Some young children sported among the tombs, and hid from each other, with laughing faces.

She passed the church, gazing upward at its old tower, went through the wicket gate, and so into the village. The old sexton, leaning on a crutch, was taking the air at his cottage door, and gave her good morrow.

"You are better?" said the child, stopping to speak with him.

"Ay surely," returned the old man. "I'm thankful to say, much better."

"You have been into the church?" he asked.

"I am going there now," the child replied.

"There's an old well there," said the sexton, "right underneath the belfry; a deep, dark, echoing well. If you lower the bucket and let out nearly all the cord, you'll hear it clanking and rattling on the ground below; the sound of being so far down, that your heart leaps into your mouth, and you start away as if you were falling in."

"A dreadful place to come on in the dark!" exclaimed the child, who had followed the old man's looks and words until she seemed to stand upon its brink.

"What is it but a grave!" said the sexton.

The child shortly afterwards departed. She soon reached the church. It was easy to find the key to the outer door, for each was labelled. Its very turning in the lock awoke a hollow sound, and when she entered with a faltering step, the echoes that it raised in closing, made her start.

If the peace of the simple village had moved the child more strongly, because of the dark and troubled ways that lay beyond, what was the deep impression of finding herself alone in that solemn building, where the very light, coming through sunken windows, seemed old and grey! Here was the broken pavement, worn, so long ago, by pious feet. Here were the rotten beam, the sinking arch, the sapped and mouldering wall, the stately tomb on which no epitaph remained, all marble, stone, iron, wood, and dust – one common monument of ruin.

Some part of the building had been a baronial chapel, and here were effigies of warriors stretched upon their beds of stone with folded hands – cross-legged, those who had fought in the Holy Wars, girded with their swords, and cased in armour.

The child sat down, in this silent place, among the tombs, and gazing round with a feeling of awe, felt that now she was happy, and at rest. She took a Bible from the shelf, and read; then, laying it down, thought of the summer days and the bright springtime to come – of the rays of sun that would fall in aslant upon the sleeping forms, of the songs of birds, and growth of buds and blossoms out of doors. What if the spot awakened thoughts of death! Die who would, it would still remain the same; these sights and sounds would still go on, as happily as ever. It would be no pain to sleep amidst them.

She left the chapel very slowly, and coming to a low door, which plainly led into the tower, opened it, and climbed the winding stair in darkness. At length she gained the turret top. Oh! The glory of the sudden burst of light; the freshness of the fields and woods, stretching away on every side; the cattle grazing; the smoke coming from among the trees; the children still playing down below! It was like drawing nearer Heaven.

The children were gone when she emerged into the porch, and locked the door. As she passed the schoolhouse she could hear the busy hum of voices. Her friend had begun his labours that day.

Twice again she stole back to the old chapel, and read from the same book, or indulged the same quiet train of thought. Even when it had grown dusk, and the shadows of coming night made it more solemn still, the child remained.

They found her there, at last, and took her home. She looked pale but very happy, until they separated for the night; and then, as the poor schoolmaster stooped down to kiss her cheek, he thought he felt a tear upon his face.

CHAPTER 47

When the bachelor had given her some history to almost every tomb and flat grave-stone, he took her down into the old crypt, and showed her how it had been lighted up in the time of the monks, and how, amid lamps, and swinging censers exhaling scented odours, and pictures, and precious stuffs, and jewels all flashing and glistening through the low arches, the chant of aged voices had been many a time heard there, at midnight, in old days, while hooded figures knelt and prayed around, and told their rosaries of beads. Thence, he showed her, high up in the old walls, small galleries, where the nuns had been wont to glide along. All that he told the child she treasured in her mind.

The old man who had seen her toiling by his side through so much difficulty and suffering, and had scarcely thought of her other than as the partner of miseries which he felt severely in his own person, suddenly awoke to a sense of what he owed her, and what those miseries had made her. Never, no, never once, in one unguarded moment from that time to the end, did any care for himself, any thought of his own comfort distract his thoughts from the gentle object of his love.

He would follow her up and down, waiting till she should tire and lean upon his arm; he would sit opposite her in the chimney corner, content to watch, and look, until she raised her head and smiled upon him as of old; he would secretly carry out those household duties too heavy for her; he would rise, in the cold dark nights, to listen to her breathing in her sleep, and sometimes crouch for hours by her bedside only to touch her hand. He who knows all, can only know what a change had fallen on the poor old man. Sometimes – weeks had crept on, then – the child, exhausted, though with little fatigue, would pass whole evenings on a couch beside the fire. At such times, the schoolmaster would bring in books, and read to her aloud. The old man sat and listened – with little understanding but with his eyes fixed upon the child. When the bachelor told some tale that pleased her, the old man would painfully try to store it in his mind.

But these were rare occasions, happily; for the child yearned to be out of doors. Parties, too, would come to see the church; and those who came, speaking to others of the child, sent more; so even at that season of the year they had visitors almost daily. The old man would follow them through the building, listening to the voice he loved so well.

They always praised the child, her sense and beauty, and he was proud to hear them! But what was that, so often added, which wrung his heart, and made him sob and weep alone, in some dull corner! Alas! Even careless strangers – they who had no feeling for her, but the interest of the moment, who would go away and forget next week that such a being lived – even they saw it – even they pitied her – even they bade him good day compassionately, and whispered as they passed.

The people of the village, too, grew fond of poor Nell; even among them, there was the same feeling; a tenderness towards her. The schoolboys, light-hearted and thoughtless as they were, even they cared for her. The roughest among them was sorry if he missed her in the usual place upon his way to school, and would turn off the path to ask for her at the latticed window. Some feeling was abroad which raised the child above them all.

Nell had sought out the young children whom she first saw playing in the churchyard. One of these was her little favourite and friend, and often sat by her side in the church, or climbed with her to the tower-top. It was his delight to help her and they soon became close companions.

It happened, that, as she was reading in the old spot by herself one day, this child came running in with his eyes full of tears, and after holding her from him, and looking at her eagerly for a moment, clasped his little arms passionately about her neck.

"What now?" said Nell, soothing him. "What is the matter?"

"She is not one yet!" cried the boy, embracing her still more closely. "No! Not yet."

She looked at him wonderingly, and putting his hair back from his face, and kissing him, asked what he meant.

"You must not be one, dear Nell," cried the boy. "We can't see them. They never come to play with us. Be what you are. You are better so."

"I don't understand," said the child. "Tell me what you mean."

"Why, they say," replied the boy, looking up into her face, "that you will be an Angel, before the birds sing again. But you won't be, will you? Don't leave us, Nell!"

The child dropped her head, and put her hands before her face.

"She cannot bear the thought!" cried the boy, exulting through his tears. "You will not go. You know how sorry we should be. Dear Nell, say that you'll stay with us. Oh! Pray, tell me you will."

The little creature folded his hands, and knelt down at her feet.

"Only look at me, Nell," said the boy, "and tell me that you'll stop, and then I shall know that they are wrong."

Still the drooping head and hidden face, and the child quite silent – save for her sobs.

"After a time," pursued the boy, trying to draw away her hand, "the kind angels will be glad to think that you stayed here with us. Willy," he spoke of his brother – "went away, to join them; but if he had known how I should miss him in our little bed at night, he never would have left me, I am sure."

Yet the child could not answer, and sobbed as though her heart would break.

"Why would you go, dear Nell? They say that Willy is in Heaven now, and yet I'm sure he grieves when I lie down upon his garden bed, and he cannot turn to kiss me. But if you do go, Nell," said the boy, pressing his face to hers, "be fond of him for my sake. Tell him how I love him still, and how much I loved you; and when I think that you two are together, and are happy, I'll try to bear it, and never give you pain by doing wrong!"

There was a tearful silence, but it was not long before she looked upon him with a smile, and promised him that she would stay, and be his friend, as long as Heaven would let her. He clapped his hands for joy, and thanked her many times; and being charged to tell nobody what had passed between them, gave her an earnest promise that he never would.

Nor did he, so far as the child could learn. He was her quiet companion in all her walks and musings, and never again discussed the theme, which he felt had given her pain, although he was unconscious of its cause.

One day the sexton took Nell down to the crypt, pausing among the gloomy arches.

They threw back the cover to the well.

"A black and dreadful place!" exclaimed the child.

"Look in," said the old man, pointing downward with his finger.

The child gazed down into the pit.

"It looks like a grave itself," said the old man.

"It does," replied the child.

"I have often had the fancy," said the sexton, "that it was dug to make the old place more gloomy, and the old monks more religious. It's to be closed up, and built over."

The child still stood, looking thoughtfully into the vault.

"We shall see," said the sexton, "on what gay heads other earth will have closed, when the light is shut out from here. God knows! They'll close it up, next spring."

"The birds sing again in spring," thought the child, as she leaned at her window, and gazed at the declining sun. "Spring! A beautiful time!"

CHAPTER 48

A day or two after the Quilp tea-party at the Wilderness, Mr Swiveller walked into Sampson Brass's office at the usual hour, and being alone in that Temple of Probity, placed his hat upon the desk.

He sat himself in the clients' chair, and moments later there came a ring at the office bell.

"Is the gentleman upstairs at home?" said Kit.

"Why?" rejoined Dick.

"Because if he is, I have a letter for him."

"From whom?" said Dick.

"From Mr Garland."

"Oh!" said Dick, with extreme politeness. "Then you may hand it over, sir. And if you're to wait for an answer, sir, you may wait in the passage, sir."

"Thank you," returned Kit. "But I am to give it to himself."

The single gentleman was heard to call violently down the stairs.

"Didn't I see somebody for me, come in?" he cried.

"Yes, sir," replied Dick. "Certainly, sir."

"Then where is he?" roared the single gentleman.

"He's here, sir," rejoined Mr Swiveller. "Now young man, don't you hear you're to go upstairs?"

Kit hurried off, and moments later Dick was again disturbed, this time by the entrance of Mr Sampson and his sister, Sally.

Mr Brass and his lovely companion appeared to have been consulting upon some matter of great interest and importance. On these occasions, they generally appeared in the office some half an hour after their usual time, and in a very smiling state. In the present instance, they seemed particularly gay.

"Well, Mr Richard," said Brass. "How are we this morning? Are we pretty fresh and cheerful sir -- eh, Mr Richard?"

"Pretty well, sir," replied Dick.

"That's well," said Brass. "Ha, ha! We should be as gay as larks, Mr Richard – why not? It's a pleasant world we live in, sir. There are bad people in it, Mr Richard, but if there were no bad people, there would be no good lawyers. Ha, ha! Any letters by the post this morning, Mr Richard?"

Mr Swiveller answered in the negative.

"Ha!" said Brass, "no matter. If there's little business today, there'll be more tomorrow. Anybody been here, sir?"

"Only somebody to the lodger," replied Dick.

"Oh indeed!" cried Brass. "Somebody to the lodger, eh?"

"Yes," said Dick, a little disconcerted by his excessive buoyancy. "With him now."

"With him now!" cried Brass. "Ha, ha! There let 'em be merry and free, toor rul lol le. Eh, Mr Richard?"

"Oh certainly," replied Dick.

"And who," said Brass, shuffling among his papers, "is the lodger's visitor – not a lady visitor, I hope, eh?"

"Another young man, who belongs to Witherden's, or half belongs there," returned Richard. "Kit, they call him."

"Kit, eh!" said Brass. "Ha ha! Kit's there, is he? Oh!"

Dick looked at Miss Sally, wondering why she didn't check his

151

exuberance; but as she made no attempt to do so, he concluded that they had just been cheating somebody, and receiving the bill.

"Will you have the goodness, Mr Richard," said Brass, taking a letter from his desk, "to step over to Peckham Rye with that? There's no answer, but it should go by hand."

Mr Swiveller solemnly put on his coat, pocketed the letter, and departed. As soon as he was gone, up rose Miss Sally Brass, and smiling sweetly at her brother (who nodded and smote his nose in return) withdrew also.

Sampson Brass was no sooner left alone, than he set the office door wide open, and sitting at his desk, so that he could not fail to see anybody who came downstairs and passed out the street door, began to write with extreme cheerfulness, humming as he did.

Every so often he stopped to listen. At length, in one of these pauses, he heard his lodger's door opened and shut, and footsteps coming down the stairs. Then Mr Brass left off writing entirely, and with his pen in his hand hummed his very loudest.

As Kit arrived before his door, Mr Brass stopped his singing, and nodded affably, at the same time beckoning to him with his pen.

"Kit," said Mr Brass, in the pleasantest way imaginable, "how do you do?"

Kit made a suitable reply, and had his hand upon the street door when Mr Brass called him softly back.

"You are not to go, if you please, Kit," said the attorney in a mysterious and yet business-like way. "You are to step in here, if you please."

"I respect you, Kit," said Brass with emotion. "Though your station is humble, and your fortune lowly. It isn't the waistcoat that I look at. It is the heart. The checks in the waistcoat are but the wires of the cage. But the heart is the bird."

This poetic figure, which Kit took to be a special allusion to his own checked waistcoat, quite overcame him.

"Well, well," said Sampson, "You're to take that, if you please." As he spoke, he pointed to a couple of half-crowns on the desk.

Kit looked at the coins, and then at Sampson, and hesitated.

"For yourself," said Brass.

"From – "

"No matter about the person they came from," replied the lawyer. "Say me, if you like. We have eccentric friends overhead, Kit, and we mustn't ask questions, you understand? You're to take them, that's all; and between you and me, I don't think they'll be the last. I hope not. Good bye, Kit. Good bye!"

With many thanks, Kit took the money and made the best of his way home. Mr Brass remained airing himself at the fire, and resumed his vocal exercise, and his seraphic smile, simultaneously.

"May I come in?" said Miss Sally, peeping.

"Oh yes, you may come in," returned her brother.

"Ahem!" coughed Miss Brass interrogatively.

"Why, yes," returned Sampson, "I should say as good as done."

CHAPTER 49

The friendship between the single gentleman and Mr Garland flourished. They were in constant communication; and the single gentleman labouring at this time under a slight attack of illness, meant that one of the inmates of Abel Cottage, came backwards and forwards between that place and Bevis Marks, almost every day.

By now the pony refused to be driven by anybody but Kit, so it generally happened that whether old Mr Garland came, or Mr Abel, Kit was of the party. Of all messages and inquiries, Kit was the bearer. So while the single gentleman remained indisposed, Kit visited Bevis Marks every morning with as much regularity as the General Postman.

Mr Sampson Brass soon learnt to distinguish the pony's trot and the clatter of the little chaise at the corner of the street. Whenever the sound reached his ears, he would instantly lay down his pen.

"Ha ha!" he would cry. "Here's the pony again! Most remarkable pony, extremely docile, eh, Mr Richard, eh sir?"

Dick would return some matter-of-course reply, and Mr Brass standing on the bottom rail of his stool, so as to see the street, would observe the visitors.

"The old gentleman again!" he would exclaim, "charming countenance, extremely calm. Ah!"

Whenever Kit came alone, and without the chaise, Sampson Brass was always reminded of some mission and sent Mr Swiveller to some pretty distant place. Mr Swiveller out of sight, Miss Sally immediately withdrew. Mr Brass would then set the office-door wide open, and smile seraphically as before. Kit coming downstairs would be called in; entertained with some moral and agreeable conversation; perhaps entreated to mind the office for an instant while Mr Brass stepped over the way; and afterwards presented with one or two half-crowns as the case might be.

This occurred so often, that Kit, believing that they came from the single gentleman, could not enough admire his generosity. He bought many presents for his family, and for Barbara to boot.

While these acts and deeds were in progress, Richard Swiveller, being often left alone, began to find the time hang heavy on his hands. He therefore provided himself with a cribbage-board and pack of cards, and would play at cribbage with a dummy, for twenty, thirty, or sometimes even fifty thousand pounds aside.

As these games were very silently conducted, Mr Swiveller began to think that on those evenings when Mr and Miss Brass were out, he heard a kind of hard-breathing sound from the door, which it occurred to him must proceed from the small servant. Looking intently that way one night, he plainly distinguished an eye at the keyhole; and having his suspicions confirmed, he stole softly to the door, and pounced upon her before she was aware of his approach.

"Oh! I didn't mean any harm indeed, upon my word," cried the small servant, struggling. "It's so very dull, downstairs. Please don't tell on me."

"Tell on you!" said Dick. "Do you mean to say you were looking through the keyhole for company?"

"Yes," replied the small servant.

"How long have you been looking through?" said Dick.

"Oh ever since you first began to play them cards, and long before."

Vague recollections of several fantastic exercises with which he had refreshed himself after the fatigues of business, and to all of which, no doubt, the small servant was a party, rather disconcerted Mr Swiveller, but he recovered himself speedily.

"Well, come in," he said, after a little consideration. "Here – sit down, and I'll teach you how to play."

"Oh! I durstn't do it," rejoined the small servant. "Miss Sally 'ud kill me, if she know'd I come up here."

"Have you a fire downstairs?" said Dick.

"A very little one," replied the small servant.

"Miss Sally couldn't kill me if she know'd I went down there, so I'll come," said Richard, putting the cards into his pocket. "Why, how thin you are!"

"It ain't my fault."

"Could you eat any bread and meat?" said Dick, taking down his hat. "Yes? Ah! I thought so. Did you ever taste beer?"

"I had a sip once," said the small servant.

"Here's a state of things!" cried Mr Swiveller, raising his eyes. "It can't be tasted in a sip! Why, how old are you?"

"I don't know."

Mr Swiveller opened his eyes wide, thoughtful for a moment; then, bidding the child mind the door, vanished straightway.

Presently, he returned, followed by the boy from the public house, who held a plate of bread and beef, and a great pot of some very fragrant beer.

"There!" said Richard, putting the plate before her. "Clear that off, and then you'll see what's next."

The small servant needed no second bidding, and the plate was soon empty.

"Next," said Dick, handing the pot, "take a pull at that; but take it slowly, for you're not used to it. Well, is it good?"

"Oh! Isn't it?" said the small servant.

Mr Swiveller appeared gratified beyond all expression by this reply, and took a long draught himself. He then applied himself to teaching her the game, which she soon learnt tolerably well, being both sharp-witted and cunning.

"Now," said Mr Swiveller, putting two sixpences into a saucer, when the cards had been cut and dealt, "those are the stakes. If you win, you get 'em all. If I win, I get 'em. To make it seem more real and pleasant, I shall call you the Marchioness, do you hear?"

The small servant nodded.

"Then, Marchioness," said Mr Swiveller, "fire away!"

The Marchioness, holding her cards in both hands, considered which to play, and Mr Swiveller took another pull at the tankard, and waited for her lead.

CHAPTER 50

Mr Swiveller and his partner played several rubbers with varying success, until the gradual sinking of the porter, and the striking of ten o'clock, reminded the gentleman of the flight of Time, and the expediency of withdrawing before Mr Sampson and Miss Sally Brass returned.

"With which object in view, Marchioness," said Mr Swiveller gravely, "I shall ask your ladyship's permission to put the board in my pocket, and to retire when I have finished this tankard. Marchioness, your health. You will excuse my wearing my hat, but the palace is damp, and the marble floor is – if I may say – sloppy."

Mr Swiveller slowly sipped the last choice drops of nectar.

"Do they often leave you here?"

"Oh, yes; they do," returned the small servant. "They sometimes go to see Mr Quilp. They go to many places, bless you!"

"I suppose," said Dick, "that they consult together, a good deal, and talk about a great many people – about me for instance, sometimes, eh, Marchioness?"

The Marchioness nodded amazingly.

"Complimentary?" said Mr Swiveller.

The Marchioness shook her head from side to side.

"Humph!" Dick muttered. "Would it be any breach of confidence, Marchioness, to relate what they say –?"

"Miss Sally says you're a funny chap," replied his friend. "And that you an't to be trusted."

"Why, really Marchioness," said Mr Swiveller, thoughtfully; "I'm sure I don't know why. Mr Brass agrees, I suppose?"

His friend nodded again, but added imploringly, "But don't you ever tell upon me, or I shall be beat to death."

"Marchioness," said Mr Swiveller, rising, "the word of a gentleman is as good as his bond – sometimes better, as in the present case. I am your friend, and I hope we shall play many more rubbers together. But, Marchioness," added Richard, wheeling slowly round upon the small servant, who followed with the candle. "You must be constantly airing your eye at keyholes, to know all this."

"I only wanted," replied the trembling Marchioness, "to know where the key of the safe was hid; and I wouldn't have taken much, if I had found it – only enough to squench my hunger."

"You didn't find it then?" said Dick. "But of course you didn't, or you'd be plumper. Good night, Marchioness. Fare thee well."

Mr Swiveller emerged from the house and returned to his lodgings, and to his bed. His apartments (for he still retained the plural fiction) were not far from the office, so he was soon seated in his own bedchamber, where he fell into deep cogitation.

"This Marchioness," said Mr Swiveller, folding his arms, "is a very extraordinary person – surrounded by mysteries, ignorant of the taste of beer, unacquainted with her own name, and taking a limited view of society through the keyholes of doors."

He awoke in the morning, much refreshed; and having taken half an hour's exercise at the flute, and graciously received a notice to quit from his landlady, repaired to Bevis Marks; where the beautiful Sally was already at her post.

Mr Swiveller acknowledged her presence by a nod, and took his seat at the desk.

"I say," quoth Miss Brass, abruptly breaking silence, "you haven't seen a silver pencil-case this morning, have you?"

"Haven't I this moment come?" said Mr Swiveller.

"Well, all I know is," replied Miss Sally, "that it's not to be found, and that it disappeared one day this week."

"Halloa!" thought Richard, "I hope the Marchioness hasn't been at work here."

"It's a very unpleasant thing, Dick," said Miss Brass, refreshing herself with a pinch of snuff; "but between you and me – for if Sammy knew it, I should never hear the last of it – some of the office-money, too, that has been left about, has gone in the same way. In particular, I have missed three half-crowns at three different times."

"You don't mean that?" cried Dick. "Be careful what you say, old boy, for this is serious." And then out loud, "Are you quite sure?"

"There can be no mistake at all," said Miss Brass emphatically.

"Then by Jove," thought Richard, laying down his pen, "I am afraid the Marchioness is done for!"

The more he thought about it, the more probable it appeared to Dick that the miserable little servant was the culprit. When he considered how neglected she was, and how her natural cunning had been sharpened by necessity and privation, he scarcely doubted it. And yet he pitied her so much, that rather than receive fifty pounds down, he would have the Marchioness proved innocent.

While plunged in serious meditation upon this theme, Miss Sally sat shaking her head with an air of great mystery and doubt, when the voice of her brother Sampson was heard in the passage, and that gentleman himself appeared.

"Mr Richard, sir, good morning! Here we are again, sir, entering upon another day, with our bodies strengthened by slumber and breakfast, and our spirits fresh and flowing."

While he addressed his clerk in these words, Mr Brass was, somewhat ostentatiously, engaged in minutely examining a five-pound bank note.

Mr Richard not receiving his remarks with anything like enthusiasm, his employer looked at him.

"You're out of spirits, sir," said Brass. "Mr Richard, sir, we should fall to work cheerfully, and not in a despondent state – "

Here Sarah heaved a loud sigh.

"Dear me!" said Mr Sampson, "you too! Is anything the matter? Mr Richard, sir – "

Dick, glancing at Miss Sally, saw her making signals to him, to acquaint her brother with the subject of their recent conversation. As his own position was not a very pleasant one until the matter was set at rest one way or other, he did so.

The countenance of Sampson fell, and anxiety overspread his features. He walked on tiptoe to the door, opened it, looked outside, shut it softly, and said in a whisper, "this is most extraordinary – Mr Richard, sir. The fact is, that I myself have missed several small sums from the desk, of late, and have refrained from mentioning it, hoping that accident would discover the offender. Sally – Mr Richard, sir – this is a particularly distressing affair!"

As Sampson spoke, he laid the bank note upon the desk among some papers, and thrust his hands into his pockets. Richard Swiveller pointed to it, telling him to take it up.

"No, Mr Richard, sir," rejoined Brass with emotion, "I will let it lie there, sir. To take it up, Mr Richard, sir, would imply a doubt of you. We

158

will let it lie there, sir, if you please." With that, Mr Brass patted him twice or thrice on the shoulder.

Mr Swiveller felt a great relief to be assured that he was not wrongfully suspected. He remained in a thoughtful state; fearing every moment to hear the Marchioness impeached, and unable to resist the conviction that she must be guilty.

They had all been pondering for some minutes, when Miss Sally all at once gave a loud rap upon the desk with her clenched fist, "I've hit it!" she cried.

"Well," cried Brass anxiously. "Go on, will you!"

"Why," replied his sister with an air of triumph, "hasn't there been somebody coming in and out of this office for the last three or four weeks; hasn't he been left alone sometimes – thanks to you; isn't that somebody the thief!"

"What somebody?" blustered Brass.

"Why, what do you call him – Kit?"

"Mr Garland's young man?"

"To be sure."

"Never!" cried Brass. "I'll never believe it of him. Never!"

"I say," repeated Miss Brass, taking more snuff, "that he's the thief."

"I say," returned Sampson violently, "that he is not. What do you mean? How dare you? He's the honestest and faithfullest fellow that ever lived, with an irreproachable good name. Come in!"

These last words were addressed to some person who had knocked at the office-door; and they had hardly passed the lips of Mr Brass, when Kit himself looked in.

"Is the gentleman upstairs, sir, if you please?"

"Yes, Kit," said Brass, still fired with an honest indignation, and frowning with knotted brows upon his sister. "Yes Kit, he is. I am glad to see you, Kit. Look in again, as you come downstairs, Kit. That lad a robber!" cried Brass when he had withdrawn, "with that open countenance! I'd trust him with untold gold. Mr Richard, sir, have the goodness to step directly to Wrasp and Co.'s in Broad Street, and inquire if they have had instructions to appear in Carkem and Painter. *That* lad a robber," sneered Sampson, flushed. "Am I blind, deaf, silly? Kit a robber! Bah!"

CHAPTER 51

When Kit came downstairs a quarter of an hour later, Mr Sampson Brass was alone, with his back to the fire, and looking so strange that Kit thought he was ill.

"Is anything the matter, sir?" said Kit. "You are so pale."

"Mere fancy," cried Brass, stooping to throw up the cinders. "Never better, Kit, never better in all my life. How's our friend above-stairs, eh?"

"A great deal better," said Kit.

"I'm glad to hear it," rejoined Brass. "An excellent gentleman – an admirable lodger. Mr Garland – he's well I hope, Kit. Ha ha!"

Kit gave a satisfactory account of the little household at Abel Cottage. Mr Brass, who seemed inattentive, beckoned him to come nearer and took him by the buttonhole.

"I have been thinking, Kit," said the lawyer, "that I could throw some little emoluments in your mother's way. You have a mother, I think? If I recollect right, you told me – "

"Oh yes, sir, yes certainly."

"A widow, I think? An industrious widow? – Put down your hat, Kit."

"Thank you sir, but I must be going directly."

"Put it down while you stay, at any rate," said Brass, taking it from him and muddling the papers, in finding a place for it. "I was thinking, Kit, we're obliged to put people into houses to take care of 'em. What's to prevent our employing your mother? There's lodging, pretty well all year round, rent free, a weekly allowance besides. Now what do you think of that?"

As Brass spoke, he moved the hat twice or thrice, shuffling among the papers, as if searching for something.

"How can I see any objection to such a kind offer, sir?" replied Kit with his whole heart.

"Why then," said Brass, suddenly turning upon him and thrusting his face close to Kit's, with such a repulsive smile that the latter drew back, quite startled. "It's done."

Kit looked at him in some confusion.

"Done, I say," added Sampson, rubbing his hands in his usual oily manner. "Ha ha! And so you shall find, Kit, so you shall find. But dear me," said Brass, "what a time Mr Richard is gone! A sad loiterer to be sure! Will you mind the office one minute, while I run upstairs?"

Talking as he went, Mr Brass bustled out of the office, and moments later returned. Mr Swiveller came back, almost at the same instant. As Kit was leaving the room hastily, he also met Miss Brass in the doorway.

"Oh!" sneered Sally, looking after him as she entered. "There goes your pet, Sammy, eh?"

"Ah! There he goes," replied Brass. "My pet, if you please. An honest fellow, Mr Richard. He has minded the office again, he has had my confidence, and he shall continue to have it; he – why, where's the – "

"What have you lost?" inquired Mr Swiveller.

"Dear me!" said Brass, slapping all his pockets, one after another, and looking into his desk, wildly tossing the papers about, "the note, Mr Richard, sir, the five-pound note – what can have become of it? I laid it down here – God bless me!"

"What!" cried Miss Sally, starting up, and scattering the papers on the floor. "Gone! Now who's got it? Never mind five pounds – what's five pounds? He's honest, you know, quite honest. It would be mean to suspect him. Don't run after him!"

"Is it really gone?" said Dick, looking at Brass.

"Upon my word, Mr Richard, sir," replied the lawyer, feeling in all his pockets. "It's certainly gone, sir. What's to be done?"

Mr Swiveller and Sampson Brass looked from Miss Sally to each other, in a state of bewilderment, and then snatched up their hats and rushed out into the street – as though running for their lives.

Kit had been running too, though not so fast, and was a good distance ahead. As they were pretty certain of the road he must have taken, they came up with him, at the moment he took breath.

"Stop!" cried Sampson, laying his hand on one shoulder, while Mr Swiveller pounced upon the other. "Not so fast sir. You're in a hurry?"

"Yes, I am," said Kit, looking from one to the other in surprise.

"I – I – can hardly believe it," panted Sampson, "but something of value is missing from the office. I hope you don't know what."

"Know what! Good Heaven, Mr Brass!" cried Kit, trembling from head to foot; "you don't suppose – "

"No, no," rejoined Brass quickly, "I don't suppose anything. You'll come back quietly, I hope?"

"Of course I will," returned Kit. "Why not? I am sure you'll be sorry for having suspected me, sir. Let us make haste back."

"Certainly!" cried Brass, "the quicker, the better. Mr Richard – have the goodness, sir, to take that arm. I'll take this one."

When they reached Bevis Marks, they ushered him into the presence of the charming Sarah, who immediately locked the door.

"Now, you know," said Brass, "if this is a case of innocence, it is a case of that description, Christopher, where the fullest disclosure is the best satisfaction for everybody. Therefore if you'll consent to an examination," he demonstrated by turning back his own cuffs, "it will be easier for all parties."

"Search me," said Kit, proudly holding up his arms. "But mind, sir – I know you'll be sorry for this, to the last day of your life."

"It is certainly a very painful occurrence," said Brass with a sigh, as he dived into one of Kit's pockets, and fished up a miscellaneous collection of small articles. "Very painful. Nothing here, Mr Richard, sir, all perfectly satisfactory. Nor in the waistcoat, Mr Richard, nor in the coat tails. So far, I am rejoiced, I am sure."

Richard Swiveller, holding Kit's hat in his hand, watched the proceedings with great interest, when Sampson turning hastily to him, bade him search the hat.

"Here's a handkerchief," said Dick.

"No harm in that sir," rejoined Brass, checking the other sleeve. "No harm in a handkerchief sir, whatever."

An exclamation, at once from Richard Swiveller, Miss Sally, and Kit himself, cut the lawyer short. He turned his head, and saw Dick standing with the banknote in his hand.

"In the hat?" cried Brass in a sort of shriek.

"Tucked beneath the lining," said Dick, aghast at the discovery.

Mr Brass looked at him, at his sister, around the room – everywhere but at Kit, who stood quite stunned.

"And this," cried Sampson, clasping his hands, "is human natur, is it! Oh natur, natur! Even now, I feel so much for this lad, as to wish to let him go! But," added Mr Brass with greater fortitude, "I am a lawyer, and bound to set an example. Sally my dear, catch hold of him on the other side. Mr Richard, sir, run for a constable. The weakness is past and over sir, and moral strength returns. A constable, sir, if you please!"

CHAPTER 52

Kit stood with his eyes wide, regardless alike of the tremulous hold which Mr Brass maintained on one side, and of the firmer grasp of Miss Sally upon the other. He remained in this posture, quite unresisting, until Mr Swiveller returned, with a police constable.

This functionary took Kit into custody.

"We had better," he said, "get to the office while there's a magistrate sitting. I shall want you to come along with us, Mr Brass, and the lady. Likewise the young man that found the property."

"Mr Richard, sir," said Brass in a mournful voice. "A sad necessity."

"But, hear me speak a word," cried Kit, raising his eyes and looking imploringly about him. "I am no more guilty than any one of you. Upon my soul I am not. Oh, Mr Brass, you know me better."

"I give you my word, constable – " said Brass. "I give you my oath, constable, that down to a few minutes ago, when this fatal discovery was made, I had such confidence in that lad, that I'd have trusted him with – a hackney-coach, Mr Richard, sir."

"Who is there that knows me," cried Kit, "that would not trust me – that does not? Ask anybody whether they have ever doubted me; whether I have ever wronged them of a farthing."

Suddenly the voice of the single gentleman was heard, demanding what was the cause of all that noise. Kit made an involuntary start towards the door anxious to answer, but detained by the constable, had the agony of seeing Sampson Brass run out to tell the story in his own way.

"And he can hardly believe it, either," said Sampson, when he returned. "I wish I could doubt the evidence of my senses. Now, Sarah, I hear the coach; we'll be off. A sad errand!"

"Mr Brass," said Kit. "Do me one favour. Take me first to Mr Witherden's."

Sampson shook his head irresolutely.

"Do," said Kit. "My master's there. For Heaven's sake, take me there, first."

"Well, I don't know," stammered Brass, who perhaps had his reasons for wishing to show as fair as possible in the eyes of the Notary. "How do we stand for time, constable, eh?"

The constable replied that if they left immediately they would have time enough, but that if they stood there any longer, they must go straight to the Mansion House.

Mr Richard Swiveller having arrived inside the coach, Mr Brass declared himself quite ready. Therefore, the constable, pushing Kit on a little before him, thrust him into the vehicle and followed. Miss Sally entered next. Sampson Brass got upon the box.

Still completely stunned, Kit sat gazing out of the coach window, almost hoping to see something that would convince him that he was in a dream. Alas! Everything was too real and familiar. Dream-like as it was – he stood charged with robbery; the note had been found upon him, though he was innocent in thought and deed; and they were taking him, a prisoner.

Absorbed in these painful ruminations, poor Kit was looking out of the window, aware of nothing, when all at once he saw the face of Quilp.

And what a leer was upon the face! It looked from the open window of a tavern. Mr Brass, on recognising him, immediately stopped the coach. The dwarf saluted the party. "Aha!" he cried. "Where now, Brass? Sally with you too? Sweet Sally! And Dick? Pleasant Dick! And Kit! Honest Kit!"

"He's extremely cheerful!" said Brass to the coachman. "Ah, sir – a sad business! Believe in honesty no more, sir."

"Why not?" returned the dwarf. "Why not, you rogue of a lawyer?"

"Banknote lost in our office, sir," said Brass, shaking his head. "Found in his hat, sir – he previously left alone there – no mistake at all, sir – chain of evidence complete."

"What!" cried the dwarf. "Kit a thief! Ha, ha, ha! Why, he's an uglier-looking thief than can be seen anywhere for a penny. Eh, Kit – eh?" And with that, he gave a yell of laughter. "Ha ha ha ha! What a disappointment for little Jacob, and for his darling mother! Drive on coachey. Bye bye, Kit; keep up your spirits; my love to the Garlands. Say I inquired after 'em, will you? Blessings on 'em, on you, and on everybody, Kit."

When they reached the Notary's, Mr Brass dismounted and entered the office with his sister, to prepare the good people within for the mournful intelligence that awaited them. Mr Swiveller accompanied them.

The Notary stood before the fire in the outer office, talking to Mr Abel and the elder Mr Garland. This posture of affairs Mr Brass observed through the glass-door as he was turning the handle, and seeing that the Notary recognised him, he began to sigh deeply.

"Sir," said Sampson, taking off his hat, "my name is Brass – of Bevis Marks, sir. I have had the honour and pleasure, sir, of being concerned against you in some little testamentary matters. How do you do, sir?"

"My clerk will attend to any business you may have come upon, Mr Brass," said the Notary, turning away.

"Thank you sir," said Brass, "thank you, I am sure. Allow me, sir, to introduce my sister. And Mr Richard, sir, have the goodness to come foward if you please – No really," said Brass, stepping between the Notary and his private office (towards which he had turned), "really sir, I must request a word or two with you, indeed."

"Mr Brass," said the other. "You see that I am occupied with these gentlemen. Communicate your business to my clerk, and you will receive every attention."

"Gentlemen," said Brass, "I believe one of these gentlemen is Garland."

"Both are," said the Notary.

"Indeed!" rejoined Brass, cringing excessively. "Extremely happy, I am sure, to have the honour, although the occasion is a most painful one. One of you gentlemen has a servant called Kit?"

"What of him?"

"This of him, sir," rejoined Brass, dropping his voice impressively. "That young man, sir, that I have felt unbounded confidence in, has this morning committed a robbery in my office, and been taken almost in the fact."

"It is not possible," said Mr Abel.

"I'll not believe one word of it," exclaimed the old gentleman.

Mr Brass looked mildly at them, and rejoined, "I'm truly sorry to be the messenger of such unpleasant news. The lad himself desired to be brought here, and I yielded to his prayers."

Kit was brought in, bursting into the rude eloquence with which Truth at length inspired him, calling Heaven to witness that he was innocent! Such a confusion of tongues, before the circumstances were related, and the proofs disclosed! Such a dead silence when all was told, and his three friends exchanged looks of doubt and amazement!

"Is it not possible," said Mr Witherden, after a long pause, "that this note may have found its way into the hat by some accident – such as the removal of papers on the desk, for instance?"

But this was clearly shown to be quite impossible. Mr Swiveller, though an unwilling witness, showed from the position in which it was found, that it must have been purposefully hidden.

"It's very distressing," said Brass, "I am sure. When he comes to be tried, I shall be very happy to recommend him to mercy on account of his previous good character. I did lose money before, certainly, but it doesn't quite follow that he took it."

"I suppose," said the constable, looking round, "that no gentleman here can give evidence as to whether he's been flush of money of late. Do you happen to know, sir?"

"He has had money from time to time, certainly," returned Mr Garland, to whom the man had put the question. "But he told me it was given him by Mr Brass himself."

"Yes to be sure," said Kit eagerly. "You can bear me out in that, sir?"

"Eh?" cried Brass, looking around in stunned amazement.

"The half-crowns that you gave me – from the lodger," said Kit.

"Oh dear me!" cried Brass, frowning heavily. "This is bad, I find."

"Ask him, somebody. Ask him whether he did or not!" cried Kit.

"Did you, sir?" asked the Notary.

"Did I, sir," replied Brass, in a very grave manner. "Of course I never did."

"Gentlemen," cried Kit, on whom a light broke suddenly. "Master, Mr Abel, Mr Witherden, every one of you – he did it! What I have done to offend him, I don't know, but this is a plot to ruin me. I will say with my dying breath that he put that note in my hat himself!"

Kit was led back to the hackney-coach. They then drove to the justice-room with all speed, followed by the Notary and his two friends in another coach.

At the justice room, they found the single gentleman, who had gone straight there, and was expecting them with desperate impatience. But not fifty single gentlemen rolled into one could have helped poor Kit, who half an hour later was committed for trial, and was assured by a friendly officer on his way to prison that he shouldn't be cast down, for the sessions would soon be on, and his little affair would be disposed of, and he'd be comfortably transported, in less than a fortnight.

CHAPTER 53

Kit was innocent; and knowing this, and feeling that his best friends deemed him guilty – that even his own mother might believe him to be the wretch he seemed – knowing and feeling all this, he experienced, at first, an intense agony of mind, and walked up and down his little cell that night, beside himself with grief.

It was a long night, but at last morning dawned, and there was the jail itself – cold, black, and dreary. He was able to walk in a small paved yard, and learnt from the turnkey that there was a regular time for visiting, and that if his friends came to see him, he would be taken to the grate. When he had given him this information, and a tin porringer containing his breakfast, the man locked him up.

This turnkey had told him that he was lodged alone because he was not thought to be utterly depraved, and had never occupied apartments in that mansion before. Kit was thankful for this indulgence, and sat reading the church catechism very attentively until he heard the key in the lock.

"Now then," said the turnkey, "come on!"

"Where to, sir?" asked Kit.

The man led him through several winding ways and strong gates, into a passage, where he placed him at a grating and turned upon his heel. Beyond this grating, about four or five feet away, was another exactly like it. In the space between, sat a turnkey reading a newspaper. Beyond the further railing, Kit saw his mother holding the baby, Barbara's mother and poor little Jacob.

Little Jacob thrust his arms between the rails to hug him, could get no nearer, so began to cry most piteously; whereupon, Kit's mother and Barbara's mother, who had restrained themselves, burst out sobbing afresh. Poor Kit could not help joining them. During this melancholy pause, the turnkey read his newspaper until, taking his eyes away for an instant, it occurred to him that somebody was crying.

"Now, ladies," he said, looking round with surprise, "I'd advise you not to waste time like this. You mustn't let that child make that noise either. It's against all rules."

"I'm his poor mother, sir," sobbed Mrs Nubbles, "and this is his brother, sir. Oh dear me!"

"Well!" replied the turnkey, folding his paper. "He ain't the only one in this fix. You mustn't make a noise about it!"

With that he went on reading.

"Oh! My darling Kit," said his mother, "that I should see my poor boy here!"

"You don't believe that I did what they accuse me of, mother?" cried Kit, in a choking voice.

"I – believe it!" exclaimed the poor woman, "I that never knew you tell a lie, or do a bad action from your cradle! I – believe it of the son that's been a comfort to me since the hour of his birth! How can I believe it of you Kit!"

"Why then, thank God!" said Kit, clutching the bars, "I can bear it, mother! Come what may, I shall always have one drop of happiness in my heart when I think that you said that."

At this the poor woman fell a-crying again, but drying her eyes, took from the ground a small basket, and submissively addressed the turnkey.

"I have brought him a little something to eat," said the good woman. "If you please, sir, might he have it?"

"Yes, he may. There's no rule against that. Give it to me when you go, and I'll take care he has it."

"No, but if you please sir, don't be angry with me sir, I am his mother, and you had a mother once – if I might only see him eat a little bit, I should go away, so much more satisfied that he was all comfortable."

The turnkey looked as if he thought the request a strange one, but nevertheless he laid down his paper, took the basket from her, and after inspecting its contents, handed it to Kit, and went back to his place. Even though the prisoner had no great appetite, he sat on the ground, and ate, while, at every morsel he took, his mother sobbed.

While thus engaged, Kit asked after his employers, and whether they had expressed any opinion concerning him. He was told that Mr Abel had himself told his mother, with great kindness, late the previous night, but had himself expressed no opinion of his innocence or guilt. Kit was about to ask Barbara's mother about Barbara, when his turnkey reappeared, a second turnkey appeared behind his visitors, and he with the newspaper cried "Time's up!" before plunging deep into his newspaper again. Kit was taken off in an instant, with a blessing from his mother, and a scream from little Jacob, ringing in his ears.

CHAPTER 54

A faint light, twinkling from the window of the counting house, warned Mr Sampson Brass as he neared the cabin, that the excellent proprietor, his esteemed client, was inside.

"A treacherous place to pick one's steps in, of a dark night," muttered Sampson, as he stumbled for the twentieth time over some stray lumber, and limped in pain. "I hate coming to this place without Sally. She's more protection than a dozen men."

He stood on tiptoe, trying to see inside. "What's he about, I wonder? Drinking, I suppose – heating his malice and mischievousness till they boil. It scares me to come here alone, when his account's pretty large. I don't believe he'd mind throttling me, and dropping me into the river – indeed he'd consider it a pleasant joke. Hark! Now he's singing!"

Mr Quilp was certainly entertaining himself, but it was rather a kind of chant than a song; being a monotonous repetition of one sentence in a very rapid manner. "The worthy magistrate, after remarking that the prisoner would find some difficulty in persuading a jury to believe his tale, committed him to take his trial at the approaching sessions; and directed the customary recognisances to be entered into for the pros-e-cu-tion."

Every time he came to this concluding word, Quilp shrieked with laughter, and began again.

"He's dreadfully imprudent," muttered Brass, after he had listened to two or three repetitions of the chant. "I wish he were dumb and deaf. I wish he were blind. Hang him," cried Brass, as the chant began again. "I wish he were dead!"

Mr Sampson then composed himself, and waiting for the shriek to die away, knocked at the door.

"Come in!" cried the dwarf.

"How do you do tonight, sir?" said Sampson, peeping in. "Ha ha ha! How do you do, sir?"

"Come in, you fool!" returned the dwarf, "and don't stand there shaking your head. Come in, you false witness, you perjurer, you suborner of evidence, come in!"

"He has the richest humour!" cried Brass, shutting the door, "the most amazing vein of comicality! But isn't it rather injudicious, sir –?"

"What?" demanded Quilp. "What, Judas? What's injudicious, hey?"

"Scarcely worth mentioning sir; but I thought that song – admirably humorous in itself – was perhaps rather – "

"Yes," said Quilp, "rather what?"

"Remotely verging upon the confines of injudiciousness perhaps, sir," returned Brass, looking timidly at the dwarf.

"What's your meaning?" retorted Quilp.

"I shouldn't have mentioned the subject, sir. Let us change it, if you please. You were asking, sir, Sally told me, about our lodger. He has not returned, sir."

"No?" said Quilp.

"He is still, sir," returned Brass, "with the Garland family. He has only been home once, sir, since the day of the examination of that culprit. He informed Mr Richard, sir, that he couldn't bear the house after what had taken place and that he looked upon himself as being in a certain kind of way the cause of the occurrence. A very excellent lodger sir."

"You may now discharge your clerk," said Quilp.

"Discharge Mr Richard, sir?" cried Brass.

"Have you more than one clerk, you parrot, that you ask the question? Yes."

"Upon my word, sir," said Brass, "I wasn't prepared for this – "

"How could you be?" sneered the dwarf, "when I wasn't? How often must I tell you that I brought him to you that I might have my eye on him and know where he was – and that I had a plot, a little quiet piece of enjoyment afoot, of which the very cream and essence was, that this old man and grandchild (who have sunk underground I think) should be, while he and his precious friend believed them rich, in reality as poor as frozen rats?"

"I quite understood that, sir," rejoined Brass. "Thoroughly."

"Well, sir," retorted Quilp, "and do you understand now, that they can't be poor, if men such as your lodger are searching for them, scouring the country far and wide?"

"Of course I do, sir," said Sampson.

"Of course you do," retorted the dwarf, viciously snapping at his words. "Do you understand then, that it's no matter what comes of this fellow."

"I have frequently said to Sarah, sir," returned Brass, "that he is of no use at all in the business. I've actually found that fellow blurting out the truth, though expressly cautioned. The aggravation of that chap, sir, has exceeded anything you can imagine. Nothing but the respect and obligation I owe to you, sir – "

Mr Quilp politely tapped him on the crown of his head with a saucepan, and requested that he hold his peace.

"Practical, sir, practical," said Brass, rubbing the place.

"Hearken to me, will you?" returned Quilp, "or I'll be a little more pleasant, presently. There's no chance of his friend returning. The scamp has had to fly abroad for some knavery. Let him rot there."

"Certainly, sir. Quite proper!" cried Brass.

"I hate him," said Quilp between his teeth, "and have always hated him, for family reasons. Besides, he was an intractable ruffian; otherwise he would have been of use. This fellow is pigeon-hearted and light-headed. I don't want him any longer,"

"By all means, sir," returned Brass. "When would you wish him to leave?"

"As soon as this trial's over," said Quilp, "Send him about his business."

"It shall be done, sir," returned Brass. "It will be rather a blow to Sarah, sir, but she has all her feelings under control. It is time for me to go sir, goodbye, sir."

"Won't you stop all night?" said the dwarf. "Do stop all night!"

"I couldn't indeed, sir," replied Brass, almost dead from nausea and the closeness of the room. "If you'd have the goodness to show me a light, so that I may see my way across the yard, sir – "

"To be sure," Quilp said, taking up a lantern, which was now the only light in the place. "Be careful how you go, my dear friend. There's a dog in the lane. He bit a man last night. Mind you take care. I'll never forgive you if you don't. There – the light's out – never mind – you know the way – straight on!" Quilp had slyly shaded the light, and listened to the lawyer stumbling up the yard, now and then falling heavily down. At length, however, he was out of hearing.

The dwarf shut himself up, and sprang again into his hammock.

171

CHAPTER 55

Eight days later, the sessions commenced. Christopher Nubbles was called upon to plead Guilty or Not Guilty to an Indictment that he the said Christopher did feloniously abstract and steal from the dwelling-house and office of one Sampson Brass, gentleman, one Bank Note for Five Pounds.

To this indictment, Christopher Nubbles, in a low and trembling voice, pleaded Not Guilty.

Sampson Brass is called to the witness-box. Up comes Mr Brass, very brisk and fresh. He looks at his gentleman as much as to say, "Here I am – full of evidence – Tap me!" And the gentleman does just that, drawing off the evidence little by little, and making it run quite clear in the eyes of all present. Then, Kit's gentleman takes him in hand, but can make nothing of him; and after a great many long questions and short answers, Mr Brass goes down in glory.

To him succeeds Sarah, who in like manner is easy to be managed by Mr Brass's gentleman. Kit's gentleman can again get nothing out of her, and therefore lets her go, in some confusion. Then Mr Brass's gentleman calls Richard Swiveller, who appears accordingly.

"Mr Swiveller," says Brass's gentleman to Dick, when he had told his tale with evident reluctance and a desire to make the best of it: "Pray sir, where did you dine yesterday?" – "Where did I dine yesterday?" – "Aye, sir, where did you dine yesterday, was it near here, sir?" – "Yes, just over the way." – "Yes. Just over the way," repeats Mr Brass's gentleman, with a glance at the court. – "Alone, sir? Did you dine alone? Did you treat anybody, sir? Come!" – "Yes, I did," says Mr Swiveller with a smile. – "Have the goodness to banish a levity, sir, and attend to me. You dined over the way. You treated somebody. Now, was that somebody brother to the prisoner at the bar?" – Mr Swiveller is proceeding to explain – "Yes or No, sir," cries Mr Brass's gentleman – "But will you allow me – " – "Yes or No, sir" – "Yes it was, but – " – "Yes it was," cries the gentleman, taking him up short. "And a very pretty witness *you* are!"

Judge, jury and spectators now have visions of his lounging about, with a dissolute young fellow six feet tall. The reality is, little Jacob, with the calves of his legs exposed to the open air. Nobody knows the

172

truth; and all because of the ingenuity of Mr Brass's gentleman.

Then come the witnesses to character, and it turns out that Mr Garland had no recommendation of Kit but from his own mother, and that he had been suddenly dismissed by his former master for unknown reasons. "Really Mr Garland," says Mr Brass's gentleman, "for a person who has arrived at your time of life, you are, to say the least, singularly indiscreet, I think." The jury thinks so too, and finds Kit guilty. He is taken off, humbly protesting his innocence.

Kit's poor mother waits at the grate below stairs, and a sad interview ensues. The newspaper-reading turnkey tells them all. He don't think it will be transportation for life, because there's time to prove the good character yet. He wonders why he did it.

"He never did it!" cries Kit's mother.

"Well," says the turnkey, "it's all one, now."

Kit's mother can reach his hand through the bars, and she clasps it. Kit bids her keep a good heart.

"Some friend will rise up for us, mother," cried Kit, "I am sure. If not now, before long. My innocence will come out, mother. Oh! Is there no good gentleman here, who will take care of her!"

The hand slips out of his, for the poor creature sinks down upon the earth, insensible. Richard Swiveller comes hastily up, takes her and, nodding to Kit, for he has a coach waiting, bears her swiftly off.

Richard took her home and stayed till she was recovered, and, having no money to pay the coach, went back to Bevis Marks, bidding the driver wait at the door while he went in for "change".

"Mr Richard, sir," said Brass cheerfully, "Good evening!"

Monstrous as Kit's tale had appeared, at first, Mr Richard did, that night, half suspect his affable employer of some deep villany. He said in as few words as possible, what he wanted.

"Money?" cried Brass, taking out his purse. "Ha ha! To be sure, Mr Richard. All men must live. You haven't change for a five-pound note, have you, sir?"

"No," returned Dick, shortly.

"Oh!" said Brass, "here's the very sum. You're very welcome I'm sure. – Mr Richard, sir – " Dick, who had by this time reached the door, turned round.

"You needn't," said Brass, "trouble yourself to come back any more, sir. The fact is, that a man of your abilities is lost in our dry line. It's terrible drudgery. I should say, now, that the stage, or the – or the – the army Mr Richard, was what would call out the genius of such a man as you. I hope you'll look in to see us now and then. Sally, sir, will be delighted I'm sure. She's extremely sorry to lose you Mr Richard, but a sense of her duty to society reconciles her."

To this, Mr Swiveller answered not one word, but, returning for the aquatic jacket, marched out of the office in profound silence.

He paid the coachman, and turned his back on Bevis Marks, with designs of comforting Kit's mother and helping Kit himself.

But the lives of gentlemen devoted to such pleasures as Richard Swiveller, are extremely precarious. That very night, Mr Richard was seized with an alarming illness, and in twenty-four hours was stricken with a raging fever.

CHAPTER 56

Tossing to and fro upon his fevered bed, tormented by an unquenchable thirst, unable to find a moment's peace or ease – in these slow tortures of his dread disease, the unfortunate Richard lay wasting inch by inch, until at last, when he seemed to fight and struggle to rise up, and to be held down by devils, he sank into a deep sleep, and dreamed no more.

He awoke. With a sensation of most blissful rest, better than sleep itself, he began gradually to remember something of these sufferings. Raising his hand, he was astonished at how heavy it seemed, and yet how thin and light it really was. Having no strength of curiosity to pursue the subject, he remained in the same waking slumber until his attention was attracted by a cough. He wondered whether he had locked his door last night. Still, he lacked energy to follow up this train of thought.

He heard the cough again, and holding the curtain open, he looked out. The same room certainly, and still by candlelight; but all those bottles, and basins, and articles of linen airing by the fire – all clean and neat, so different from when he went to bed! Also the cool smell of herbs and vinegar; and – the – the Marchioness?

Yes; playing cribbage. There she sat, intent upon her game, coughing now and then. Mr Swiveller briefly watched, and releasing the curtain, laid his head on the pillow again.

"I'm dreaming," thought Richard, "that's clear. When I went to bed, my hands were not made of eggshells; and now I can almost see through 'em. I have no doubt I'm asleep. Not the least."

Here the small servant had another cough.

"Very remarkable!" thought Mr Swiveller. "I never dreamt such a real cough as that before."

Mr Swiveller raised the curtain again, determined to address his companion. The Marchioness dealt, turned up a knave, and omitted to take the usual advantage. Mr Swiveller called out as loud as he could – "Two for his heels!"

The Marchioness jumped up quickly and clapped her hands, then laughed, then cried; declaring she was "So glad, she didn't know what to do."

"Marchioness," said Mr Swiveller, "be pleased to draw nearer. Pray tell me what has happened?"

The Marchioness cried again.

"I take it, Marchioness," said Richard after a pause, and smiling with a trembling lip, "that I have been ill."

"You have!" replied the small servant, wiping her eyes.

"Very ill, Marchioness?" said Dick.

"Dead, all but," she replied. "I never thought you'd get better. Thank Heaven you have!"

Mr Swiveller was silent a long while, and then asked how long he had been there.

"Three weeks tomorrow," replied the servant.

"Three what?" said Dick.

"Three long, slow weeks," returned the Marchioness emphatically.

The thought of having been in such extremity made Richard silent again. The Marchioness arranged the bedclothes, and felt that his forehead was quite cool. She then applied herself to getting tea ready, and making some thin dry toast.

Mr Swiveller looked on with a grateful heart, attributing this attention to Sally Brass, whom, in his own mind, he could not thank enough. The Marchioness gently propped him up with pillows, and looked on with

175

unutterable satisfaction while the patient, stopping occasionally to shake her by the hand, took his poor meal with great appetite.

"Marchioness," said Mr Swiveller, "how's Sally?"

The small servant screwed her face up and shook her head.

"What, haven't you seen her lately?" said Dick.

"Seen her!" she cried. "Bless you, I've run away!"

Mr Swiveller immediately laid down flat again, and so remained for about five minutes. Gradually he resumed his sitting posture, and inquired: "And where do you live, Marchioness?"

"Here!"

"Oh!" said Mr Swiveller.

And with that he fell down flat again. Thus he remained, until she had finished, and tidied away. Then he motioned her to bring a chair to the bedside.

"And so," said Dick, "you have run away?"

"Yes," said the Marchioness.

"Tell me," said he, "why you thought of coming here."

"Why, when you was gone, I hadn't any friend at all. The lodger never come back, and I didn't know where him or you was to be found. But one morning, when I was – "

"Near a keyhole?" suggested Mr Swiveller, seeing her falter.

The small servant nodded. "When I was near the office keyhole I heard a lady say that you lodged at her house, and that you was took very bad, and wouldn't nobody come and take care of you. Mr Brass, he says, 'It's no business of mine,' and Miss Sally, she says, 'He's a funny chap, but it's no business of mine.' The lady went away. So I run away that night. I come here, and said you was my brother. I've been here ever since."

"This poor little Marchioness has been wearing herself to death!" cried Dick.

"No I haven't," she returned, "don't you mind about me. I like sitting up, and I've slept in one of them chairs. But I'm so glad you're better."

"I strongly suspect I should have died, Marchioness, but for you," said Dick thoughtfully. He took the small servant's hand in his.

"The doctor," she told him, "said you was to be kept quite still, and there was to be no noise. Now, rest, and then we'll talk again."

Richard Swiveller fell into a slumber, and waking about half an hour later, inquired the time.

"Just gone half after six," replied his small friend.

"Marchioness," said Richard, passing his hand over his forehead and turning suddenly round, "what has become of Kit?"

"He has been sentenced to transportation for a great many years," she said. "But, there's something I could tell you – but I won't now."

"Yes, do," said Dick. "It will amuse me."

"Oh! Wait till you're better and then I'll tell you."

Dick looked very earnestly at his little friend: and he urged her to tell him.

"Is it to do with things you were not intended to hear?" he asked, in a breathless state. "Conversations between Brass and Sally?"

"Yes," cried the small servant.

Richard Swiveller gripped her hand, and drawing her close, bade her out with it. She, seeing that he was greatly agitated, promised compliance, on condition that he kept himself perfectly quiet.

"Do go on, there's a darling," pleaded Dick.

His companion spoke thus: "Before I run away, I slept in the kitchen. I hated being locked there, because if there was a fire, I thought they might forget about me. So, whenever I see an old rusty key, I pick it up and try it in the door, and at last I found a key that fit."

"I used to come out at night," she continued, "and feel about in the dark for bits of biscuit, or sangwitches that you'd left in the office. Well, one or two nights before all that precious noise in the office – when the young man was took, I mean – I come upstairs while Mr Brass and Miss Sally was a-sittin' at the office fire."

"And Mr Brass says, 'Upon my word, it might get us into a world of trouble, and I don't half like it.' She says, 'You're the chickenest-hearted, feeblest man I ever see, and I ought to have been the brother, and you the sister. Isn't Quilp our principal support?' 'He certainly is,' says Mr Brass. 'And an't we,' she says, 'constantly ruining somebody or other in the way of business?' 'We certainly are,' says Mr Brass. 'Then does it signify,' she says, 'about ruining this Kit when Quilp desires it?' 'It certainly does not signify,' says Mr Brass. Then they whispered about there being no danger if it was well done, and then Mr Brass pulls out his pocketbook, and says, 'Well,' he says, 'here it is – Quilp's own five-pound note. Kit's coming tomorrow morning, I know. While he's upstairs, you'll get out of the way, and I'll clear off Mr Richard. I'll hold

177

Kit in conversation, and put this in his hat. I'll arrange it that Mr Richard finds it, and is the evidence. And if that don't get Christopher out of Mr Quilp's way, and satisfy Mr Quilp's grudges,' he says, 'the Devil's in it.' Miss Sally laughed, and as they seemed to be moving, I went downstairs again. There!"

The small servant was as worked up as Mr Swiveller, and therefore made no effort to restrain him when he sat up in bed and hastily demanded whether this story had been told to anybody.

"I was almost afraid to think about it," replied his nurse, "and hoped the young man would be let off. When I heard they found him guilty of what he didn't do, you was gone, and so was the lodger. Since I come here, you've been out of your senses, and what would have been the good of telling you then?"

"Marchioness," said Mr Swiveller, plucking off his nightcap and flinging it to the other end of the room; "where are my clothes?"

"I've been obliged to sell them, to get what the doctor ordered for you. But anyway," urged the Marchioness, as Dick fell back. "You're too weak to stand."

"I am afraid," said Richard, "that you're right. What is to be done!"

The first step would be to communicate with one of the Mr Garlands instantly. Swiftly, the small servant had the address on a piece of paper; and a verbal description of father and son, which would enable her to recognise either, without difficulty. She hurried away, commissioned to return with one or the other.

"I suppose," said Dick, as she left, "I suppose there's nothing left – a waistcoat even?" The Marchioness shook her head.

"It's embarrassing," said Mr Swiveller, "but you did quite right, dear Marchioness. I should have died without you!"

CHAPTER 57

The Marchioness dived into the first dark by-way that presented itself, and endeavoured to put two good miles of brick and mortar between herself and Bevis Marks.

Then she began to shape her course for the Notary's office, shrewdly inquiring of traders at street-corners, rather than in lighted shops. By the time she reached the street, she was fairly exhausted.

Lights still burned in the office window. So the Marchioness stole softly up the steps, peeping in through the glass door.

Before the ashes of the fire stood two gentlemen, one she rightly judged to be the Notary, and the other, buttoning his great-coat, was Mr Abel Garland.

The small spy resolved to wait in the street until Mr Abel came out. She slipped out and sat down upon a doorstep just opposite.

A moment later there came dancing up the street, a pony, pulling a little phaeton behind him, and a man in it. He had obvious problems getting the pony to stop!

Mr Abel left the building opposite, walking up to the carriage.

"He's a very good fellow if you know how to manage him," he said, getting in, and taking the reins. "This is the first time he has been out for a while, since he lost his old driver."

After one or two strange plunges, quite of his own invention, the pony yielded to Mr Abel, and trotted gently off. The Marchioness could do nothing else but run after the chaise, and call to Mr Abel to stop. Being out of breath, she couldn't make him hear. The pony was quickening his pace. The Marchioness hung on behind for a few moments, and, feeling that she could go no farther, clambered into the hinder seat.

Mr Abel having enough to do to keep the pony going, went jogging on without looking round, little dreaming of the strange figure close behind him, until the Marchioness, uttered close into his ear, the words – "I say, sir – "

He turned quickly, and stopping the pony, cried with some trepidation, "God bless me, what is this!"

"Don't be frightened, sir," replied the still panting messenger. "Oh, I've run such a way after you!"

"What do you want with me?" said Mr Abel.

"Oh, please drive on, sir," replied the Marchioness. "Towards the city, will you? There's somebody wants to see you. He sent me to say would you come directly, and that he knowed all about Kit, and could prove his innocence."

"What do you tell me, child?"

179

"The truth, upon my word and honour I do. But please drive on – please! I've been such a time gone, he'll think I'm lost."

Mr Abel involuntarily urged the pony forward. The pony burst into a great pace, and didn't indulge in any eccentric performances, until they arrived at the door of Mr Swiveller's lodging, where, incredibly, he stopped when Mr Abel checked him.

"See! It's the room up there," said the Marchioness, pointing to one showing a faint light. "Come!"

Mr Abel, a timid creature, naturally hesitated for he had heard of people being lured into strange places to be robbed and murdered, and for all he knew, by guides very like the Marchioness. His regard for Kit, however, overcame every other consideration. So he suffered his companion to lead him up the dark and narrow stairs.

He was not a little surprised to find himself conducted into a dimly lighted sick chamber, where a man slept peacefully in bed.

"An't it nice to see him lying there so quiet?" said his guide, in an earnest whisper. "Oh! If you had only seen him two days ago."

Mr Abel made no answer, but kept far from the bed and very near the door. His guide, who appeared to understand his reluctance, approached the bed. As she did so, the sleeper started up, and he recognised in the wasted face the features of Richard Swiveller.

"Why, how is this?" said Mr Abel kindly, as he hurried towards him. "You have been ill?"

"Very," replied Dick. "Nearly dead. You might have heard of your Richard on his bier, but for the friend I sent to fetch you. Another shake of the hand, Marchioness, if you please. Sit down, sir."

Mr Abel seemed rather astonished to hear of the quality of his guide, and took a chair by the bedside.

"I have sent for you, sir," said Dick. "She told you why?"

"She did. I really don't know what to say," replied Mr Abel.

"Marchioness," said Dick. "Tell this gentleman all that you told me; and be particular. Don't you speak another word, sir."

The story was repeated, exactly as before, without any deviation or omission. Richard Swiveller kept his eyes on his visitor and when it was concluded, spoke again.

"You have heard it all. You and your friends will know what to do. After this long delay, every minute is an age. Go home fast tonight. Don't stop to say one word to me. She will be found here, whenever she's wanted; and as to me, you're pretty sure to find me at home, for a week or two."

Mr Abel needed no more persuasion. He was gone in an instant; and the Marchioness, returning from lighting him downstairs, reported that the pony had dashed away at full gallop.

"That's right!" said Dick. "But get some supper and a mug of beer, for I am sure you must be tired. Do have a mug of beer. It will do me as much good to see you take it as if I might drink it myself."

Nothing but this assurance could have prevailed upon the small nurse to indulge in such a luxury. Having eaten and drunk to Mr Swiveller's contentment, given him his drink, and put everything in neat order, she wrapped herself in an old coverlet and lay down before the fire.

Mr Swiveller murmured, "Good night, Marchioness!"

CHAPTER 58

On awaking in the morning, Richard Swiveller became slowly aware of whispering in his room. Looking out, he saw Mr Garland, Mr Abel, the Notary, and the single gentleman, gathered round the Marchioness, and talking to her in subdued tones. He swiftly let them know he was awake, and all four approached his bedside.

Dick's little nurse, pushing the visitors aside, set his breakfast before him, and insisted on his taking it first. Mr Swiveller, perfectly ravenous, consented to eat and drink on one condition.

"And that is," said Dick, "that you answer me this question truly, before I take a bit or drop. Is it too late?"

"For completing the work you began so well last night?" said the old gentleman. "No. Set your mind at rest. It is not, I assure you."

Comforted, the patient applied himself to his food. While he ate, Mr Swiveller constantly kept in his right hand, one palm of the Marchioness tight locked; and to kiss this imprisoned hand, he would stop every now and then. Whenever he put anything into his mouth, the face of the Marchioness lighted up beyond all description.

At length, Mr Swiveller had despatched as much toast and tea as in that stage of his recovery it was discreet to let him have. Then she brought a basin of water, and laved his face and hands, and brushed his hair, as if he were a very little boy, and she his grown-up nurse. To these various attentions, Mr Swiveller submitted in a kind of grateful astonishment beyond the reach of language.

"Gentlemen," said Dick, "you'll excuse me. Men who have been brought so low as I, are easily fatigued. I am fresh again now, and fit for talking."

"What can we do for you?" said Mr Garland, kindly.

"If you could make the Marchioness yonder, a Marchioness, in truth," returned Dick, "I'd thank you to get it done. But as you can't, pray sir, let me know what you intend doing."

"It's chiefly on that account that we have come just now," said the single gentleman. "We feared you would be anxious to know our intentions, and therefore came to you first."

"Gentlemen," returned Dick, "I thank you. Anybody in the helpless state that you see me in is naturally anxious. Don't let me interrupt you, sir."

"Then, you see, my good fellow," said the single gentleman, "that while we have no doubt of the truth of this disclosure, which has so providentially come to light – "

"Meaning hers?" said Dick, pointing towards the Marchioness.

" – Meaning hers, of course. While we have no doubt that it would procure Kit's immediate pardon and liberation, we doubt whether it would, by itself, enable us to reach Quilp, the chief villain. I should tell you that this has been confirmed by the best opinions we have been enabled, in this short space of time, to take upon the subject. You'll agree with us, that to give him even the slightest chance of escape would be monstrous. You agree, no doubt, if somebody must escape, let it be anyone but he."

"Yes," returned Dick. "Certainly."

The single gentleman proceeded to explain that they would endeavour to extort a confession from the gentle Sarah.

"When she finds how much we know, and how we know it," he said, "and that she is clearly compromised, we strongly hope that through her we will be able to punish the other two effectually. If we could do that, she might go scot-free for aught I cared."

Dick pointed out that they would find the old buck (meaning Sarah) more difficult to manage than Quilp himself – that she was of a kind of brass not easily melted or moulded into shape – in short, that they were no match for her, and would be signally defeated.

But it was in vain to urge them to adopt some other course.

They told Mr Swiveller how they had not lost sight of Kit's family; how they had never once even lost sight of Kit himself; and how he, Richard Swiveller, might keep his mind at rest. Then Mr Garland, the Notary, and the single gentleman took their leaves.

Mr Abel remained behind, looking at his watch and at the door, until Mr Swiveller was roused from a short nap by the setting-down on the landing-place outside of some giant load. Directly this sound reached his ears, Mr Abel started up, and hobbled to the door, and opened it; and behold! There stood a strong man, with a mighty hamper, which, being hauled into the room and unpacked, disgorged such treasures as tea, coffee, wine, rusks, oranges, grapes, and fowls ready trussed for boiling, and calves'-foot jelly, and other delicate restoratives, that the small servant stood silently rooted to the spot, with her mouth and eyes watering in unison. But, not so Mr Abel, or the nice old lady who appeared suddenly, and who began to make chicken broth in saucepans, and to cut up oranges for the sick man, and to ply the small servant with glasses of wine. The sudden appearance of such bounty was so unexpected and bewildering, that Mr Swiveller, when he had taken two oranges and a little jelly, knowing that it was all for his use and benefit, was fain to lie down and fall asleep again.

Meanwhile, the single gentleman, the Notary, and Mr Garland, went to a coffee-house, and wrote to Miss Sally Brass, requesting her, in terms mysterious and brief, to favour an unknown friend with her company there. Within ten minutes of the messenger's return and report of its delivery, Miss Brass herself arrived.

"Pray ma'am," said the single gentleman, whom she found alone, "take a chair."

Miss Brass sat herself stiffly down, a little astonished to find that the lodger and mystery correspondent were one and the same.

"You did not expect to see me?" said the single gentleman.

"I didn't think much about it," returned the beauty. "I suppose it's professional business?"

183

"It is connected with the law, certainly."

"Very well," returned Miss Brass. "My brother and I are just the same. I can take any instructions, or give you any advice."

"As there are other parties interested besides myself," said the single gentleman, rising and opening the door of an inner room, "we had better confer together. Miss Brass is here, gentlemen." Mr Garland and the Notary walked in; and, drawing up chairs, either side of the single gentleman, formed a kind of fence round Sarah, and penned her into a corner. She – all composure – calmly took a pinch of snuff.

"Miss Brass," said the Notary, "we professional people understand each other, and can say what we have to say, in very few words. You advertised a runaway servant, the other day?"

"Well," returned Miss Sally, a sudden flush overspreading her features, "what of that?"

"She is found, ma'am," said the Notary.

"Who found her?" demanded Sarah hastily.

"We did, ma'am – we three. Only last night, or you would have heard from us before."

"And now I have heard from you," said Miss Brass, folding her arms, "what of it? You have got something into your heads about her, of course. Prove it, will you. I can tell you that she is the most artful, lying, pilfering little minx ever born. Is she here?" she added, looking round.

"No, she is not," returned the Notary. "But she is quite safe. Did it occur to you when you found she had run away, that there were two keys to your kitchen door?"

Miss Sally took another pinch.

"One of which gave her the opportunities of roaming through the house at night when you supposed her locked up, and of overhearing confidential consultations, in particular one to be described today before a justice. One that you and Mr Brass held together, on the night before that most innocent young man was accused of robbery, by a horrible device which may be characterised by the epithets you have applied to this wretched little witness."

Sally took another pinch. Although wonderfully composed, it was clear that she had expected something very different.

"Come, come, Miss Brass," said the Notary, "you are sister to one of the greatest scoundrels unhung. But connected with you is a villain of the name of Quilp, the prime mover of the whole diabolical device, who I believe to be worse. Miss Brass, do us the favour to reveal the whole history of this affair. Let me remind you that doing so will place you in a safe and comfortable position. Against your brother and you we have quite sufficient evidence already. Time," said Mr Witherden, pulling out his watch, "in a business like this, is exceedingly precious. Favour us with your decision as speedily as possible, ma'am."

With a smile upon her face, Miss Brass took two or three more pinches of snuff, and said – "I am to accept or reject at once, am I?"

"Yes," said Mr Witherden.

The charming creature was about to reply, when the door was hastily opened and Sampson Brass came into the room.

"Excuse me," he said. "Wait a bit!"

So saying, and quite indifferent to the astonishment his presence caused, he shut the door, and made a most abject bow.

"Sarah," said Brass, "hold your tongue if you please, and let me speak. Gentlemen, if I could express the pleasure it gives me to see three such men in a happy unity of feeling and concord of sentiment, I think you would hardly believe me."

"If you're not an idiot," said Miss Brass harshly, "hold your peace."

"Sarah, my dear," returned her brother, "I know what I am about, my love, and will express myself accordingly."

Brass, with a scratched face, a green shade over one eye, looked round with a pitiful smile. "Gentlemen – regarding your present conversation – I happened to see my sister on her way here, and wondered where she could be going to. Being of a suspicious turn, I followed her. Since then, I have been listening."

"If you're not mad," interposed Miss Sally, "say no more."

"Sarah, my dear," rejoined Brass with undiminished politeness, "I thank you kindly, but will still proceed. Mr Witherden, sir, as we have the honour to be members of the same profession, suffer me to speak, I beg."

Mr Witherden was silent, and Brass went on.

"If you will look at this," he said, holding up the green shade, and revealing an eye most horribly discoloured, "you will naturally ask how did I get it. Gentlemen," said Brass, "I answer – Quilp!"

The three gentlemen looked at each other, saying nothing.

"I say," pursued Brass, glancing aside at his sister, as though for her information, "Quilp. Quilp, who lures me into his infernal den, and takes delight in looking on while I injure myself. Quilp, who has in all our communications, treated me as a dog. Quilp, whom I have always hated. He gives me the cold shoulder on this very matter as if he had had nothing to do with it, instead of being the first to propose it. I can't trust him. Now," said Brass, replacing the shade, "where does all this lead?"

Nobody spoke. Brass stood smirking for a little while and then said: "To be short, it leads me to this. If the truth has come out, as it plainly has in a manner that there's no standing up against, I had better turn upon this man than let this man turn upon me. It's clear to me that I am done for. Therefore, if anybody is to split, I had better be the person and have the advantage of it. Sarah, my dear, comparatively speaking you're safe. I relate these circumstances for my own profit."

With that, Mr Brass, in a great hurry, revealed the whole story; bearing as heavily as possible on his amiable employer, and making himself out to be rather a saint-like and holy character, though subject – he acknowledged – to human weaknesses. He concluded thus: "You must do with me what you please. If you wish to have this in writing, we'll reduce it into manuscript immediately. I am quite confident you will be tender with me. You are men of honour. Punish Quilp, gentlemen. Weigh heavily upon him. Grind him down. He has done as much by me, for many and many a day."

Having now arrived at the conclusion of his discourse, Sampson smiled as only parasites and cowards can.

"And this," sneered Miss Brass, surveying him from head to foot, "this is my brother, is it! This is my brother, that I have worked and toiled for, and believed to have had something of the man in him!"

"Sarah, my dear," returned Sampson, rubbing his hands feebly; "you disturb our friends. You're disappointed, Sarah, and not knowing what you say."

"You pitiful dastard," retorted the lovely damsel, "I understand you. You feared that I should speak. Do you really think I would have said a word! Not if they had tempted me for twenty years!"

"He, he!" simpered Brass. "You think so, Sarah. But do not forget that it was a maxim with Foxey – our revered father, gentlemen – 'Always suspect everybody.' If you were not actually about to purchase your own safety when I showed myself, I suspect you'd have done it by now. And therefore I've done it myself, and spared you the trouble as well as the shame. The shame, gentlemen," added Brass, "if there is any, is mine. It's better that a female should be spared it."

But had Mr Brass not been so over-suspicious, and left his sister to manage the conference on their joint behalf, he would probably have found himself much better off in the end.

The three gentlemen spoke together apart for a few moments. Then the Notary pointed to the writing materials, and informed Mr Brass that if he wished to make any statement in writing, he had the opportunity of doing so. He also told him that they would require his attendance, presently, before a justice of the peace, and that in what he did or said, he was guided entirely by his own discretion.

"Gentlemen," said Brass, "I will justify the tenderness with which I know I shall be treated; and you may depend upon it I will make a clean breast."

Mr Brass then sat down to write.

The lovely Sarah paced the room with manly strides while he wrote. She continued to pace up and down until quite tired, and then fell asleep on a chair near the door.

It has been since supposed, with some reason, that this slumber was a sham, as she slipped away unobserved in the dusk of the afternoon. She did not return.

Mr Brass's task was not finished until evening; but, being done at last, he and the three friends travelled to the private office of a justice, who, detaining Mr Brass in a secure place that he might have the pleasure of seeing him on the morrow, dismissed the others with the cheering assurance that a warrant for the apprehension of Mr Quilp would be prepared, and that a proper application and statement of all the circumstances to the secretary of state (who was fortunately in town), would no doubt procure Kit's free pardon and liberation without delay.

Their business ended, the three gentlemen hastened back to Mr Swiveller, whom they found progressing favourably in his recovery. Mr Abel still sat with him. After telling him all they had done, the two Mr Garlands and the single gentleman took their leaves for the night, leaving the invalid alone with the Notary and the small servant.

"As you are so much better," said Mr Witherden, sitting down at the bedside, "I may give you a piece of legal news."

Dick's countenance fell, as he considered the one or two threatening letters he had received concerning outstanding accounts. He replied, "I hope it's nothing of a very disagreeable nature?"

"If I thought it so, I should choose some better time for communicating it," replied the Notary. "Let me tell you, first, that my friends know nothing of it, and that their kindness to you has been quite spontaneous, with no hope of return. It may do a thoughtless, careless man, good, to know that."

Dick thanked him, and said he hoped it would.

"I have made some inquiries about you," said Mr Witherden, "little thinking that I should find you under these circumstances. You are the nephew of Rebecca Swiveller, spinster, deceased, of Dorsetshire."

"Deceased!" cried Dick.

"Deceased. If you had been another sort of nephew, you would have come into possession of some five-and-twenty thousand pounds. As it is, you have fallen into an annuity of one hundred and fifty pounds a year. I think I may congratulate you upon that."

"Sir," said Dick, sobbing and laughing together, "you may. For, please God, we'll make a scholar of the poor Marchioness yet! And she shall walk in silk attire, or may I never rise from this bed again!"

CHAPTER 59

Mr Quilp was in his hermitage, extremely well satisfied with his machinations. He had not strayed from his den for two whole days. The third day found him little disposed to stir abroad.

It was the day after Mr Brass's confession.

Having no intuitive perception of the cloud lowering upon his house, the dwarf was in his ordinary state of cheerfulness; varying the day's monotonous routine with a little screeching, or howling, or some other innocent relaxation of that nature.

The day, in the highest and brightest quarters of the town, was damp, dark and gloomy. In that low and marshy spot, the fog filled every corner with a thick dense cloud. Every object was obscure at one or two yards' distance. The warning lights and fires upon the river were powerless, and now and then but for the cry of some bewildered boatman resting on his oars, trying to make out where he was, the river itself might have been miles away.

The mist was of a keenly searching kind. No muffling up in furs and broadcloth kept it out. It seemed to penetrate into the very bones. Everything was wet and clammy to the touch. The warm blaze alone defied it. It was a day to be at home, crowding about the fire.

The dwarf ordered Tom Scott to pile the little stove with coals, and dismissed him. He lighted up fresh candles, and having dined off a beefsteak and brewed a great bowl of hot punch, lighted his pipe and sat down to spend the evening.

At this moment, a low knocking at the door arrested his attention. He softly opened the little window, and demanded who was there.

"Only me, Quilp," replied a woman's voice.

"Only you!" cried the dwarf. "And what brings you here, you jade? How dare you approach the ogre's castle, eh?"

"I have brought a letter," cried the meek little woman.

"Toss it in at the window here, and go your ways," said Quilp, interrupting her, "or I'll come out and scratch you."

"No, but please, Quilp – do hear me speak," urged his submissive wife, in tears.

"Speak then," growled the dwarf with a malicious grin. "Be quick about it."

"It was left at our house this afternoon," said Mrs Quilp, trembling. "The boy said he didn't know from whom it came, but that it must be brought on to you directly, for it was of the greatest consequence. Please," she added, as her husband reached for it, "please let me in. You don't know how wet and cold I am. Let me dry myself at the fire for five minutes. I'll go away directly you tell me to, Quilp."

Her amiable husband hesitated a moment; but, considering that the letter might require answering, closed the window, opened the door, and bade her enter. Mrs Quilp obeyed and, kneeling down before the fire to warm her hands, delivered into his a little packet.

"I'm glad you're wet," said Quilp, snatching it. "I'm glad you're cold. I'm glad your eyes are red with crying. It does my heart good to see your little nose so pinched and frosty."

"Oh Quilp!" sobbed his wife. "How cruel it is of you!"

"Did she think I was dead?" said Quilp, wrinkling his face. "Did she think she was going to have all the money, and to marry somebody she liked?"

The poor little woman remained on her knees, warming her hands, and sobbing, to Mr Quilp's great delight.

"I'll read the letter. Humph!" he muttered. "I ought to know this writing. Beautiful Sally!"

Opening it, he read, in a fair, legal hand, as follows: "Sammy has broken confidence. It has all come out. Strangers will call upon you. They mean to surprise you. Don't lose time. I didn't. I am not to be found anywhere. If I was you, I wouldn't either. S. B."

For a long time he said nothing; but, after a time, during which Mrs Quilp was almost paralysed by his looks, he contrived to gasp out, "If I had him here. If I only had him here – "

"Oh Quilp!" said his wife, "what's the matter?"

" – I should drown him," said the dwarf, not heeding her. "Too easy a death, too quick – but the river runs close by. Oh! If he were here! Just to take him to the brink, holding him by the buttonhole – joking with him, – and, with a sudden push, send him splashing down! Drowning men come to the surface three times they say. Ah! To see him, and mock him as his face came bobbing up, – oh, what a rich treat that would be!"

"Quilp!" stammered his wife, venturing to touch his shoulder. "What has gone wrong?"

"Such a bloodless cur!" said Quilp, rubbing his hands very slowly. "I thought his cowardice and servility were the best guarantee for his silence. Oh Brass, my dear, good, affectionate, faithful, complimentary friend – if I only had you here!"

He hurried to the door to call Tom Scott, who appeared immediately.

"There!" said the dwarf, pulling him in. "Take her home. Don't come tomorrow, for this place will be shut up. Come back no more till you hear from me. Do you mind?"

Tom nodded sulkily, and beckoned Mrs Quilp to lead the way.

"As for you," said the dwarf, addressing her, "ask no questions about me, make no search for me, say nothing concerning me. I shall not be dead, mistress, and that'll comfort you."

"But, Quilp? What is the matter? Where are you going?"

"I have told you what to do. Woe betide you if you fail to do it, or disobey me by a hair's breadth. Will you go!"

Tom Scott dragged his charge away as swiftly as he could.

"It will be a good night for travelling anonymously," he said, as with great exertion he closed the two old gates and barred them with a heavy beam. He shook the matted hair from his eyes, and tried to push them – strong and fast.

"The fence between this wharf and the next is easily climbed," said the dwarf. "There's a back lane, too, from there. That shall be my way out. I need fear no unwelcome visitors while this lasts."

Almost groping his way with his hands (it had grown so dark and the fog had so much increased), he returned to his lair and busied himself in preparations for a speedy departure.

While collecting a few necessaries and cramming them into his pockets, he never once ceased murmuring in a low voice.

"Oh Sampson!" he muttered, "good worthy creature – if I could but hug you! If I could only hold you in my arms and squeeze you. If we ever do cross each other again, Sampson, we'll have a greeting not easily to be forgotten, trust me. Oh, if we were face to face in this room again, my white-livered man of law, how well contented one of us would be!"

He stopped and drank a long deep draught of punch.

"There's Sally," he said, with flashing eyes; "the woman has spirit, determination, purpose. She could have stabbed him – poisoned him safely. She might have seen this coming on. Why does she warn me when it's too late? When he sat there, over there, with his white face, and red head, and sickly smile, why didn't I know what was passing in his heart? It should have stopped beating, that night. – What's that?"

A loud and violent knocking at the gate. Then, a pause as if they stopped to listen. Then, the noise again.

"So soon!" said the dwarf. "And so eager! I am afraid I shall disappoint you. I'm quite prepared. Sally, I thank you!"

As he spoke, he extinguished the candle. The noise at the gate still continuing, he felt his way to the door, and stepped into the open air.

The knocking ceased. Thick cloud rested upon the earth, and shrouded everything from view. He darted forward for a few paces; then, thinking he had gone wrong, changed the direction of his steps; then stood still, not knowing where to turn.

191

"If they would knock again," said Quilp, trying to peer into the gloom by which he was surrounded, "the sound might guide me! Come! Batter the gate once more!"

He stood listening intently, but the noise was not repeated. Nothing was to be heard but, at intervals, the distant barkings of dogs. It was no guide, for he knew it often came from shipboard.

"If I could find a wall or fence," said the dwarf, stretching out his arms, and walking slowly on, "I should know which way to turn. A good, black, devil's night this!"

As the words passed his lips, he staggered and fell – and next moment was fighting with the cold dark water!

For all its bubbling up and rushing in his ears, he could hear the knocking at the gate again – could hear a shout that followed it – and recognised the voice. He realised they had lost their way, and had wandered back to the point from which they started; that they were close at hand, but could not make an effort to save him; that he himself had shut and barred them out. He answered the shout. It was of no avail. The strong tide filled his throat, and bore him on, upon its rapid current.

Another mortal struggle, and he was up again, beating the water with his hands, and looking at some black object he was drifting close upon. The hull of a ship! He could touch its smooth and slippery surface with his hand. The resistless water bore him down, and, driving him under it, carried away a corpse.

It toyed with its ghastly freight, now bruising it against the slimy piles, now hiding it in mud, now dragging it heavily over rough stones and gravel, until, tired of the ugly plaything, it flung it on a swamp and left it there to bleach. And there it lay alone.

CHAPTER 60

Lighted rooms, bright fires, cheerful faces, the music of glad voices, words of love and welcome, and tears of happiness – what a change is this! But it is to such delights that Kit is hastening. They are awaiting him, he knows. He fears he will die of joy, before he gets among them.

192

He is not to be carried off tomorrow with the rest, they tell him. By degrees they let him know that doubts have arisen, that inquiries are to be made, and perhaps he may be pardoned after all. At last, they bring him to a room where some gentlemen are assembled. Foremost among them is his good old master, who takes him by the hand. He hears that his innocence is established, and that he is pardoned.

They crowd about him, and tell him that the truth has gone abroad, and that all the town and country ring with sympathy for his misfortunes. He has no ears for this. His thoughts, as yet, have no wider range than home. Does she know it? What did she say? Who told her? He can speak of nothing else.

They make him drink a little wine, and talk kindly to him for a while. He is free to go. Mr Garland thinks if he feels better, it is time they went away. The gentlemen cluster round him, and shake hands with him. He feels very grateful to them, but the power of speech is gone.

The last door shuts behind them. They have passed the outer wall, and stand in the open street. It seems busier than it used to be. The night is bad, and yet how cheerful in his eyes! One gentleman had pressed some money into his hand. When they have gone a few paces beyond the box for poor Prisoners, he hastily returns and drops it in.

Mr Garland has a coach waiting, and, taking Kit inside, bids the man drive home. At first, they can only travel at a foot pace, because of the heavy fog. But, as they get farther from the river, they are able to proceed more swiftly. On the road, hard galloping would be too slow for Kit; but, drawing near their journey's end, he begs they may go more slowly, but there is no stopping, for the old gentleman speaks stoutly to him, and they are at the garden-gate. Next minute, they are at the door. There is a noise of tongues, and tread of feet, inside. It opens. Kit rushes in, and finds his mother clinging round his neck.

And there, too, is the ever faithful Barbara's mother, still holding the baby; and there is little Barbara – poor little Barbara, so much thinner and paler, and yet so very pretty – trembling like a leaf; and there is Mrs Garland, neater and nicer than ever; and there is Mr Abel, violently blowing his nose, and wanting to embrace everybody; and there is the single gentleman hovering round them all; and there is thoughtful little Jacob, sitting all alone by himself on the bottom stair.

In the parlour there are decanters of wine, and all that sort of thing, set out as grand as if Kit and his friends were first-rate company. Kit no sooner comes in, than that single gentleman charges all the glasses, and drinks his health, and tells him he shall never want a friend while he lives; and so does Mr Garland, and so does Mrs Garland, and so does Mr Abel. Then the single gentleman forthwith pulls from his pocket a massive silver watch, engraved with Kit's name; in short it is Kit's watch, bought expressly for him, and presented to him on the spot. Kit is the happiest of the happy.

Kit takes the first opportunity to slip to the stable. The moment he lays his hand upon the latch, the pony neighs his greeting; when Kit goes up to caress and pat him, the pony rubs his nose against his coat. Kit fairly puts his arm round Whisker's neck and hugs him.

But how comes Barbara in the stable, of all places in the world? Since Kit has been away, the pony took his food from nobody but her, and Barbara, just looking in, to see that everything was right, has come upon him unawares. Blushing little Barbara!

It may be that there are even better things to caress than ponies. Kit leaves him for Barbara at any rate. "We have hardly had time to shake hands, Barbara," says Kit. Barbara gives him hers.

Kit is so near her when they shake hands, that he can see a tiny tear, yet trembling on an eyelash. It's natural that he should look at it, unknown to Barbara, who raises her eyes unconsciously. Is it natural that at that instant, Kit should kiss Barbara? He does, whether or no. Barbara says "for shame," but lets him do it – twice.

Later that evening Mr Garland called Kit to him, and told him that he had something to say that would surprise him greatly. Kit looked so pale on hearing this, that the old gentleman quickly asked him if he would be ready next morning for a journey.

"With me and my friend in the next room. Can you guess why?"

Kit turned paler yet, and shook his head.

"Oh yes. I think you do already," said his master.

Kit murmured something rather unintelligible, but plainly pronounced the words "Miss Nell," shaking his head as he did so, as if to say there was no hope of that.

But Mr Garland told him that he had guessed right.

"The place of their retreat is indeed discovered," he said, "at last. And that is our journey's end."

Kit faltered out such questions as, where was it, and how had it been found, and how long since, and was she well and happy?

"Happy she is, beyond all doubt," said Mr Garland. "And well, I – I trust she will be soon. She has been ailing, I've learnt, but she was better when I heard this morning. Sit, and hear the rest."

Mr Garland then related to him, how he had a brother who lived a long way off, with an old clergyman who had been his early friend. How they had not met for many years, but had communicated by letter from time to time, always looking forward to when they should meet again. How this brother was greatly beloved by the people among whom he dwelt, who called him the Bachelor. How he seldom mentioned his village friends; but in a letter received a few days before, he had dwelt upon a child and an old man who had come to live among them, and had told such a tale of their wandering, and mutual love, that few could read it without being moved to tears. How he, the recipient of that letter, believed that these must be the very wanderers for whom they searched, and whom Heaven had directed to his brother's care. How he had written for further information. It had that morning arrived and confirmed his first suspicion. This was the reason for the journey.

"In the meantime," said the old gentleman rising, and laying his hand on Kit's shoulder, "rest; for a day like this would wear out the strongest man. Good night, and may our journey have a prosperous ending!"

CHAPTER 61

Kit sprang from his bed before dawn, to prepare for his welcome expedition. His sleep had been so troubled that it was rest to rise.

Before he had been up a quarter of an hour the whole house were astir and busy. Everybody hurried to do something towards facilitating the preparations. The single gentleman, it is true, could do nothing himself, but he overlooked everybody else and was more locomotive than anybody. The work of packing and making ready went briskly on, and by daybreak every preparation for the journey was completed.

Now, Barbara seemed to take least pleasure in the bustle of the

195

occasion; and when Kit, in the openness of his heart, told her how overjoyed it made him, Barbara became more downcast still.

"You have not been home so long, Christopher," said Barbara, "that you need to be glad to go away again."

"But for such a purpose," returned Kit. "To bring back Miss Nell! I am so pleased too, to think that you will see her, Barbara, at last."

Barbara gave a little toss of her head.

"Barbara," said Kit, detaining her gently, "let us part friends. I always thought of you, in my troubles. I should have been more miserable than I was, if it hadn't been for you. When I want you to be pleased to see Miss Nell, it's because I like you to be pleased with what pleases me – that's all."

Little Barbara melted into tears.

At that moment the wheels of the carriage were heard.

Soon the single gentleman and Mr Garland were in the carriage, and Kit, well wrapped and muffled up, was in the rumble behind; and all were crying out, "Good bye!" In another minute, the carriage was out of sight.

It was a bitter day. A keen wind blew, shaking the white frost from the trees and hedges, and whirling it away like dust. But little cared Kit for weather. There was a freedom in the wind, as it came howling by. As it swept on, bearing down the dry twigs and withered leaves, carrying them away pell-mell, it seemed as though everything was in a hurry.

All day long, it blew without cessation. The night was clear, but the wind had not fallen, and the cold was piercing.

The two gentlemen inside the carriage were little disposed to sleep, passing the time with conversation.

In one of the pauses, the single gentleman, who had gradually become more thoughtful, turned to his companion and said abruptly: "Are you a good listener?"

"Like most other men, I suppose," returned Mr Garland, smiling.

"I have a short narrative on my lips," rejoined his friend, "and will try you with it. It is very brief."

Pausing for no reply, he laid his hand on the old gentleman's sleeve, and proceeded thus: "There were once two brothers, who loved each other dearly. There was a disparity in their ages – some twelve years. Wide as the interval was, they became rivals too soon. The deepest affection of both their hearts settled upon one object.

"The youngest was the first to find this out. I will not tell you what misery he underwent. He had been a sickly child. His brother, patient and considerate, had many a day denied himself the sports he loved, to sit beside his couch, telling him stories till his pale face lighted up; to carry him in his arms to some green spot, where he could see the bright summer day; to be, in any way, his fond and faithful nurse. When the time of trial came, the younger brother's heart was full of those old days. Heaven strengthened it to repay the sacrifices of inconsiderate youth by one of thoughtful manhood. He left his brother to be happy, quitting the country, hoping to die abroad.

"The elder brother married her. She was in Heaven before long, leaving him with an infant daughter. In this daughter the mother lived again. He who lost that mother almost in the winning, clung to this girl, her breathing image. She grew to womanhood, and gave her heart to one who knew not its worth. Well! Her fond father could not see her unhappy. They were married.

"Through all the misery that followed; through all the cold neglect; through all the poverty he brought upon her, she toiled on, in the deep devotion of her spirit, as only women can. Her means wasted; her father nearly beggared by her husband, and the witness (for they lived now together) of her ill-usage and unhappiness – she never bewailed her fate. Patient to the last, she died a widow of some three weeks' date, leaving to her father's care two orphans; one a son of ten or twelve years old; the other an infant girl as she had been herself.

"The elder brother, grandfather to these two children, was now a broken man. He began to trade – in pictures first, and then in curious ancient things.

"The boy grew like his father in mind and person; the girl like her mother. The wayward boy soon spurned the shelter of his roof, and sought associates more congenial to his taste. The old man and the child dwelt alone together.

"It was then, that the love of two dead people who had been nearest and dearest to his heart, was all transferred to this slight creature; it was then that there began to beset him, a gloomy dread of poverty and want. His fear was for the child. It haunted him night and day.

"The younger brother had travelled in many countries, and had made his pilgrimage through life alone. Communication between him and the elder was difficult, and often failed; but still he learnt – with long gaps between each interval – all that I have told you now.

"Then, dreams of their young, happy life visited his pillow and every night, a boy again, he was at his brother's side. With the utmost speed he could exert, he settled his affairs; converted into money all the goods he had; and, with honourable wealth enough for both, arrived one evening at his brother's door!"

The narrator, whose voice had faltered lately, stopped.

"The rest," said Mr Garland, pressing his hand, "I know."

"Yes," rejoined his friend. "You know the result of my search. Pray God, we are not too late again!"

"We cannot be," said Mr Garland. "This time we must succeed."

"I have believed and hoped so," returned the other. "But a heavy weight has fallen on my spirits, my good friend, and the sadness that gathers over me, will yield to neither hope nor reason."

"That does not surprise me," said Mr Garland; "it is a natural consequence of the events you have recalled; and of this dismal night! Hark! How the wind is howling!"

CHAPTER 62

Day broke, and found them still upon their way. Since leaving home, they had halted here and there for necessary refreshment. They had made no other stoppages, but the weather continued rough. It would be night again before they reached their destination.

Kit, hardened with the cold, went on manfully. The short daylight of winter soon faded away, and it was dark again.

As it grew dusk, the wind fell; its distant moanings were more low and mournful. By degrees it died away, and then it came on to snow.

The flakes fell fast and thick, soon covering the ground some inches deep, and spreading abroad a solemn stillness. The rolling wheels were noiseless, and the sharp clatter of the horses' hoofs became a muffled tramp.

Shading his eyes from the falling snow, Kit often tried to catch the earliest glimpse of twinkling lights, denoting their approach to some not distant town.

He descended slowly from his seat – for his limbs were numbed – when they arrived at a lone posting-house, and inquired how far they had to go. It was a late hour in such by-places; but a voice answered from an upper window, Ten miles. After another brief delay they were again in motion. It was a country road, full of holes, and the horses were held to a footpace. All three men got out and plodded behind the carriage. The walk was most laborious. As each was thinking that the driver must have lost his way, a church bell, close by, struck the hour of midnight, and the carriage stopped. It had moved softly enough, but when it ceased to crunch the snow, the silence was startling.

"This is the place, gentlemen," said the driver, dismounting, and knocking at the door of a little inn. "Halloa! Past twelve o'clock is the dead of night here."

The knocking was loud, but failed to rouse the drowsy inmates. All continued dark and silent. They looked up at the windows, but no light appeared. They spoke together in whispers; unwilling to disturb again the dreary echoes.

"Let us go on," said the younger brother, "and leave this good fellow to wake them. I cannot rest until I know that we are not too late. Let us go on!"

They did so, leaving the postilion to order such accommodation as the house afforded, and to renew his knocking. Kit accompanied them.

The road wound gently downward. As they proceeded, they lost sight of the church, and of the small village clustering round it. The knocking, they could plainly hear.

The old church tower, clad in a ghostly garb of pure cold white, again rose up before them.

A wicket gate was close at hand, but more than one path led across the churchyard, and, uncertain which to take, they came to a stand again.

The village street was close by. A faint light shone in a chamber window not far off, and Kit ran towards that house to ask the way.

His first shout was answered by an old man who demanded who was abroad at that unseasonable hour.

"'Tis hard weather this," he grumbled, "and not a night to call me up in. What do you want?"

199

"I am sorry to call you from your bed," said Kit, "but we seek the parsonage-house. You can direct us?"

"I should be able to," answered the old man, in a trembling voice. "The right hand path, friend, is the road. – No ill news for our good gentleman, I hope?"

Kit thanked him, and hastily answered in the negative; he was turning back, when his attention was caught by the voice of a child.

"Has my dream come true?" cried the child, from a neighbouring window. "Pray tell me."

"Poor boy!" said the sexton, before Kit could answer, "how goes it, darling?"

"Has my dream come true?" exclaimed the child again. "But no, that can never be! How could it be!"

"I guess his meaning," said the sexton. "To bed again, poor boy!"

"Ay!" cried the child, in a burst of despair. "I knew it could never be, before I asked! But, all tonight, and last night too, it was the same. I never fall asleep, but that cruel dream comes back."

"Try to sleep again," said the old man, soothingly. "It will go in time."

"No no, I would rather that it stayed – cruel as it is," rejoined the child. "I am not afraid to have it in my sleep, but I am so very sad."

The old man blessed him, the child in tears replied Good night, and Kit was again alone.

He hurried back, moved by what he had heard, though more by the child's manner, as the meaning was hidden from him. They took the path, and soon arrived before the parsonage wall. Turning to look about them, they saw, among some ruined buildings, one single solitary light.

It shone from an old oriel window, and, being surrounded by the deep shadows, sparkled like a star.

"What light is that!" said the younger brother.

"It is surely," said Mr Garland, "in the ruin where they live. I see no other ruin hereabouts."

"They cannot," returned the brother hastily, "be waking at this late hour – "

Kit begged that, while they rang, he should make his way to this light and try to ascertain if any people were about. He darted off, and made straight towards the spot.

He soon arrived within a few yards of the window. He approached as softly as he could. There was no sound inside. Touching the glass with his cheek, he listened. No sound.

A strange circumstance, a light in such a place at that time of night, with no one near it.

A curtain was drawn, and he could not see into the room. Again and again he listened; again and again the same wearisome blank.

Leaving the spot with cautious steps, and skirting the ruin for a few paces, he came at length to a door. He knocked. No answer. But there was a curious noise inside. It bore a resemblance to the low moaning of one in pain, but it was far too regular and constant. Now it seemed a kind of song, now a wail. It was unlike anything he had ever heard; and in its tone there was something fearful, chilling, and unearthly.

The listener's blood ran colder now than ever it had done in frost and snow, but he knocked again. There was no answer, and the sound went on. He laid his hand upon the latch, and put his knee against the door. It yielded to the pressure, and turned upon its hinges. He saw the glimmering of a fire upon the old walls, and entered.

CHAPTER 63

The dull glow of a fire showed him a figure, seated with its back towards him, bending over the fitful light. The stooping posture and the cowering form were there, but no hands were stretched out to meet the grateful warmth. With limbs huddled together, head bowed down, and arms crossed upon the breast, it rocked to and fro upon its seat without a moment's pause, accompanying the action with the mournful sound he had heard.

The heavy door had closed behind him, with a crash that made him start. The figure neither spoke, nor turned to look, nor gave in any other way the faintest sign of having heard the noise. It was an old man. He, and the failing light and dying fire, the solitude, the wasted life, and gloom, were all in fellowship. Ashes, and dust, and ruin!

Kit tried to speak, but still the same terrible low cry went on – still the same rocking in the chair, heedless of his presence. He had his hand upon the latch, when something in the form – distinctly seen as one log blazed up – stopped him. He advanced a pace – another still. And he saw the face. Yes! Changed as it was, he knew it well.

"Dear master!" he cried, stooping on one knee and catching at his hand. "Speak to me!"

The old man turned slowly towards him and muttered, "This is another! How many of these spirits there have been tonight!"

"No spirit, master. None but your old servant. You know me now, I am sure? Miss Nell – where is she?"

"They all say that!" cried the old man. "They all ask the same question. A spirit!"

"Where is she?" demanded Kit. "Oh tell me but that, dear master!"

"She is asleep – yonder – in there."

"Thank God!"

"Aye! Thank God!" returned the old man. "I have prayed to Him, many a livelong night, when she has been asleep, He knows. Hark! Did she call?"

"I heard no voice."

"You did. Do you tell me that you don't hear *that*?"

He started up, and listened again.

"Nor that?" he cried, with a triumphant smile. "Can anybody know that voice so well as I? Hush!" Motioning to him to be silent, he stole away into another chamber. After a short absence, when he could be heard speaking in a soothing tone, he returned, carrying a lamp.

"She still sleeps," he whispered. "You were right. She did not call – unless she did so in her slumber. She has called to me in her sleep before now, I have seen her lips move. I feared the light might wake her, so I brought it here."

He spoke rather to himself than to the visitor.

"She sleeps soundly," he said, "but no wonder. Angel hands have strewn the ground deep with snow."

Again he stopped to listen, scarcely drawing breath.

"Why dost thou lie so idle there, dear Nell," he murmured, "when there are bright red berries waiting for thee to pluck them! Why dost thou lie so idle there, when thy little friends come creeping to the door, crying, 'Where is sweet Nell?' And sob, and weep, because they do not see thee."

Kit could not speak. His eyes were filled with tears.

202

"When she is well again, she will rise early, as she used to do, and ramble abroad in the healthy morning time. I often tried to track the way she had gone, but her small footstep left no print upon the dewy ground. Who is that? Shut the door. Quick! Have we not enough to do to drive away that marble cold, and keep her warm!"

The door was indeed opened, for the entrance of Mr Garland and his friend, accompanied by two other persons. These were the schoolmaster, and the bachelor. The former held a light in his hand. He softened again at sight of these two friends, and, laying aside the angry manner, resumed his former seat, and subsided into the old, dull, wandering sound.

Of the strangers, he took no heed whatever. He had seen them, but appeared quite incapable of interest. The younger brother stood apart. The bachelor drew a chair towards the old man. After a long silence, he ventured to speak.

"Another night, and not in bed!" he said softly. "I hoped you would remember your promise to me. Why not take some rest?"

"Sleep has left me," returned the old man. "It is all with her!"

"It would pain her to know that you were watching thus," said the bachelor. "You would not give her pain?"

"She has slept so very long. It is a good and happy sleep – eh?"

"Indeed it is," returned the bachelor. "Indeed, indeed, it is!"

"That's well! – And the waking – " faltered the old man.

"Happy too. Happier than tongue can tell, or heart of man conceive."

They watched him as he rose and stole to the other chamber where the lamp had been replaced. They listened as he spoke again within its silent walls. They looked into the faces of each other, and no man's cheek was free from tears. He came back, whispering that she was still asleep, but that he thought she had moved. It was her hand, he said – a very, very little – but he was pretty sure she had moved it – perhaps in seeking his. And then he dropped into his chair again, and clasping his hands above his head, uttered a cry never to be forgotten.

The poor schoolmaster and the bachelor gently unlocked his fingers, which he had twisted in his grey hair, and pressed them in their own.

"He will hear me," said the schoolmaster, "I am sure. He will hear either me or you if we beseech him."

"I will hear any voice she liked to hear," cried the old man. "I love all she loved!"

"I know you do," returned the schoolmaster. "I am certain of it. Think of her – think of all the sorrows and afflictions you have shared together; and all the peaceful pleasures you have jointly known. Think of nothing else tonight – open your heart to old affections and old times. It is in her name that I speak now."

"You do well to speak softly," said the old man. "We will not wake her. I should be glad to see her smile again. There is a smile upon her young face now, but it is fixed. We will not wake her."

"Let us not talk of her in her sleep, but as she used to be when you were journeying together, far away – as she was, in the old cheerful time," said the schoolmaster.

"She was always cheerful," cried the old man, looking at him.

"We have heard you say," pursued the schoolmaster, "that she was like her mother. You can think of, and remember her?"

He maintained his steadfast look, but gave no answer.

"And the one before her," said the bachelor. "It is many years ago, but you have not forgotten her whose death contributed to make this child so dear to you? Say, that you could carry back your thoughts to very distant days – to the time of your early life – when you did not pass your youth alone. Say, that you could remember, long ago, another child who loved you dearly. Say, that you had a brother, long forgotten, long separated from you, who now, at last, in your utmost need came back to comfort and console you – "

"To be to you what you were once to him," cried the younger, falling on his knee before him; "to repay your old affection, brother dear, by constant care, and love; to be, at your right hand, what he has never ceased to be when oceans rolled between us. Give me but one word of recognition, brother – and never in the brightest moment of our youngest days, when, poor silly boys, we thought to pass our lives together – have we been half as dear and precious to each other as we shall be from this time hence!"

The old man looked from face to face, and his lips moved; but no sound came in reply.

"If we were knit together then," pursued the younger brother, "what will be the bond between us now! Our love and fellowship began in childhood, and will be resumed. And even," he added in an altered voice, "even if what I dread to name has come to pass – even so, still, dear brother, we are not apart, and have that comfort."

Gradually the old man had drawn towards the inner chamber, while these words were spoken. He pointed there, as he replied, with trembling lips.

"You plot among you to take me from her. You never will do that – never while I have life. I have no relative or friend but her – I never had – I never will have. She is all to me. It is too late to part us now."

Waving them off with his hand, and calling softly to her as he went, he stole into the room. Those left behind drew close together, and after a few whispered words, followed him. They moved so gently, that their footsteps made no noise; but there were sobs from among the group.

For she was dead. There, upon her little bed, she lay at rest. She was dead. No sleep so beautiful and calm, so free from pain, so fair to look upon. She seemed fresh from the hand of God, waiting for the breath of life; not one who had lived and suffered death.

Her couch was dressed with here and there some winter berries and green leaves. "When I die, put near me something that has loved the light, and had the sky above it always." Those were her words.

She was dead. Dear, gentle, patient, noble Nell was dead.

Where were the traces of her early cares, her sufferings, and fatigues? All gone. Sorrow was dead indeed in her, but peace and perfect happiness were born; imaged in her tranquil beauty and profound repose.

The old man had a small hand tight folded to his breast, for warmth. It was the hand she had stretched out to him with her last smile – the hand that had led him on, through all their wanderings. He hugged it to his breast, murmuring that it was warmer now; and, as he said it, he looked, in agony, to those who stood around, as if imploring them to help her.

She was dead, and past all help, or need of it. The ancient rooms she had seemed to fill with life, even while her own was waning fast – the garden she had tended – the peaceful haunts – the paths she had trodden – could know her no more.

"It is not," said the schoolmaster, as he bent down to kiss her on the cheek, "on earth that Heaven's justice ends. Think what earth is, compared with the World to which her young spirit has winged its early flight; and say, if one deliberate wish expressed in solemn terms above this bed could call her back to life, which of us would utter it!"

CHAPTER 64

When morning came, and they could speak more calmly on the subject of their grief, they heard how her life had closed.

She had been dead two days. They were all with her, knowing that the end was drawing on. She died soon after daybreak. They had read and talked to her, but as the night hours crept on, she sunk to sleep. They could tell, by what she faintly uttered, that her dreams were of her journeyings with the old man; not of painful scenes, but of people who had helped them, for she often said "God bless you!" with great fervour. Waking, she never wandered in her mind but once, and that was of beautiful music that she said was in the air. God knows. It may have been.

Opening her eyes from a very quiet sleep, she begged that they would kiss her once again. That done, she turned to the old man with a lovely smile upon her face, such, they said, as they had never seen, and never could forget, and clung with both her arms about his neck. They did not know that she was dead, at first.

She never murmured or complained; but with a quiet mind and manner, faded like the light upon a summer's evening.

The child who had been her little friend came there, almost as soon as it was day, with an offering of dried flowers. It was he who had come to the window, and they saw in the snow traces of small feet, where he had lingered near the room in which she lay, before he went to bed. He had a fancy, it seemed, that they had left her alone; and could not bear the thought.

He told them of his dream of her being restored to them, just as she used to be. He begged hard to see her, saying that he would be very quiet, and would not be alarmed, for he had sat by his young brother all day when he was dead, and had felt glad to be so near him. They let him have his wish; and indeed he kept his word, and was a lesson to them all.

The old man had not spoken once, except to her, or stirred from the bedside, but when he saw her little favourite, he pointed to the bed, and burst into tears for the first time.

Soothing him with his artless talk, the child persuaded him to rest, to walk abroad, to do almost as he desired. And the day came, when she must be removed forever, the child led him away, that he might not know when she was taken from him.

They gathered fresh leaves and berries for her bed. It was Sunday – a bright, clear, wintry afternoon, and as they traversed the village street, those walking in their path gave them a softened greeting. Some shook the old man kindly by the hand, some stood uncovered while he tottered by, and many cried, "God help him!" as he passed along.

The bell rang its remorseless toll for her, so young, so beautiful, so good. Decrepit age, and vigorous life, and blooming youth, and helpless infancy, poured forth to gather round her tomb.

Along the crowded path they bore her now; pure as the newly fallen snow that covered it. Under the porch, where she had sat in that peaceful spot, she passed again; and the old church received her in its quiet shade.

They carried her to one old nook, where she had many a time sat musing, and laid their burden softly on the pavement. The light streamed on it through the coloured window – a window, where the boughs of trees rustled in the summer, and where the birds sang sweetly all day long.

Earth to earth, ashes to ashes, dust to dust! Many a young hand dropped in its little wreath, many a stifled sob was heard. Some – and they were not a few – knelt down. All were sincere and truthful in their sorrow.

The service done, the mourners stood apart, and the villagers closed round to look into the grave before the pavement-stone should be replaced. One called to mind how he had seen her sitting on that very spot, her book fallen on her lap, and she gazing upon the sky. Another told, how he had wondered that she had never feared to enter the church alone at night, but had loved even to climb the tower stair, with no more light than that of the moon. Thus, coming to the grave in little knots, and glancing down, and falling off in whispering groups of three or four, the church was cleared in time, of all but the sexton and the mourning friends.

They saw the vault covered, and the stone fixed down. Then, when the dusk of evening had come on, and not a sound disturbed the sacred stillness of the place, when the bright moon poured in her light upon her quiet grave – then, with tranquil and submissive hearts they turned away, and left the child with God.

It was late when the old man came home. The boy had led him to his own dwelling on their way back and he had sunk into a deep sleep by the fireside. He was perfectly exhausted, and they were careful not to rouse him. When he finally awoke the moon shone.

The younger brother, uneasy at his protracted absence, was watching at the door for his coming, when he appeared in the pathway with his little guide. He advanced to meet them, and conducted the old man with slow steps towards the house.

He went straight to her chamber. Not finding what he had left there, he returned with distracted looks to the room in which they were assembled. Then he rushed to the schoolmaster's cottage, calling her name. They followed close upon him, and when he had vainly searched, brought him home.

With such persuasive words as pity and affection could suggest, they prevailed upon him to sit among them, and dwelling with many fervent words upon the happy lot to which she had been removed, they told him, at last, the truth. At their words he fell down among them like a murdered man.

For many hours, they had little hope of his surviving; but grief is strong, and he recovered.

For many days, the old man pined and moped away the time, and wandered here and there as seeking something, and had no comfort.

Whatever power of thought or memory he had was all bound up in her. He never understood, or seemed to care to understand, about his brother. To every endearment he continued listless.

On the one theme, which was in his and all their minds, it was impossible to touch. Dead! He could not bear the word. In what hope he lived, no man could tell; but that he had some hope of finding her again was plain to all. He was a broken-hearted man.

At length, they found, one day, that he had risen early, and, with his knapsack on his back, his staff in hand, her own straw hat, and little basket, was gone. As they were making ready to pursue him, a frightened schoolboy came who had seen him, but a moment before, sitting in the church – upon her grave.

Going softly to the door, they espied him in the attitude of one who waited patiently. They did not disturb him, but kept watch. When it grew quite dark, he rose and returned home, and went to bed, murmuring, "She will come tomorrow!"

He was there again from sunrise until night; and still at night he laid him down to rest, and murmured, "She will come tomorrow!"

And thenceforth, every day, all day long, he waited at her grave. He never told them what he thought, or where he went. He would sit with them at night, pondering with a secret satisfaction, they could see, upon the flight that he and she would take; and still he whispered in his prayers, "Lord! Let her come tomorrow!"

The last time was a pleasant spring day. He did not return and they went to seek him. He was lying dead upon the stone.

They laid him beside she whom he had loved so well; and, in the church where they had often prayed, the child and the old man slept together.

CHAPTER 65

Mr Sampson, detained by the justice upon whom he called, remained under his protection for a considerable time, so that he was quite lost to society for some time. His name was also erased out from the roll of attorneys.

Of Sally Brass, there were conflicting rumours. Some said that she had gone down to the docks in male attire, and had become a female sailor; others that she had enlisted as a private in the second regiment of Foot Guards. But the truth appears to be that, after some five years, two wretched people were more than once seen at dusk in the area of St Giles's, shuffling and cowering as they went in search of food. It was whispered that they were Sampson and his sister Sally.

The body of Quilp being found – though not for some days – an inquest was held near to where it had been washed ashore. The general supposition was that he had committed suicide, and the verdict was to that effect. He was left to be buried with a stake through his heart in the centre of four lonely roads.

Being cast upon the world by his master's death, Tom Scott began to tumble for his bread. He assumed an Italian name and tumbled with extraordinary success, and to overflowing audiences.

Little Mrs Quilp never quite forgave herself the one deceit that lay so heavy on her conscience. Her husband had no relations, and she was rich. Having married the first time at her mother's instigation, she consulted in her second choice nobody but herself. It fell upon a smart young fellow; and as he made it a preliminary condition that Mrs Jiniwin should be thenceforth an out-pensioner, they lived together after marriage with no more than the average amount of quarrelling, and led a merry life upon the dead dwarf's money.

Mr and Mrs Garland, and Mr Abel, went on as usual and in due time the latter went into partnership with his friend the Notary, on which occasion there was a ball. Unto this ball there happened to be invited the most bashful young lady that was ever seen, with whom Mr Abel happened to fall in love. In due course they were married; and they were the happiest of the happy.

The pony preserved his character for independence down to the last moment of his life. He often went to and fro between Mr Garland's and his son's, and, as the old people and the young were frequently together, had a stable of his own at the new establishment. He did no work for two or three years before he died, but lived in clover; and his last act (like a choleric old gentleman) was to kick his doctor.

Mr Swiveller, receiving his annuity, put the Marchioness to school forthwith, honouring the vow he had made upon his sickbed. He decided on the name Sophronia Sphynx for her, as being genteel, and indicative of mystery. The Marchioness repaired, in tears, to the school of his selection. And although these expenses kept him in straitened circumstances for half a dozen years, he never slackened in his zeal, and always held himself sufficiently repaid by the accounts he heard (with great gravity) of her advancement.

Mr Swiveller kept the Marchioness there until she was, at a moderate guess, nineteen years old – good-looking, clever, and good-humoured; then he began to consider seriously what to do next. On one of his periodical visits, while considering this question, the Marchioness came to him, alone, looking more smiling than ever. Then, it occurred to him, but not for the first time, that if she married him, how comfortable they might be! So Richard asked her and they were married that day week.

They found a little cottage at Hampstead and became its tenants. And let it be added, to Dick's honour, that he called her the Marchioness from first to last.

Young Frederick Trent rioted abroad for a brief term. He drowned in the river in Paris, after a fight and scuffle. His body was never claimed.

210

The younger brother, or the single gentleman, would have drawn the poor schoolmaster from his retreat, to be his companion. But the humble village teacher was fond of his dwelling in the old churchyard. Calmly happy in his school, and in the attachment of Her little mourner, he pursued his quiet course in peace.

The single gentleman, or younger brother, whichever you will, went forth into the world. For a long, long time, it was his chief delight to travel in the steps of the old man and the child (so far as he could trace them from her last narrative). Those who had been kind to them did not escape his search. Mrs Jarley of the waxwork, Codlin, Short – he found them all.

Kit's story having got abroad, raised him up a host of friends, and a good post was procured for him, by some of the gentlemen who had believed him guilty, and who had acted upon that belief. Through the same kind agency, his mother was secured from want, and made quite happy. Thus, as Kit often said, his great misfortune turned out to be the source of all his subsequent prosperity.

Of course Kit married, and who should be his wife but Barbara? And the best of it was, he married so soon that little Jacob was an uncle, before the calves of his legs were ever encased in broadcloth pantaloons. Kit's mother and Barbara's mother took up their abode together, and were a most harmonious pair of friends from that time forth.

When Kit had children six and seven years old, there was a pretty Barbara among them. There was a copy of little Jacob. Of course there was an Abel, godson to Mr Garland; and there was a Dick, whom Mr Swiveller did especially favour. The little group would often gather round him of a night and beg him to tell again that story of good Miss Nell who died. This, Kit would do and he would teach them how she had gone to Heaven, as all good people did; and how, if they were good, like her, they might hope to be there too, one day.

He sometimes took them to the street where she had lived; but the old house had been long ago pulled down, and a fine broad road was in its place. At first he would draw with his stick a square upon the ground to show them where it used to stand. But he soon became uncertain of the spot, and could only say it was thereabouts, he thought, and that these alterations were confusing.